MAID FOR THE MARQUESS

MELANIE MORELAND
SCARLETT SCOTT

DEDICATION

To our readers,
Even when fear stands in your way, may you find the courage—and
the believer—who help you reach your dreams.

PROLOGUE

ALEXANDER

Outside my town house, London made its displeasure with the weather known.

The streets were deserted, the roads absent of the sounds of carriages, ladies strolling and chatting. The only souls out were servants scurrying to complete their errands so they could hurry back to the heat and dryness of a kitchen hearth and perhaps a cup of weak tea to warm themselves with before getting busy with their tasks.

Shops were mostly empty, the downpour bouncing off the roads, settling the constant dust but creating puddles of muck instead. Those out in the weather tried to dodge the vast puddles without much success, their feet, skirts, and trouser legs wet and muddy.

The steady beat of the rain on the glass was almost soothing as I bent over the numerous ledgers and piles of correspondence awaiting my attention. An empty plate and cup were balanced on one end of the desk, precarious and forgotten from the small meal sent to me by the cook. She insisted I needed to eat and I refused to leave my study, so a compromise was made. I didn't have to tell her she was correct and the small repast had cleared my head so I could continue to work. She knew, and I had no desire to see the smug smile on her face. She was already far too settled in her role here and knew I would rather cut off my arm than dismiss her.

A fire danced merrily in the hearth, warming the room and eschewing the dampness seeping in from outside. It was pleasant and quiet, the faint sounds of the servants going about their tasks a low noise in the background.

A sharp rap on my study door sounded out, disturbing my concentration. I didn't cease in my endeavors, recognizing the knock. I had heard it innumerable times before now.

"Enter," I called out.

The sound of steady footsteps confirmed my judgment.

"Sit, and I will be with you momentarily. You know where the scotch is."

A chuckle sounded. "That would be most welcome, my lord."

I finished the column in the ledger, pleased with the number. I shut the tome and sat back, regarding my visitor. Edward Warwick observed me, his gaze steady and calm. His shoulders were damp from the rain outside. No doubt too broad to fit under an umbrella. They filled the chair across from my desk, and his hair was wet. But his boots were clean, no doubt dried before he entered the hall. My housekeeper was as frightening as my cook, and he knew better than to tread on the Axminster with wet soles.

He had his ankle crossed over his knee, appearing relaxed, but I knew better. There was a tightening of his jaw, an erratic beat to his foot. The hand that held his crystal glass was fisted tightly. He was my right hand, my land steward, and my closest friend. I had known him most of my life and trusted him completely. He had news.

I sat back. "Tell me."

He grinned, showing off his wide smile. "I bring news of the empty acreage between Wheaton and Milton Manor."

Simply the subject sent a rush of fretfulness through me. "What of it?"

"Rumor has it that the piece of land your father sold will finally be made available."

I leaned forward, eager. "How?"

"Lord Barnett is in deep financial trouble."

I could barely hide my disdain simply hearing that name.

"How deep?"

"He is barely holding on. And, as such, is hosting a game. I have heard he plans to recoup his losses and pay his debts."

I rubbed my bottom lip thoughtfully. "Is your source reliable?"

He tilted his head, studying me. "Isn't it always?" he asked, raising his eyebrow in shock that I would question him.

"Is his situation well-known?"

"No. It is simply a chance for a high-stakes game for those who can afford it. I understand he has a very extravagant event planned to cover up his real reason for the gathering."

"So he is going further into debt to cover it."

"Yes."

"It would seem that he is still naught but a simpleton with more ideas than brains."

Edward inclined his head in agreement.

"And we have all his tricks memorized and ready to counter?"

"I am unsure, my lord. Do you?" he replied with a grin.

I laughed, enjoying our back-and-forth as I always did.

Edward and I had a relationship that was rare. It mattered not to either of us that I was a marquess and he non-titled. We never had anything but honesty and friendship between us—even if I paid him a handsome sum for his services. He was fast to put me in my place if needed, and I respected that honesty above all else.

"I have practiced with you so often, I can't imagine him defeating me," I mused. "The trick will be to lead him on, letting him think he is winning. And to know when to press my luck with my own trick."

Edward made a low noise of agreement in his throat.

"I have memorized the markings on the cards. Both the deck he will play with and the one we will swap out." I had studied them for so long, the hard-to-see markings were burned into my memory. "His accomplice did an incredible job," I observed. "If your spy hadn't told us about them, we'd be none the wiser." I scowled in anger. "Nor would anyone else he has ever fleeced."

"Yes. You will have to lose some but stay in the game." He stood, pouring us each a scotch. He handed me a glass, and I sipped the smoky liquid, savoring the richness of the liquor. It was worth having it smuggled in. "And you must show little interest in the land beside Wheaton."

"He knows it is I who had been trying to buy it."

"But he thinks you changed your mind and decided it was worthless."

I lit a cheroot—a terrible habit, but one I only fell back on when angry or upset.

"It is worthless the way he has let it decay."

"Now is your chance to win it back."

I nodded, lifting my glass. "When?"

"A fortnight."

"And you are sure I will receive an invite?"

"I saw the guest list myself. All wealthy, titled gentlemen. He despises you, but he wants your money."

"He shall be disappointed."

Edward grinned and raised his glass. "Indeed."

"Then let us prepare."

CHAPTER 1

ALEXANDER

I surveyed the trunks strapped to the carriage, resisting the urge to refuse to take them or the items they contained. But I knew I would have to keep up appearances for the duration of the invitation, which meant several clothing options. I sighed, thinking how much I would prefer to be headed directly to Wheaton rather than Cliffwood, Barnett's estate.

Edward appeared beside me with a grin. "At least we shall be out of London," he observed, reading my mind.

He was correct. I preferred the country. The soft sounds of the wind in the trees and the scent of the earth rich in my nose. The quiet that permeated the walls of my favorite place in the world—my own country estate, Wheaton. I loved to work the dirt with my farmers, sit and discuss crop rotation and planting. I enjoyed using my hands to build. To put my body to the test with the manual labor most gentlemen of my standing would never dream of doing. It was at Wheaton I felt most like the man I wished to be. I had no airs to put forth, no false face to present.

I only came to London when absolutely necessary. I found the smells and crowds displeasing. The constant invitations, the mamas ever hopeful I would cast an eye toward their daughter to be my marchioness. The too-loud and smoke-filled rooms of the clubs frequented by my peers. It was all wearisome. It made me ill-tempered and snappish. I knew behind my back I was called cold. Removed. Unfeeling.

I let the gossipmongers have their say—I wasn't bothered by it.

Edward found my nonchalance amusing.

"Are the horses ready?"

"Of course. I made sure Knight was prepared."

"Excellent. He'll be happy to return to Wheaton as well. We can run for miles there."

My favorite steed was a massive black stallion with a streak of gray across his face and the same color in his mane. He stood tall and proud, headstrong and powerful. We rode well together. I was looking forward to doing so once we left London behind us. The carriage could catch up as we stopped to rest.

I clapped my hand on Edward's shoulder. "Then let us depart and finish this game we have been playing for too long. I want my property back intact, and I want Barnett back where he belongs. In the dust."

Edward regarded me seriously. "Once this is done, you can move on to the next important step in your life."

I groaned. He had been at me for months about my marital state and the need for an heir. I knew he was right, yet I was in no hurry to change my status or take on a wife. I found the young women in London empty-headed and boring, if I was honest. The thought of marrying one of them, having babes and being trapped for the rest of my life, made me shudder. It was another reason I avoided

London. Spare me from the simpering chits. And their overanxious mamas.

"We will put that aside for the time being," I responded. "I have too much on my mind at this point."

Edward chuckled. "Let us be off, then."

I climbed from my carriage, stretching my muscles. I had ridden most of the journey, but the last part of it had been foggy and gray and I'd chosen the inside of the carriage for comfort and the effect of arriving as a marquess should. Edward preferred to ride—he always did. He insisted the carriage was too confining and only for softer sorts.

He never said that when we sparred and I was soundly thrashing him.

Edward's mother had been my dear mama's lady's maid. We had practically grown up together. I owed him my life. When I was ten, a tree branch I was shimmying down broke, and I fell into the river, striking my head. It was Edward who jumped in and saved me from drowning. When I woke, my mother's worried countenance and my father's frown greeted me. My head ached for days, the deep cut constantly reminding me of my misfortune. I carried the scar still, hidden under my hairline. My mother insisted a debt was owed to Edward, and he received a good education at my side until our later years. Once my mother passed, I argued time and again with my father to allow him to stay in school with me, but he would not have it. He preferred spending his money gambling and drinking, not repaying Edward for saving the life of his son who would never be what he wished for him to be.

I looked around at the estate, spotting the neglect immediately. The grounds needed tending, the brambles growing up and covering what used to be lovely stone. The façade was dirty, crumbling in places. As we entered the house, I noticed bare patches on the walls, empty spots where paintings and tapestries once hung. Items had been rearranged, attempting to disguise the fact that the more expensive pieces were absent, and some might not notice.

But I was observing and taking notice of all of it.

There was a lack of servants as well. I could see it in the upkeep of the home, making note of the dust in places that should shine, the Axminster threadbare in spots.

I judged that the rumors of Barnett's debts were understated, given what I was seeing.

Inwardly, I smiled. That made him more desperate. And desperate men became careless.

I planned on making him very careless.

"Ah, Lord Wheaton."

I turned at the sound of my name, keeping my face impassive. I met the cold, rheumy eyes of Baron Barnett, his appearance exactly as I expected. His clothing was slightly out of fashion and not well cared for. His gray hair a trifle long. He walked as if unsure of his own stability, and I wondered if it was age, illness, or drink causing his odd gait. Still, he bowed and greeted me as if we were old friends, not mere acquaintances, barely on speaking terms.

He also felt he was my equal. I could see it in his

slightly upturned nose, the way his voice thinned out as he spoke, and the rather displeased look when he bowed.

As if I were the one below him in rank.

I chose to pretend that I didn't notice anything amiss. I wanted him to feel as if he had the upper hand this entire visit.

Until I struck.

"I trust your rooms are to your liking," he inquired.

"Quite," I muttered, not bothering to mention the dust, the lack of paintings or comfortable furniture, nor the fact that there were hardly enough servants to offer the proper care to guests.

"You will have to forgive the estate," he offered with a cold smile. "I am in the midst of a large plan of refurbishment, and as you know, these things get behind."

"Think nothing of it. I am interested in naught but cards and conversation," I lied. "Good brandy and some fine food are all I require."

I had a feeling I would be getting neither, but I didn't care. The only thing I wanted was the land beside Wheaton.

An odd look crossed his face, but he indicated I should follow him. I walked slowly, observing the evident decay of the rooms. What once was a great house was slowly falling into ruin.

And I didn't plan on helping him rebuild it.

CHAPTER 2

MADELEINE

*J*ust as they always did when my father hosted his house parties, the kitchens bustled with activity around me. But this time, I sensed an unmistakable difference, tension drawn about us as tightly as a hangman's noose, the inevitable feeling of doom hovering in the air.

My stomach growled angrily as I moved past a tray of honey cakes Cook had prepared earlier. I hadn't eaten since the night before with the other servants at dinner. The urge to take one was strong, despite the punishment I knew I would face if I were caught.

"Madeleine!"

I winced as the strident voice of the housekeeper, Mrs. Wells, echoed off the kitchen walls, cracking with the warning of a whip.

Leaving the honey cakes, I skirted a scarred table and emerged from behind a towering collection of pots that were all in need of cleaning. Fewer hands in the kitchen meant more work for everyone, and we were down to just one scullery maid.

I curtsied before Mrs. Wells, knowing that the slightest hint of tarrying or lack of deference would earn me a vicious reprimand.

"Yes, Mrs. Wells?" I asked, careful to keep my voice low and subservient, to avert my gaze in humility.

"There has been a spill in the drawing room. You are to hasten there at once and clean it."

"Of course, Mrs. Wells."

My stomach rumbled again, and I felt warmth creeping up my throat. I hoped the sound wasn't loud enough to carry to the housekeeper. There hadn't been time for breaking my fast this morning with the seemingly endless tasks heaped upon me, given the arrival of so many guests, and then morning had loomed into afternoon. I had scarcely had time to open the windows, clean the ashes from the hearths, and sweep and beat the carpets in the main rooms before I was needed in the kitchens.

Mrs. Wells's eyes narrowed. "Return to me when you've completed your task. There is a great deal more to be done."

"Yes, Mrs. Wells."

I curtsied again and wasted no time in fetching some cloths, water, and soap. I was certainly in no hurry to get back to the drudgery awaiting my return belowstairs, but my father would expect the spill to be treated forthwith. Appearances were of the utmost importance to him.

I emerged from the servant stairs, careful to keep water from sloshing onto the floor. The low rumble of masculine voices in the drawing room grew more pronounced as I approached. In preparation for the card games my father was hosting during the house party, a large table had been moved into place in the center of the chamber. It was ringed with chairs I had rubbed with cold-drawn linseed oil to restore some of their luster a few days ago.

Those chairs were now occupied with an assortment of gentlemen, all of whom were unfamiliar to me except one. My father didn't spare me a glance as I entered the room with another curtsy. No one else did either. They were far too concerned with their amusements to take note of a mere chambermaid.

I preferred it that way. For a woman in my position, no male attention could possibly be good male attention. Keeping my head lowered, I moved silently, in search of the spill.

"Over there, girl," my father said harshly, making a dismissive gesture with his right hand.

The signet ring he ordinarily wore on his smallest finger was absent. I wondered if he had lost it to one of the gentlemen seated at the table as I moved to the Axminster and discovered a large puddle of what appeared to be red wine soaking into the intricate floral design. I suppressed a sigh at the sight. If my father would have allowed me to have a drugget placed beneath the table as I had recommended, the stain would have soaked into the removable textile instead of the costly carpet he couldn't afford to replace.

I set to work blotting up the stain with my cloths, soaking up as much of the wine as I was able. As I pressed my hands into the carpets, grateful for the protection of my gloves against the burn of the harsh soap and water on my palms, I slowly became aware that I was being watched. A furtive glance in my father's direction sent relief cascading through me. He was ruminating upon the cards he held in his hand.

But all my relief fled when I flicked my glance two seats down and my gaze briefly clashed with a dark-eyed stare. My breath caught in my throat. Good heavens. The gentleman was elegantly dressed and solidly built, with broad shoulders and brown hair that was long enough to be constrained at his nape in a queue. He possessed a wide, strong jaw and high cheekbones, and a nose that was almost sharp. Intelligence sparkled in his curious gaze.

Curiosity was every bit as dangerous as male attention was.

I jerked my head back down and continued with a fresh cloth. Wine seeped into the clean rag, rising from the Axminster. I applied some water and soap, but it was obvious I would need to return to the stain later with other means of lifting the wine. Foolishly, I chanced another glance in the mysterious stranger's direction, but his attention had returned to the card game. Disappointment rose, swift and equally irrational. Why should a gentleman like him take notice of a lowly chambermaid?

"You're taking far too long, girl," my father snapped, cutting through my thoughts and making me flinch. "Leave the rest until we've finished our games."

"Forgive me." I rose, taking my soiled cloths and water with me, excusing myself from the room.

An icy frisson of dread curled down my spine as I left, knowing I would bear the brunt of his displeasure later.

As I slipped back into the servant stairs, I collided with a fellow maid. The small pail of water I'd been carrying tipped toward me, soaking my gown. I gasped at the unpleasant sensation of water dampening my shift as I realized I had run into Lydia, who, along with an older maid named Geraldine, was one of my few friends here at Cliffwood.

"Oh, Maddie," she said on a rush, her blue eyes wide under her mobcap, "I'm so sorry!"

"You needn't apologize," I reassured her at once, mustering a smile for her benefit. "The fault was mine. I was rushing when I should have been taking my time."

In truth, I'd been so flustered by the dark-eyed gentleman in the drawing room that I had been fairly racing away like a horse galloping down a track. Only, instead of winning a purse, all I managed to do was make a mess of myself. Mrs. Wells would be quite vexed if I were to return to the kitchens in such a state.

I glanced up from the rapidly spreading wetness on my gown and made another discovery. Lydia's cheek was reddened, and now that some of my distraction had dissipated, I realized the whites of her eyes were pink, her nose a similar shade.

As if she had been weeping.

"What's happened to you?" I asked, although I needn't have.

I knew the answer.

"Mrs. Wells," Lydia said.

Impotent fury rose within me.

"I'll speak with my father," I blurted, knowing I couldn't and yet wanting to aid her in some way.

"No, please." Lydia shook her head, dashing at a lone tear on her cheek with the back of her hand. "You mustn't. I fear doing so will only make both our predicaments worse."

"Why did she strike you this time?" I asked.

"I stole a honey cake," my friend admitted, frowning. "So, you see? It was deserved. I knew it was a risk that she would see."

Like me, she had been far too burdened with tasks this morning and afternoon to consume any of the scant food allotted to us. Perhaps this evening, we would have some spare bits of roast to tuck into our weary bellies if enough remained after my father's houseguests had supped. More likely than not, we would go to bed after naught but thin porridge and bread. We'd been given such meager fare lately in order to prepare for the guests. They were not allowed to be hungry, but we did not matter.

"I was similarly tempted," I told Lydia, new guilt seeping through me for the sin I had nearly committed.

I deserved the punishment I next received.

The sound of footfalls on the stair below had us both stiffening our spines and resuming our duties. There would be more opportunity to speak later, when the house was asleep for the night. No need to further incite the wrath of Mrs. Wells. As I hurried down the steps, clutching the soiled cloths and my now-empty water pail, however, it wasn't the housekeeper or my father who lingered most prominently in my thoughts.

It was the stranger with the broad shoulders and the casual air of command, the only gentleman in the drawing room who had seen me.

Until he'd looked away, knowing I was beneath him.

CHAPTER 3

ALEXANDER

$\mathcal{A}$ full moon was high over Barnett's unkempt gardens, illuminating the shrubbery. I inhaled deeply and exhaled, appreciative of the fresh air after spending the day trapped in a room stinking of smoke, spilled wine, pomade, and soot. Play had finished for the evening, affording me the opportunity to escape from Barnett's dubious hospitality.

Surrounding me was more evidence of his estate's ruinous decline, from box hedges in wont of a sound trim and towering syringa, to clumps of Sweet William and lavender overrun with weeds. It was a tangled mass on once carefully cultivated soil.

The crunch of gravel alerted me to Edward's presence before I turned, grateful for the companionship of my trusted steward after a day fraught with tension. For some reason, the servant girl Barnett had reprimanded rose in my mind before I banished the thought.

"How much did you lose today?" Edward inquired quietly.

No one else had ventured to the gardens at this late

hour. Likely, most of the other houseguests had already fallen into bed with bellies full of wine. But discretion was wise. I had no desire for word of my true intentions to reach the baron.

"Enough to make Barnett think I'm an easy mark."

A breeze ruffled the boughs of the trees overhead as clouds passed before the moon, blanketing us in shadow. I turned my attention toward the darkened shrubbery, an odd restlessness settling over me. I was closer than ever to obtaining what I wanted, and yet, I felt no satisfaction. There was only a hollow sense of disgust for it all—the baron, the greed, the vices. Was I the only man in that room who had taken note of the true fear in the maid's voice when she had apologized to Barnett for taking too long to clean the threadbare carpets?

I told myself it didn't signify, that *she* didn't signify. And yet it rang hollow.

"Was he using the marked cards?" Edward asked, interrupting my thoughts.

I looked away from the ruined gardens, trying to keep my mind settled upon the task at hand. "Yes. And I saw where he places them when we are finished for the day. There is a hidden drawer in the table. I lingered in the hallway watching him, and he was so busy congratulating himself over his winnings that he didn't notice my presence. We will have to slip in once the house is abed and switch them for tomorrow."

We would linger here in the gardens until it was safe to accomplish the substitution. Given the dearth of domestics, we likely wouldn't have long to wait.

Edward nodded. "How will you play the day?"

Tomorrow was another day, another opportunity to seize what I wanted. The groundwork had already been laid, and I was confident of our success.

"Off and on. I will let my luck run out a bit, then pick up again so he is not completely suspicious. Two of the crowd have already run out of their funds." I snorted derisively. "Young pups who have no business gambling. I let Barnett pick them off to get him overconfident. There are two more who will be gone before the afternoon is over. That will leave four of us for the evening."

"Everything is falling into place." Edward's voice was pleased.

And well it should have been. My victory was his victory. We were nearer to obtaining our objective than ever. Triumph was at last within reach. Yet oddly, I didn't share his sense of satisfaction.

"You're quiet," he observed. "Is aught amiss? Is there something you aren't telling me?"

I stared into the shadows, contemplating the whirlwind of the day, and sighed heavily. The girl's face rose in my mind.

"Nothing is amiss," I reassured him.

We passed a few more minutes in pleasant conversation, and I was grateful for the distraction. The last thing I needed was to dwell on a servant girl. She was Barnett's concern, not mine.

MADELEINE

I rose before dawn in the cramped garret room I shared with Lydia. Even beneath a thick layer of old counterpanes, my feet were so cold that I could scarcely feel my toes. Shivering, I emerged from my small, uncomfortable bed and made my way through the darkness to perform some hasty morning ablutions. Candles were a luxury that couldn't presently be spared for those of us who worked belowstairs. They were reserved for the baron's guests. Sun seeped through the rafters in odd gaps, enabling me a small amount of light.

Lydia was little more than an indistinct lump across the room in her own small bed. The sound of my friend's rhythmic breathing suggested she was yet asleep. I would wake her soon, but I was reluctant to intrude on the pleasant escape of slumber, so oft our only release from the drudgery of our days. Although, for me, even my dreams were haunted.

I dressed and secured my hair with pins before hiding it beneath a mobcap. I had just finished when a faint rustle and yawn from Lydia's bed told me she was awake.

"Why didn't you wake me?" she asked, her voice raspy with sleep and an edge of worry. "I didn't mean to be a slugabed."

"You've time aplenty yet," I reassured her. "I thought to let you rest for an extra few minutes. The day is sure to be a long one."

We all secretly dreaded the baron's house parties. Our work increased threefold during the revels, as drunken lords indulged in gambling and demanded feasts to satiate their seemingly endless appetites, all whilst we went without. The sole source of consolation to me was that the baron's attention was usually diverted to his guests rather than to me. I preferred hunger and exhaustion to my father's wrath.

"I'm not the only one of us who needs rest," Lydia said pointedly. "You are always fretting over everyone else. What of yourself?"

She worried about me, I knew, and I did the same for her.

I smiled, grateful for her companionship. "I don't need the extra rest. I'm accustomed to the baron's house parties."

Lydia harrumphed as if to say she disagreed, but there wasn't much time for conversation with the day's work waiting to be done. I made my bed and swept up the scarred floor while Lydia washed her face and dressed. Then we quietly made our way from the cold garret to the main floor of the house. Once there, we parted ways to attend our separate duties.

I began in the drawing room as usual, going to the hearth and turning up the threadbare carpet surrounding it for a sound sweeping. Next, I moved to the soot in the fireplace, taking up the dirty task of cleaning as much as I could before tending to the fire itself. There was an art to the proper lighting of a fire that calmed me. Perhaps it was the distraction or the careful attention to detail or the relative solitude of early morning hours. Or perhaps it was that I found comfort in the familiar.

I had learned long ago how to stack the coals and cinders and wood to avoid smoke billowing into the room, a feat that some other housemaids could not readily accomplish. It pleased the baron to keep the rooms as clean and free of soot and chimney smoke as possible, and it was my duty to make certain that he was well contented. When he wasn't, all of us paid the price.

By the time I finished my tasks, the guests had stirred from their chambers in search of the handsome breakfast that was laid in the dining room for their delectation at the same time each morning. My stomach rumbled with the reminder that I had gone to bed hungry the evening before and would need to wait a few more hours until I could break my own fast. I ignored it and made my way to the guest chambers to continue my duties.

I began with the finest room, the blue bedchamber, which had been given to the Marquess of Wheaton. Whilst some of its fine mahogany furnishings had been sold off, the linen press, dressing table, and bed remained. The Axminster had yet to become as faded and thinned as some of the parts of the household that saw more frequent wear.

There was a difference to a room when it was inhabited. The notions a chamber's occupant left behind were telling. Some were slovenly and careless. Bed linens rumpled and scattered, soiled garments flung everywhere, curtains pulled wide to admit the sun without a care for the damage it might do to the paintings on the walls and the carpets. Others were neat and tidy, leaving only the slightest hint that they had even been within the four walls.

Fortunately, the marquess was the latter. A lone book was on the table at the bedside, the counterpane had been pulled smoothly over the sheets, and the curtains were drawn. I wondered which of the gentlemen assembled at the baron's table yesterday was the marquess, and then I just as swiftly reminded myself it hardly mattered. But I couldn't shake the memory of those dark eyes that had burned into me, seeing me just for a moment.

Shaking my head to dispel all such unwanted notions, I drew aside the curtains and opened the windows to allow a bit of crisp air into the space while I freshened the room. The day beyond was gray and cold and damp. I inhaled deeply to chase the pleasant scent the marquess had left behind—leather, shaving soap, and a faint hint of lemons. The sooner I moved on to the next room, the better.

Hastily, I attended to the fire and then spread damp tea leaves on the Axminster by the hearth before sweeping them up to collect the dust. I closed the window and drew the curtains, knowing the sun, should it pierce the fog and clouds, would be at its brightest around noon. Mrs. Wells was strict in her expectations for the preservation of the rooms. And well she had to be, for the baron's profligacy seemed to increase by the day, as did his desperation. Rumors abounded belowstairs that he was in danger of losing Cliffwood to his debts since it wasn't entailed.

My thoughts weighed heavily upon me as I dusted and took my leave of the chamber. I wasn't afraid of losing the only home I'd ever known. These walls had been mostly a prison to me rather than a refuge. It was what the baron would do should he lose everything that worried me most.

I could only hope and pray that the outcome of his house party proved a boon for us all.

CHAPTER 4

ALEXANDER

Barnett eyed the pile of markers on the table, his greed evident. Only the two of us were left, the stakes high now. Our third had just lost his winnings and chosen to sit, sipping his brandy and watching. The money he had lost meant nothing to him, but he was eagerly waiting to see the outcome of the last hand. If I actually lost, the money would dent but not break my accounts. If I won, the money meant nothing. It was the land I wanted. Why the old fool wouldn't simply sell it to me, I had no idea.

Edward had joined us for the evening's play, and I was grateful for his presence now as I laid the final trap for Barnett.

"I raise," I said, knowing this was the moment, as I added my markers. I knew he didn't have any of the funds laid on the table and was playing his role well. I had purposely complained about the cards feeling off, and he had generously opened a new deck. He had no idea it was not the one he thought it to be. It was time to end this charade.

He narrowed his eyes, and I knew he was looking at the marks on my cards, thinking I was bluffing. Thanks to the special cards and the sleight of hand that Edward had taught me, I was ready for him.

"You were interested in the land I hold beside yours at one time," he said slowly.

It took everything in me not to react. I lifted one shoulder as if bored. "It was a boy's idea, which has passed. Now, the state it is in, it has become no longer useful to me."

"Your farmers could change that."

"Is that your offering?" I asked, making my voice sound disinterested. "It hardly has much value."

He nodded, instructing a servant to bring him the deed. When he set it down, I sighed, making it seem as if I was unsure.

"I will add one more thing," he said abruptly.

I frowned at the unexpected offer.

"Which is?"

"A servant for you." Something in his voice set my teeth on edge. He looked delighted, as if he had suddenly thought of a plan.

"I have no need of any servants."

He waved his hand. "This one is special. Been in my house her whole life." He paused. "Untouched. She will be yours to do with what you wish. In fact, I hope you use her then cast her aside when done."

I was shocked at his callous tone. Horrified at his suggestion. I met the eyes of Edward, who also looked dismayed.

"I beg your pardon," I snapped.

He held up his hand. "I mean no disrespect. I know you are a man who prefers experience. Consider this a gift. Whether you win or not."

I realized he fully expected to win. That, in his twisted mind, I would accept a servant in lieu of funds, never suspecting his fraud.

"Bring her in," he ordered his butler.

Once again, I met Edward's gaze, a silent conversation flowing between us. Whoever this servant was, it was obvious Barnett despised her. Wanted her gone and wished for her to suffer.

Nothing prepared me for the young woman who was dragged into the room and pushed in front of me. I automatically rose to my feet as any gentleman would do when a lady entered. I had to grab the edge of the table to remain standing. It was the chit I had seen scurrying away —the one who had captured my interest for some reason. Seeing her fully was a shock.

Draped in a gown that was threadbare and far too large on her small frame, she shrank into herself, as if used to hiding. Her head was bowed, her shaking arms wrapped around her torso. Small feet covered in torn boots peeked out from under the useless garment. It did nothing to hide her form or protect her.

I wondered what the greatest motivation behind her trembling was.

Cold or fear?

I noticed how tiny her hands were that clutched her gown. Surprisingly long fingers gripped the material— digits so slender they were noticeable even through the gloves she wore. That oddity caught me off guard, making me wonder why she would have such heavy gloves on at this time of night. Her arms were rail-thin—in fact, her entire body seemed more childlike than that of a maiden.

Unbound wild, dark hair hid her face. I crossed my arms, feigning disinterest.

"I have no need of a child," I growled, furious.

Lord Barnett leaned forward, his voice dripping in anger.

"Show yourself, girl. Push that horrid mane behind you and look up. Or bear the taste of my displeasure." When she didn't move, he stood. "Your father is speaking!" he roared.

Another jolt of shock hit me.

This was his *daughter*? Why was she being treated as a servant?

Slowly, she straightened her shoulders, using one hand to push away the heavy tresses. She lifted her head, and our gazes locked. I stepped back in disbelief, barely able to hide my horror and shock.

The face she revealed was that of a beautiful skeleton. White skin, beyond pale, stretched taut over high cheekbones. A perfectly formed nose. Small ears. A swan's neck. In contrast with her paleness, her lips were full and red, akin to a slash of crimson on snow. Hers was one of the loveliest faces I had ever beheld with my eyes.

Her hair tumbled past her slender shoulders, and my eyes were drawn to her bosom.

Her breasts were large, heavy. Far too large for her tiny frame. Even standing straight, she tried to hide them, obviously ill at ease.

Her trembling increased as I drew closer. Our eyes met, and I felt the stirrings within my chest as I took in her weary, ancient gaze.

Her eyes were blue—but not the simple blue of the sky or water. They were a shade I could not even describe, that of the ocean on a stormy day, blues and grays mixing and crashing together. Framed by long lashes, they were filled with pain and trepidation.

And pure, abject terror.

I had seen that terror in one other set of eyes. It was a

memory I carried close to my heart—which after all these years still had the power to bring me to my knees.

I hadn't been able to comprehend what I was seeing then, but I recognized it now. And I refused to turn my back on that emotion.

"She'll do."

Her eyes widened, her trembling increasing. I wanted to step forward, whisper reassurances that all would be well, but I could not. Any sign of weakness would put both her and me in danger.

My gaze flickered to Edward. I lifted one eyebrow, and his nod was evident only to me.

He would watch her until this was done.

With determination, I returned to my chair, lifting my brandy and tossing it back. "The bet is agreeable. The sum on the table, your deed to the scrub-brush piece of land, and your servant."

The greedy, inept fool grinned. It was malicious and filled with preemptive victory. "If I win, five thousand pounds is mine."

I filled a marker and tossed it in the pile. "Agreed."

MADELEINE

Dismissed from the den of vice in the drawing room by my father, I hastened through the maze of halls belowstairs, tears blurring my vision. With shaking fingers, I tucked my hair back up into my muslin cap, which had been torn from my head before I entered the room. The Marquess of

Wheaton's words echoed in my mind, fear clawing at my throat with each hurried step.

She'll do.

His voice had been deep and mellifluous, but it had been his dark, impenetrable stare that had worried me, as impossible to read as his grim, harsh countenance had been. He was a much larger man than my father, tall and broad of shoulder with a lean yet muscular build. A man who could overpower me with ease.

I was being presented as a prize to him, as if I were an object or a piece of land. As if I were incapable of feeling. As if I were less than a person. And by the man who had sired me.

I shouldn't have been surprised. My father's disdain for me was as plain as the nose on my face. But when I had been forced into the drawing room by Mrs. Wells, I hadn't anticipated the true purpose for my presence would be so horrifying.

I had not been called to clean up spilled wine or to attend to the hearth or to sweep the carpets. Instead, I had been hauled into the room as an offering.

The eyes of every man in the chamber had been upon me, assessing me as if I were a horse on the auction block at Tattersalls. But I was only being presented to one of them. To the marquess.

What manner of man was Lord Wheaton? And for what purposes would I *do*, as he had so callously stated? If the marquess emerged the victor from the gaming table, would I be forced into servitude at his estate instead of my father's?

My stomach twisted with dread. Or would I be expected to perform other duties for his lordship?

As I rounded a corner in the dank hall, the sound of a mouse scurrying away distracted me. I turned toward the noise and collided with someone. Fresh alarm crept up my spine as I jerked my head forward, struggling to keep from tumbling to my bottom.

The visage before me was concerned and kindly, thank heavens. It was Geraldine, an older and experienced maid who had been here at Cliffwood before I was born. She had been my mother's lady's maid, and though my mother was long gone, Geraldine had remained, despite the lesser position she now held as a housemaid.

"Madeleine. Where are you running to in such a state?"

My heart pounded, and my tongue was thick from shock.

I blinked furiously, struggling to catch my breath. "Forgive me, please. I didn't intend to run into you."

"You needn't apologize, dear girl." Geraldine's brow creased as she studied me with a concerned expression, her slight French accent easy to discern. "What's happened?"

"Mrs. Wells ordered me into the card room," I managed to explain, finding my voice.

"Another spill?" Shaking her head, Geraldine clicked her tongue in disapproval. "Such careless ways, those gentlemen. I suppose I ought not to be surprised, given all the spirits they've requested. We'll be needing to haul out the Axminster after this house party, to be sure. They'll be requiring more than just a sweeping or a beating with all these stains."

I shook my head. "It…it wasn't for a spill. The baron has wagered me to the Marquess of Wheaton."

Geraldine's gray brows snapped together. "Wagered you? What do you mean by that?"

I swallowed hard against a lump of rising panic. "The baron has offered me to Lord Wheaton, along with a piece of land and a sum of money."

"*Offered* you?"

Geraldine was aghast.

It was a mercy that my father's actions were still capable of astonishing her. But then, in my experience, I was alone in bearing the full brunt of his wrath.

I nodded again, incapable of answering.

"But the marquess is a gentleman," Geraldine protested. "A fine lord, I'm told, with a good reputation. Surely he wouldn't accept a maid as gaming spoils. Such a thing isn't done."

"If he were a fine lord with a good reputation, would he be at the baron's table?" I asked, giving voice to the fears churning through me.

She faltered, clearly lacking an answer.

"I think not," I said grimly.

"Oh, my dear girl."

Geraldine startled me by taking me in an embrace. Displays of emotion were not tolerated in the baron's household. If Mrs. Wells were to come upon us standing idle, putting our own concerns before those of Cliffwood, her rage would know no bounds. Geraldine did not deserve to suffer a punishment on my behalf.

But I selfishly clung to her anyway, holding her tightly. It wasn't the first occasion upon which I had needed comfort, but it was the sole time in many years that I had accepted it.

I had endured much during my time at Cliffwood. The prospect of being taken away by a man I didn't know, however, frightened me more than facing my father's wrath ever had.

"Perhaps leaving this place isn't as dreadful as it may seem, Madeleine," she sought to reassure me. "From all accounts, the Marquess of Wheaton is a man of honor. If he were to take you from Cliffwood, at least you'd finally be free of Lord Barnett."

I stiffened and slipped from her embrace. My father despised disloyalty. Any hint of it was ruthlessly punished. "You mustn't say so, Geraldine. 'Tis wrong."

"It isn't wrong if his lordship doesn't hear it. Even if the marquess were to take you as his mistress, it would be a far better life than the one you're living here. Your dear mother would have wanted more for you than being reduced to Lord Barnett's servant."

"My father would not give me to the marquess with the intention that I should become his mistress," I denied dutifully, although I had already considered the possibility.

I wasn't sure which knowledge terrified me more, that my father was capable of anything, or that my entire future now depended upon a game of chance.

CHAPTER 5

ALEXANDER

"*I*mpossible!" Barnett bellowed, pounding on the table and standing.

I lifted one eyebrow, looking confused and indignant. "How is it impossible, pray tell? My three kings beat your sequence." I paused. "Yours is a good second," I added, wanting to twist the knife a little.

"But—but you were not supposed to have a tricon," he sputtered. "Your cards—" He stopped speaking, realizing he was talking himself into a corner.

"Cards you dealt. From your own hand. Cards you opened in front of everyone. Are you saying they are wrong?" I taunted.

"No, of course not." He wiped his brow, clearly distraught. "Another hand. I insist."

"What have you left?" I asked carefully, tempted beyond measure. "Surely you are not willing to risk this fine estate," I mocked.

Edward narrowed his eyes at me, warning me not to push this.

"Milton Manor—the country estate next to yours. I have no use for it."

I had to laugh. "It has been deserted for years, Barnett. The house, or what is left of it, is crumbling—even worse than the scrub brush you have on the table at the moment. The land you have not yet sold is dry and unusable. It has no value or sentimental reason for me to risk what I have earned here." I ran my hands over the winnings. "As tempting as it is."

"You must."

"There is nothing I must do," I said, a warning note in my voice. "I won the pot. I was willing to walk earlier, and you insisted. You knew the risk."

He sat down, defeated. I glanced around, a small fissure of guilt hitting me. I had taken everything. It wasn't him I was worried about, but his servants. The innocents who would suffer. The villagers to whom he no doubt owed for this party. The butcher, the grocer. They would suffer because he had squandered all the money.

I stood. "Contact my solicitor, Barnett. Make a fair offer on the estate, and I will purchase it. Do not risk any more debt."

He glared. "I do not need your charity."

I was puzzled. "You would rather lose another hand, more money, than make an honest trade? Cash for the land and house you agree is worthless."

"And why are you being so charitable?" he demanded.

Aside from Edward and the old butler, we were alone, the last of the players having become bored and seeking brandy and their own company rather than watch the game between us. The hour was late, and I, too, was tired and wanted this evening over. I got what I came for. My land and apparently a new servant. I had no need to add more hard times to this man—even though I disliked him intensely.

"Because I have grown weary and have lost my taste for the game. Perhaps I can salvage something at Milton Manor—at least, what is left of it."

"No."

I shrugged and stood, Edward moving forward to take my winnings from the table. "I will bid you good night, then."

I left him at the table, grabbing the cards, muttering to himself. He would never figure out how the deck was misprinted. He couldn't demand retribution without showing his own misdeeds. He couldn't accuse me of anything for the same reason. It had taken us a long time to figure out the codes and break them, as well as produce an exact match to the cards so he couldn't tell them apart.

We went upstairs, shutting my door behind me.

"This could get disagreeable if he manages to figure it out."

"I am aware."

"I suggest we leave before daylight."

I nodded, scrubbing my hand over my face. "I believe you are correct, my friend."

"He can prove nothing without implicating himself. There would be a long line of angry gentlemen after him if word got out he had been duping these games. His life would be forfeit, I think."

"I know. But best to be safe."

"I will replace our deck of cards with a duplicate of his own before we leave. He will be even more baffled."

"Good." I lit a cheroot, needing the calming action. I exhaled by the window, staring into the darkness.

"And what of the girl?" he asked. "What are your plans?"

The housekeeper had come and removed her from the room once play began again. I recalled her face. The delicate beauty. The painfully thin form under the too-big gown. The terror in her eyes.

"Part of me wants to leave her here. She is not any of my concern. But…" I trailed off, once again her anxiety pushing against my thoughts. "I assume Mrs. Dougall could find a place for her within the household. Or perhaps a situation with Beckett in London. His new wife is a gentle sort. She would be safe there. Or the village. She could find work there if I vouch for her."

"I do not think she would make it on her own," Edward stated quietly. "There is something infinitely… fragile about her."

"London, then." I decided. It would be best if she weren't close. She was distracting in a different sort of way —a displeasing one. I had a feeling that distraction might be my downfall.

MADELEINE

In the storeroom, I attended to my evening duties with only half a mind on the organizing of the goods we had received earlier from the village. They were meager, and I doubted they would be sufficient to accommodate my father's guests for more than a day or perhaps two at best. But maybe the guests would be leaving soon if their sport was at an end.

The thought made a chill sweep over me just as the

familiar footsteps of Mrs. Wells cut through the stillness of the air.

The housekeeper stopped at the threshold to the small room, her face as unreadable as a mask. "Lord Barnett requires you in the drawing room again, girl."

This summons was no different from the last. However, a few hours before, I hadn't any notion of what awaited me. Now, I did. My breath caught.

Instinctively, I knew that the game was over. My fate had been decided whilst I had been tending to the flour and sugar.

"Of course, Mrs. Wells." I curtsied.

Her eyes narrowed. "You will return to completing your evening tasks after his lordship has finished with you."

"Yes, Mrs. Wells."

She nodded and then moved aside, allowing me to pass.

I buried my gloved hands into my well-worn gown, gripping my skirts tightly as I passed through the halls to the servants' stairs. My stomach roiled with each step that took me closer to the drawing room.

What if the men who had assembled were still gathered round the table? What if the Marquess of Wheaton remained? How would I face them? More importantly, how would I face *him*?

I was spared from further worry when I reached the drawing room and found it empty, save my father. He was seated alone at a table strewn with cards and markers, his thinning gray hair mussed as if he had been passing a hand through it relentlessly. His gaze was lowered, pinned upon the cards in disbelief. Tobacco smoke and sour wine heavily tinged the air.

"Mrs. Wells said you had need of me, my lord," I

managed, trepidation making my tongue stick to the roof of my mouth.

Mere hours before, I had been brought here roughly before an audience of strange men, presented as a sacrificial lamb. I feared I already knew the outcome of the game.

"You," he said harshly, his lip curling in a sneer. "Why are you lingering at the threshold? Come in, curse you."

I did his bidding, offering him a curtsy. "What may I do for you, your lordship?"

"Sit," he commanded.

I folded myself into a chair at the opposite end of the table, intentionally keeping myself beyond his reach. Although he had spoken few words, I could hear the telltale slur in his words. His eyes were glazed and bloodshot. By now, I was more than familiar with the signs of dissipation. The deeper he fell into his cups, the angrier he became. And I had no wish to bear the brunt of his rage this night.

I settled my gloved hands in my lap and waited, offering up a silent prayer that I would be spared.

"Such a slovenly baggage," he sneered. "You've been nothing but a burden to me all your life, girl."

My father was a hateful, unhappy man. But I was numbed to his vitriol.

"Forgive me. It was never my intention to burden you."

He slammed his fist down on the table with so much force that I winced. "Such unbridled cheek. Show some humility."

I bowed my head, staring at my entwined hands, trying to keep them from trembling. "Yes, your lordship."

"Mrs. Wells has warned me repeatedly that you are slothful."

The housekeeper's hatred of me was not new. I had

learned that I could not change it. No matter how diligently I worked, she was never satisfied. Still, I knew better than to argue with my father.

I kept my head lowered. "Yes, my lord."

"Mrs. Wells has also reported that your appearance is never that befitting a maid in a grand household such as Cliffwood. She says that you have invited sinful gazes from the footmen."

I lifted my chin, daring to meet my father's irate glare. "I have never behaved in an indecorous fashion, my lord."

"Silence!" he bit out, rapping on the table again, sending the wine yet in his goblet sloshing violently. "Have I given you leave to speak?"

I bit my lip.

"Hold your tongue, girl. You have disgraced me, burdened me, and taken advantage of my generosity for long enough. As of this evening, you will no longer be a millstone around my neck."

I inhaled sharply at his cutting revelation.

It was over, then. My father had lost me in a game of cards. I was to be sent away with the marquess.

"Father," I entreated. "Please, you cannot mean to send me from Cliffwood."

His nostrils flared. "I haven't a choice in the matter. Wheaton defeated me. The bastard cheated, I've no doubt of it. But as a gentleman of honor, I have no recourse other than to acknowledge him as the victor."

Panic seized me in its relentless hold. I wouldn't miss my father. But I would mourn Lydia and Geraldine. I didn't want to go with Lord Wheaton. I couldn't. I had to find a way to remain.

"If he cheated," I began, "then surely there is something that can be done."

"Do you dare to gainsay me?" my father snarled.

"Nothing can be done, and Cliffwood will be the better for your absence."

"No," I whispered. "I beg of you, please don't send me from here."

"It is done," he said with cold finality. "You belong to the marquess. Now be gone from my sight. I never want to see you again."

Trying to stifle a sob, I rose from the chair and curtsied again. As I retreated, a string of vile curses followed me. I had no doubt that my father would spend the rest of the evening getting thoroughly soused.

But there would be no such oblivion for me.

My life had just been forever altered, and there was nothing I could do to stop it.

ALEXANDER

"The preparations have been made for departing Cliffwood in the morning before dawn," Edward reported as we reconvened in my chamber.

I nodded. "Excellent."

"The cards have been changed. It took me a while, as the old fool obviously had a fit of anger and tossed them all about. I had to be sure to find all ours and replace them with the ones we switched out. But it is done, and there is nothing he can do to prove he was not too in his cups to read his own fake cards correctly."

"That is good news indeed, my friend."

"We will be gone soon."

Relief settled over me. It was nigh to midnight.

Nearly two hours had passed since my victory in the drawing room, and I itched with the need to leave this place.

A soft knock startled us, and Edward went to the door, opening it, then admitting an older servant.

She dipped into a curtsy. "Forgive the intrusion, my lord."

"The hour is late. What is it that could not wait until morning?"

"Only the master is furious. In his study, drinking and cursing. That never bodes well for Madeleine."

"Madeleine?"

"Miss Madeleine Smythe, the girl he wagered to you," she said with a sad shake of her head. "Please, my lord, I beg of you, take her when you go. If you leave her here, I fear for her."

"She is his daughter. Surely—"

She interrupted me. Something that surprised me since few dared to do so. "She will suffer even more so because of that," she pleaded. She grabbed my elbow, looking terrified. "You have no idea, my lord. Please take her. Even being ruined is better than the life she has."

I was shocked at her forwardness and sickened at the thought of what this young girl's life must be like. I made a fast decision. "I will take her, but you must accompany us. I refuse to ruin her."

She shook her head in wonder. "You are a good man, my lord. And the little mistress is a rare gem."

"We will leave an hour before dawn. She can take only what she can carry."

"She has little to take, my lord. I have only a small bag."

"Be at the stable, then, at the appointed hour."

She turned, then paused and looked at me, tears in her

eyes. "Bless you, sir. You have saved her. You have saved both of us."

Edward smirked at me after she departed. "It is a good thing we brought the carriage and the horses, then."

I waved my hand. "I will ride with you. The women can have the carriage. I will assist you loading it. We will have to be quiet."

"The amount of drink consumed tonight, I doubt we will disturb many."

"I pray you are right."

"We return to Wheaton?"

"Yes. I have no desire to venture to London. The marriage season is winding up, and I want nothing to do with the anxious mamas and their darling debutantes. God spare me."

Edward laughed.

"The country suits me best."

He nodded in agreement, clapping me on the back.

"Both of us, my lord. Both of us." He rolled his shoulders. "I'll go now to rest a while. Dawn will come early."

"Thank you, Edward."

He threw me a wink. "Always, my lord."

CHAPTER 6

MADELEINE

*T*he carriage swayed over the road, each revolution of its wheels taking me farther from the only home I had ever known. My stomach was knotted with a peculiar combination of anticipation and dread.

He was taking me.

The dark-eyed stranger. The man my father gave me to as if I were of no greater import than a painting on the wall or a mahogany chair. As if I were an object rather than a daughter of flesh and blood and bone. But then, perhaps to the baron, that had been all I ever was. One more possession, his to do with as he liked until he grew weary of me and passed me off to the next household.

You will no longer be a millstone around my neck.

And the stranger, Lord Wheaton. The man who had examined me before callously declaring I would *do*.

For what purpose?

I still didn't know.

I was afraid to ask. All I had to rely upon was Geraldine's assurance that the marquess had told her he had no intention of ruining me. It had been at her urging that I packed what few belongings I possessed in a bandbox and climbed into Lord Wheaton's carriage at dawn.

"You're trembling."

Geraldine's voice pierced my thoughts. At least I had her for accompaniment. I wouldn't be entirely alone. But my heart ached as I thought of Lydia, the sister of my heart, and our tearful parting earlier that morning. I would miss her dreadfully, as I knew she would miss me.

I twisted my gloved hands in my lap and met Geraldine's kind gaze. "The day has been a trying one thus far. I'm a bit overset."

Overset was a woefully inadequate means of describing the maelstrom within me, but my emotions were in such a tumult that I didn't think I could properly make sense of them myself, let alone attempt to explain them to someone else.

"I expect you shall be far safer in the marquess's care than in the baron's," Geraldine said, no doubt seeking to reassure me.

I wanted to believe her. But hope was a dying ember within me, scarcely capable of making flame. It had been for years now.

"Have you learned anything else of Lord Wheaton?" I asked her, wondering yet again about the man I had been given to.

He had at least provided us with the comfort of his carriage for the journey, and a more handsome conveyance I had never beheld. The squabs were sumptuous and comfortable, covered in fine Morocco leather a deep shade of claret with silk trim. The matching linings were of superfine cloth. It was clearly new, a crest proudly emblazoned upon the door, and a far cry from the shabby old carriage the baron kept for his trips to London.

Wealth, however, did not suggest kindness.

"Little more than belowstairs gossip," Geraldine told me, "but I've seen enough with my own two eyes to know that he's nothing like the baron."

Before I could respond, a commotion rose from beyond the carriage, masculine shouts followed by the whinnying of a horse. The conveyance drew to an abrupt halt.

Concern laced through me. For a breath, I suspected the baron had set off after us, changing his mind. I would be removed from the carriage and returned to Cliffwood. I wasn't sure which I feared more, going back to my life of servitude or proceeding to whatever awaited me at Lord Wheaton's mercy.

But suddenly, the door to the carriage burst open to reveal the marquess's steward, his expression grave.

"Is something amiss?" Geraldine asked, reacting before I could.

"I'm afraid so," the steward said. "It's Lord Wheaton."

ALEXANDER

I cursed as I tried to stand, my foot almost collapsing under my weight. But my concern was for Knight. I had not been paying as close attention as I should, and he had stumbled on a large unseen divot in the roadside. He lurched, throwing me from the saddle, and I landed with my foot bent at an odd angle. I ascertained it wasn't broken, but ye gods, it ached.

Edward was at my side immediately, and I waved him off. "Check Knight."

He knelt beside my horse, examining his leg with a trained eye. He rose with a nod. "Lamed, but not broken." He shook his head. "Much like you, my lord."

The carriage had stopped, my servants waiting my direction.

"You need to ride in the carriage. It will be full, but there is not another option. You cannot ride Knight, nor can he carry you." He flashed a smile, wanting to jest with me. "Unless of course, I walk and you ride."

"Do not tempt me," I grunted, not pleased with the idea of being trapped with the servant and the terrified girl. Every time she looked at me, I felt her trepidation and dread. I had not had the time to speak with her, soothe her worry, assure her that she would be safe.

Edward strode forward, opening the carriage door and leaning in to say something. Movement caught my eye, and I was shocked to see a strange girl rise from between the trunks and bags on the carriage roof. Her anxious gaze met my surprised one, and I shouted out.

"Edward! Above you!"

He stepped back from the carriage as the startled girl lurched, her arms acting like windmills as she tried to steady herself and failed. She toppled from the roof, and it was only by some sort of miracle that Edward caught her, holding her in his arms.

For a moment, the air was silent as he stared down at her. Then he set her on her feet.

"Who are you?" he demanded. "What are you on about? Did Barnett send you?"

"No, sir," she gasped. "Never."

Miss Smythe appeared at the door of the carriage, looking shocked and confused. "Lydia?"

The girl, Lydia, I presumed, turned and gasped. "Oh, Maddie!"

"What are you doing here? Where have you come from?" Miss Smythe climbed from the carriage, embracing the girl. The two began a fast conversation I could not hear. Edward, however, seemed to know what they were saying, his countenance going from puzzled to shocked to almost delighted.

I shut my eyes, trying to seek my forbearance. It had been a trying time since I left London. The baron and his insufferable attitude. His rude guests. The blasted card game and the acquisition of a guest I didn't want and an older servant—both of whom I was now responsible for. Sneaking away like a thief under the cloak of darkness. Knight's accident. Now, with the appearance of Lydia, I was at the end of my tether.

I was exhausted and sat down in the dirt on the side of the road, not caring about my breeches, my station, or anything else. It pained me too much to keep standing, and I had no idea what was about to occur next.

A moment later, Edward came over, hunching beside me. "Are you well, Alexander?"

"Explain to me what has occurred."

"Lydia is, *was*, a servant at Barnett's. When she heard Miss Smythe was leaving, she refused to stay. She wedged herself up on the carriage between the trunks."

"And she planned to remain hidden the entire journey?" I asked in disbelief. It would be hot when the sun rose and awkward. Dangerous.

"She said she would rather die than stay."

I lifted my eyebrows. "A bit melodramatic," I muttered. "What is she seeking?"

"To stay with Miss Smythe. Wherever you take her."

I looked past his shoulder to where Miss Smythe stood, her arm around her fellow servant. Except she wasn't truly one of them. Yet for the first time, I saw something other than fear in her gaze. Determination. I sensed if I said no, she would refuse to travel on without her friend. And I refused to leave her on a dark, lonely road.

"Fine," I granted, in too much pain to argue. "But that makes the carriage even fuller."

"I can ride on the box," Lydia spoke up. "I hate being inside." I waved my hand, indicating for her to do exactly that, watching as she scrambled back up.

Edward helped me to my feet, and I tried not to grimace as we hobbled to the carriage. I climbed in, sitting down, scowling as Edward lifted my leg to the seat opposite. Geraldine pursed her lips but sat next to me, leaving Miss Smythe no choice but to sit beside my rapidly swelling foot.

I glanced at Edward. "Take us to Wheaton. As swiftly as possible."

Swift was impossible with Knight's injury. Inside the carriage, no one spoke. I had my eyes shut, trying to ignore the pain in my foot. Miss Smythe was pushed into the farthest corner of the seat, not looking anywhere but her lap. The only one to make any noise was Geraldine, who sat next to me, knitting. On occasion, she stopped, lifting a hand to her mouth, then with a shake of her head, continued, her countenance drawn. I was too preoccupied with fighting the ache in my foot to question her as to her welfare. When she did knit, the click-clack of the needles was somehow both soothing and irksome, but I kept my mouth shut.

The carriage stopped, and Edward came to the door.

"My lord, Knight cannot continue without risking further injury."

"Bloody hell," I growled. I did not wish him more harm.

"There is a coaching inn a short distance ahead. I can remain with Knight and a groom. Perhaps a fresh set of horses will take you on to Wheaton more swiftly. I will follow once Knight is rested and his leg attended to."

I nodded in acknowledgment.

We arrived at the inn and disembarked from the coach. I refused to stay behind as Edward spoke to the innkeeper, making the proper arrangements, while the women went inside for refreshments.

We slowly headed in that direction, my foot feeling as if it were on fire. My gait was halting and painful, and we stopped for a moment to allow me to catch my breath. Lydia appeared from the inn and hurried in our direction.

"Bollocks, what now?" I breathed out.

Lydia curtsied in front of me. "Pardon me, my lord, but Geraldine has requested she remain behind with your, ah, Mr., ah…" She trailed off, unsure.

"Mr. Warwick. Why does she wish to stay behind?"

She leaned in. "She was bilious in the carriage and cannot continue."

Edward shook his head. "I cannot attend her."

"I will remain behind as well. I can't be inside a carriage."

"Blast it. And what of Miss Smythe?" I demanded.

"I will travel with you, my lord." Her soft voice broke into our discussion. I had not noticed her approach, yet now that I saw her, she eclipsed anything else in my vision.

"You need a chaperone," I insisted, meeting her unique gaze.

"It matters not. No one knows of me. Who I am,

where I am going. I am but a lowly maid. I believe, from what Geraldine has ascertained, that you are a gentleman of the highest standing."

I frowned at her brave words.

"Your coachman and servant will be there," she added.

"And they would ignore any wrongdoing on my part," I insisted.

She lifted her chin. "I am not afraid."

The obvious solution was clear. We all would stay at the inn until Geraldine was able to travel again. I suggested it, but Lydia spoke. "Geraldine is worried that the master will awaken and regret his drunken wagers. He may be angry and perhaps chase after Maddie. She urges you to take her."

I cursed Barnett as I watched the color drain from Miss Smythe's face. It was plain that she feared her father.

And the truth was, I wanted to return to Wheaton today. To the quiet order my life had there. Away from all the excesses of the life someone of my station was forced to live with. I was weary. Tired of this journey and the constant twists and turns it had taken.

"Fine," I ground out. "We leave as soon as the horses are ready."

I settled into the soft leather of the carriage with a grateful sigh as we began to move. Across from me, Miss Smythe was once again pressed against the farthest corner, her face pale, her gloved hands fisted on her lap. I noticed how thick the gloves appeared to be—not the delicate type I was used to seeing ladies wear, but these appeared more protective. I briefly contemplated why that would be, then dismissed my thoughts. It was not my concern. Yet the words were out of my lips before I could stop them.

"Are your hands not warm in those gloves? It is a hot day."

She startled at my voice, lifting her head to meet my eyes. I saw the worry and dismay in hers, and once again, it hit me fully in my chest, making me want to ease that distress.

"I am used to them," she whispered, her fingers moving restlessly over her skirts.

"Fear me not, my lady. You are safe with me."

"I am not a lady. Not any longer. I am simply a maid. You may call me Madeleine if you desire."

I tilted my head in acknowledgment. The carriage went over a large bump, causing my foot to jump on the seat. I bit back a groan, shutting my eyes. The pain was growing in its intensity. Edward had wanted to fetch a physician, but I refused, knowing it would delay my departure. I would see my own physician, Dr. Atwood, when we arrived at Wheaton.

"You are in pain, my lord."

"Yes," I said through gritted teeth.

"Might you allow me to help you?"

I frowned in confusion. "May I ask how you propose to do that?"

She bit her lip and slid forward. "I spent a great deal of time in the stable watching the grooms work on the horses when he—my father—still had many. When an animal was hurt, they rubbed down the leg with liniment and bandaged it. I tried it once when I fell down the steps and injured my foot. It helped greatly. I practiced wrapping limbs on Lydia and Geraldine and the other servants if they were injured. Perhaps you would allow me to try to ease your discomfort?"

"You wish to rub horse liniment on my skin?" I asked, askance. It was strong and effective for animals—but humans?

"No," she assured me. "It is not for animals. It will not harm you, I assure you, my lord."

I paused. That meant she would touch me—a wildly inappropriate occurrence between an unmarried maiden and someone like me. I weighed the consequences.

"Perhaps if you thought of me as a ward and yourself my guardian, you would feel at ease?" she questioned, somehow knowing exactly my worries.

"Yes," I answered promptly. "Until I decide your future, I am your guardian." I indicated my foot. "Please begin."

CHAPTER 7

ALEXANDER

I had never known a touch as tender and gentle. Or as comforting. From a battered bandbox, Madeleine produced some rags and a tin of liniment. The box was the only item she brought with her, and she had refused to part with it, sliding it under her skirts as she sat. I didn't argue with her, already feeling dismay that her entire cache of worldly goods was in a case of such disrepair.

She turned her back, removing her gloves, not allowing her hands to be visible. She carefully set my leg on the seat beside her, pulling off my boot and inspecting my foot. I was shocked at the size of it and the large discoloration on the ankle.

"You are fortunate this did not break the bone, my lord," she murmured, running her fingers over the hot skin.

I only grunted in response, unable to form words as she applied some of the ointment and began kneading it into the skin. I could smell the liniment, the aroma of herbs not unpleasant. Her touch was so light it didn't bother me, and to my surprise, the pain eased slightly. There was a slight feeling of roughness to her skin, but I did not comment, assuming it was from years of toiling, and I did not wish to embarrass her further. I watched from under narrowed eyes as she worked. She had a small wrinkle between her eyes as she concentrated, and she hummed under her breath, a welcome sound in the carriage. I was certain she did not realize she was doing so, and I chose not to remark on it. There was none of her nervousness, or qualms about touching a strange man—she was determined and calm.

"Where did the liniment come from?" I queried.

"One of the servants had a mother who was a healer. I twisted my foot badly, and she kindly made it up for me. Between that and the bandages, it healed quickly."

"Ah." There was a healer in the village by Wheaton whom I consulted with from time to time.

"I had to hide it from my father."

"The liniment?"

"All of it. The small rags I tore for bandages. The fact that I spoke with people in the stables. Or aided the servants."

"Your father is the devil," I stated mildly.

A ghost of a smile graced her lips, but she remained quiet, stroking her fingers gently along the injured area, never hurting, only soothing. She stopped and reached into the bag again, producing some rolled rags. She tied one around my foot so it was tight, but not painful. She handed me a small bundle of linen, and I opened it to find an apple, bread, and cheese nestled inside.

"You did not eat at the inn. I thought perhaps you would need sustenance."

Something warm cracked inside my chest, leaking throughout my person. She was incredibly kind and caring. Sweet in her thoughts and gestures. Given the situation she had left behind, it was a pleasing surprise to discover that she wasn't bitter and angry.

"Thank you."

"Keep your foot relaxed and up," she encouraged. "I believe that aids the healing as well."

I munched the apple and ate the bread and cheese. I longed for a whiskey but knew that would have to wait until we reached Wheaton. Madeleine pulled on her gloves, then placed her things back in her bandbox, but as we hit another jarring bump, it fell from her hands, a few items falling to the floor and seat of the carriage. Some small pieces of paper fluttered in the air, and I pulled one down, examining it.

It was a sketch done in pencil. I was amazed at the detail in the small etching. How lifelike the petals and stems were of the flowers. I lifted my gaze, meeting hers.

"Is this your illustration?"

"Y-yes," she stuttered.

"Have you others?"

She nodded, and I held out my hand. "I would like to see them, if you please."

She hesitated and then reached into her bag, pushing a few scraps of rag paper into my hand. Each sketch was a delight for the eyes. Flowers, horses, a meadow. One of Lydia, the likeness so clear on the small scrap, it was as if I were staring at a portrait.

"Madeleine, you are talented."

She didn't respond.

I held up the minute pile. "Why on such scraps?"

"Only what my father discarded. I didn't dare take a sheet from his desk. And I had only the very stubs of pencils to use."

"I do not understand your father's mind-set. Why you have been treated as a maid."

"Nor do I, my lord." She sighed as I handed her the pretty scraps. "Sometimes I wish it were not so. Sometimes…" She trailed off.

"Sometimes?"

Her voice was so low I had to strain to hear it. "There were moments I hated my father. I wished him gone. I prayed he wasn't my real father, and I would be taken elsewhere to live a different life. I wanted to run, but I had nowhere to go. There were times I wished to spit in his tea. Infest his study with mice, which he loathed, so he would return to the city until they were gone. Add salt peter to his food. My thoughts were wicked, and my father often told me I was wicked as well. As if he knew my thoughts."

I withheld my laughter at her supposed wickedness.

"My thoughts would have been far darker," I assured her. "Nor do I believe you to be wicked."

She shook her head in disbelief, settled her bag back under her skirts, and stared out the window.

The afternoon light accentuated her profile. She would be a great beauty once she was stronger. Healthier. I suspected she had many hidden depths which needed to be encouraged. I imagined her smile would be a wondrous sight.

I was surprised to realize I would like to see that smile.

To have it directed toward me.

I was also astounded to discover that she was quite fascinating.

"Do you have other interests?" I asked.

She frowned. "At one time, I did, my lord. Many."

"Such as?"

"I played the piano, did needlepoint, had dance lessons, and studied French. My mother taught me to sew and how to garden. She was a different sort of lady, and she loved to cook. She taught me several dishes. I used to love to read and to stroll in the garden. I loved to swim. To play cards. Do figures."

I gaped at her list of accomplishments. She had been raised as a lady with some interesting twists to her personality.

"Figures?" I asked, curious.

"My grandmother was a little eccentric. When her husband died, she eschewed society. She taught my mother everything she needed, but also many things ladies are not shown. I can use a sword rather well too."

"How remarkable."

"My father didn't think so. He thought I was vapid and useless."

"Frankly, my sweet, your father is an arse."

She laughed, the sound honeyed and high, making me want to laugh with her. Then she clapped a hand over her mouth as if afraid to hear herself enjoying a light-filled moment. She was beautiful in her levity, and I found myself even more drawn to her.

"Do you ride?" I asked, needing to distance myself from my thoughts.

The light on her face dimmed. "Yes. But not since my mother passed." She swallowed and looked away. "I had a horse I loved. She was a gift from my mother, and we would ride together. When she died, Father sold Star, making me watch as she was taken away." She lifted my eyes. "I begged him not to, but he gave me a choice—sell her or he would shoot her."

I shut my eyes at the cruelty she had endured. Reaching for her hands, I held them in mine.

"How old were you?"

"Four and ten."

"May I ask how she died?"

"She was ill. One day, she seemed fine. The next, she was not. She died a few days later."

"You must have been devastated."

"I was. I still miss her. My entire life changed after she died."

I asked her some more questions, enjoying listening to her pleasant voice, discovering an intelligence she kept hidden. We discussed art, her love of the subject obvious. She admitted she loved to sing but hadn't raised her voice in song since her mother died.

"Except once," she admitted, her hands twisting again on her lap. I stifled the urge to reach over and calm the nervous gesture.

"What occurred?"

"My father heard me and locked me in my quarters for three days without food. Only water—and a very small amount, at that. I never sang again."

I felt the hatred I had toward Barnett grow. Blossom. Take on a life of its own.

His vile treatment toward his daughter was abominable. He told me to ruin her. Cast her aside, he said, his voice almost gloating in glee.

I thought of my idea of taking her elsewhere to be looked after. It felt wrong to take her to a new situation or have her work in the village. Serving others. She had done that far too long.

"Madeleine," I said gently, waiting until she met my eyes. "I wish to ask something of you, and I would like you to speak the truth to me. There will be no consequences for honesty. Can you do that?"

"Yes, my lord."

"How old are you?"

"One and twenty."

That news pleased me, a kernel of an idea growing in

my mind. Like a mist flowing over a field in the morning, it was still thin and wispy but beginning to take shape.

"Have you been to London?"

"London?" she repeated. "No, I have never been."

"I have a friend there, newly married. His wife is a gentle soul. You would be well treated there. Would that please you? To be away from your father and live in the city?"

She hesitated, then shook her head. "No, my lord. I would prefer to remain in the country. But if you feel it is for the best, I will do so, as it will be better than what my life was at my father's."

"If you could choose your future, what would it be?"

Her voice was low. "I have not been able to hope for a future for a long time. When I was younger, I wanted a home of my own in the country. A husband and a family. I wished for happiness."

I contemplated her. Thought of her upbringing. Reflected back on a conversation I'd had with Edward some time ago.

"You need a wife and an heir," he informed me. "Soon. Your future is at stake."

I had waved him off, but his words hit me soundly again, like an echo that refused to stop.

I required a future. Madeleine had none.

I found her beguiling. Her nature sweet and kind. To my astonishment, I liked her. For some reason, she delighted me. Recalling Geraldine's words of her being a rare gem, I had to agree. She deserved more than the drudgery of toiling as a servant the rest of her life. She deserved to be the lady she was born to be.

The wispy idea solidified quickly in my brain, taking shape, causing me to smile. If I saw it to its completion, not only would I have acquired the land I desired, but I would also have angered Barnett to utter distraction when the news reached him. Beaten him at his own game. Then I would work on taking Milton Manor and completely ruining him. But that would be a dividend to the entire idea.

I studied Madeleine from under partially closed eyes. She had no idea I was watching her. Tallying up her potential. I discerned a backbone in her somewhere that her father had tried to remove. I saw it when she tried to defend her friend. When she insisted on aiding my suffering.

She was stronger than I thought—and much braver and fiercer than her father ever gave her credit for.

She would make a fine wife.

My idea was perfect. And to my surprise, the thought of it suited me. I grunted in surprise.

"My lord, are you well?"

"Indeed, Madeleine," I assured her. "Very well indeed."

MADELEINE

As the carriage rolled down the approach to the marquess's country seat, I found myself shockingly grateful for the last few unexpected hours. Despite the cramped nature of the latter portion of the journey, thanks to the marquess's massive size taking up so much of the conveyance's fine interior, I had enjoyed his company. The necessity of aiding him had assuaged the fear keeping me in its relentless thrall, and I had become persuaded that Lord

Wheaton was not at all like my father. He had shown me courtesy and kindness, taking an interest in my past and accomplishments.

Our conversation had reminded me of the girl I had once been, a girl I had been forced to lock away as if she had never existed.

He was still in pain from the injury to his leg, but some of the strain had fled his countenance. The tense lines around his mouth had relaxed, suggesting that perhaps he had been similarly put at ease by our time together and my tending his foot. I didn't fool myself that I had charmed him, of course. I was the daughter of a baron, but I had spent the last few years earning my keep as a housemaid. I was below Lord Wheaton in station.

Still, speaking with him had been effortless.

"We approach Wheaton," he told me in his deep, soothing baritone.

There was pride in his voice as he spoke of his home.

"The journey wasn't as arduous as I worried it would be, my lord," I commented. "How is your injury? Is it paining you?"

"Thanks to your ministrations, I will be well enough now that I am where I belong. Wheaton is a true beauty."

He was not looking at his estate as he uttered the words, however. He was gazing upon *me*.

Warmth crept up my throat. I liked the way his dark gaze fell over me. The way he seemed to see me. These were dangerous feelings, and I knew it. Lord Wheaton wasn't courting me. I had never graced a ballroom and had spent a third of my life as a servant. The marquess was a handsome man, kind and capable and intelligent. Judging from his fine carriage, he was also wealthy. No doubt he had all the ladies in London eagerly setting their caps at him. Besides, he intended to send me away as soon as he could.

I banished the sudden pang that notion caused in the vicinity of my heart. Why should I wish to linger here? Wheaton was not my home any more than Cliffwood had been.

I cleared my throat. "I'm pleased that I was able to be of use, my lord. It's the least I can do, given your generosity."

"Generosity?" A dark brow rose. "My dear Madeleine, all I've managed to do is injure myself and allow you to tend to my lame foot."

My cheeks heated even more at his intense regard and the note of praise in his voice. I was accustomed to my father's disapproval. Lord Wheaton's appreciation for my efforts secretly thrilled me.

"It was my pleasure to help in any way I could."

"And it was my pleasure to share this carriage with you and to be afforded the opportunity to become acquainted with you."

We stared at each other, my heart quickening until I was certain he must hear it above the din of jangling tack, creaking wood, and falling hooves.

The carriage rocked to a halt.

I looked away from him, past the Venetian blinds on the carriage window, to the manor house that loomed beyond. My breath caught in my throat, for the marquess's home was at least thrice the size of Cliffwood, and its faultless exterior showed nary a hint of disrepair.

But not only was Wheaton impressive in size and grandeur, the commanding edifice was simply an architectural marvel.

"Here we are at last," the marquess said softly.

I took in the grand stairs flanking either side of the

entrance, the Doric columns, high sloped roof, and at least forty windows across the front facade alone.

"I hope you will feel at home at Wheaton," he added.

This was not a home. It was a palace.

"I am certain I shall," I managed weakly.

My mind went to the task of cleaning all those windows, of beating the carpets that would line the immense floors. Maintaining such an impressive household would require an army of domestics. Perhaps I could be incorporated into the servants here. I didn't doubt, after my time spent during the journey with the marquess, that he would be a fair man. He would not be exacting, unjust, or cruel and callous as my father had been.

Yes, mayhap I might find a place for myself here after all, if he allowed it. I truly had no wish to dwell in London. The thought of it frightened me, although I had to admit, it would be better than staying at Cliffwood.

"Madeleine, there is something I wish to discuss with you," he said, his tone shifting.

I forced my attention back to the marquess, painfully aware I had been gaping at his estate like any green country girl. What must he think of me? I was a maid he had taken as forfeit in a game of cards, and yet he had treated me as if I were a duke's daughter instead of a wastrel baron's despised offspring.

I needed to show him the deference he deserved, to remember my place.

"Of course, my lord," I said, bowing my head.

Over the course of our journey to Wheaton, I had allowed myself to forget the vast differences between us. The marquess was a wealthy, powerful gentleman in his own right, and yet he had not been haughty or cold. When we had been conversing, it had been easy to think of us as simply man and woman. His polite interest in me had quite battered the walls I ordinarily kept around myself.

"Madeleine."

I waited, thinking that now would be the time he would inform me of his true intentions. I would be sent away sooner rather than later. But I had no wish to go to London, as I had told him earlier. Perhaps I might somehow persuade him to keep me here. I could be of service. I'd already proven myself with the liniment and binding of his foot, had I not?

He cleared his throat. "Would you look at me. Please?"

I glanced up instantly, our gazes meeting, that same surge of awareness I had experienced from the first moment our paths had crossed in the drawing room cutting through me. Stealing my breath.

"You know why I have brought you with me, do you not?"

I nodded. "My father offered me to you."

"At the time Barnett had you forcibly brought into the drawing room, I had no intention of accepting."

I swallowed hard against a rush of disappointment. It sounded as if there would be no place for me here after all.

"Of course, my lord."

"My intention, after I saw your terror and the baron's intolerable treatment of you, was to see you somewhere safe."

"To your friends in London."

"Quite." He paused, his jaw hardening.

"Is it your foot, my lord? Are you in pain again?" I asked, thinking that perhaps he would require more liniment now.

"It is not my foot. It is the matter of making a rather delicate request of you that has me searching for words." He puffed out a small laugh.

A new kind of warmth settled over me. Not shame but something else. Something far more dangerous.

"You wish for me to be your mistress," I blurted.

The marquess stared at me in silence, his expression inscrutable.

Would I accept? It was far more honorable to be a maid. But the marquess was a handsome man. A fair man. A kind man. And I…

I *liked* him. I found him intriguing. And he seemed to think me equally interesting, if his questions during the carriage ride had been any indication. As Geraldine had told me in her practical, no-nonsense way, I would be better served by ruining myself than by remaining at my father's home. She hadn't been wrong when she had told me that my mother would have wanted more for me than the life of a maidservant.

"I don't want you to be my mistress, Madeleine," Lord Wheaton said, cutting through my wildly racing thoughts.

My stomach plummeted. How embarrassing. Why would a gentleman like the Marquess of Wheaton wish to take a maid as his mistress? What a fool I was to believe it even for a heartbeat.

"Forgive me for the conclusion, my lord," I hastened to say, misery churning in my belly.

"I want you to be my wife," the marquess announced.

The carriage door swung open in the next moment, which was just as well, for I found that my tongue was incapable of coherent speech.

CHAPTER 8

ALEXANDER

"Are you well, my lord?" Madeleine whispered.

"I am fine. Do not fret so," I assured her.

The footman reappeared, handing me one of my walking sticks. I stepped from the carriage gingerly, pleased at how much better my foot felt. I turned, holding out my hand for Madeleine to assist her in stepping down. She did so, and I marveled at how tiny she was next to me. She reached to my chest, and I felt the incredible draw of wanting to wrap my arms around her, rest my chin on her dark hair, and breathe her in. While seated close in the carriage, her light scent of lilacs had been constant. I found it pleasant and thought how it suited her.

She stared past me in wonder at my estate, and I followed her gaze, smiling at the look of delight on her lovely face.

"Come," I said, tugging on her hand and placing it into the crook of my arm. "I am anxious to show you my home."

"It is wondrous, my lord."

We made our way to the door, the steps making me

grateful for the support of the walking stick. Mrs. Dougall, my housekeeper, waited, patient but worried for me. "My lord, are you well?"

I waved her off. "A simple sprain." I paused, suddenly at a loss for words. How did I explain my unexpected guest? I decided brevity was the best solution.

"Mrs. Dougall, may I present Miss Madeleine Smythe? She will be staying with us."

She gave Madeleine a kind smile. "Welcome to Wheaton."

Madeleine returned her smile with a small bob and a murmured thank you. I resisted the temptation to tell her that she bowed to no one, but I decided to let it go for now. She was nervous and worried. I could see her hand twisting and grasping at her too-large gown, her unease evident in the tightness of her voice and the tension in her shoulders.

"Kindly show her to her room," I asked.

"Very good, my lord."

I allowed Madeleine to walk in ahead of me, pausing as Mrs. Dougall asked me a question.

"Which room shall I prepare?"

I withheld telling her that Madeleine would be taking over the marchioness room next to mine. "The rose room. I believe she would enjoy a bath and some quiet time. Once you have settled her, please see me in my study. I have much to discuss with you."

"Of course. And Mr. Warwick?"

"Is behind a day or two. Knight was hurt and required a rest." I rubbed my eyes. "And he will be bringing other guests."

She only nodded, not asking who or any other questions. "I will attend to it all."

"Thank you."

TWO HOURS LATER, I was in my study, surrounded by the warm familiarity of being home. I had always preferred Wheaton to town. The quiet to the bustle of London. The aroma of fresh air and good earth to the cloying scent of the crowded ballrooms and unpleasant smell of the city. Too many bodies crammed together, producing too much noise and odor for my taste.

My valet wrapped my foot, his work quick and efficient. I missed the gentle touch of Madeleine's hands on my skin, but before we separated in the lower hallway, she had pressed her small jar of liniment into my hand, instructing me to use it every few hours. Jones had added some before he bandaged the injured limb, but it was far rougher treatment than I had received earlier from Madeleine.

A knock on my door paused my thoughts, and I called for the person to enter, not surprised to see Mrs. Dougall come in. She carried a tray, setting it on the desk.

"I thought you might be in need of some food, my lord."

"Thank you for your thoughtfulness."

"I took a tray to the little mistress as well."

I was amused at her words. That was how Geraldine described her. "How is she faring?"

She pursed her lips. "Might I speak plainly, my lord?"

"Please do."

"Confused and bewildered. She thought I had taken her to the wrong room. She believed she should be in the servants' quarters, but I assured her she was in the right place. When the bath was ready, I offered to help, but she insisted she was fine. I had the feeling the bath was an unexpected treat for her."

"She is, ah, not used to being offered help or nicer things."

"I thought as much."

"Mrs. Dougall, I know this is unorthodox, but Miss Smythe has been in a situation in which I could not leave her. I brought her with me, planning on taking her to a new placement in London, but I have changed my mind."

"Do you wish me to take her under my wing?"

I sighed. "No, I find her delightful and intriguing. She was raised as a lady and deserves to be one." I met her eyes. "I intend to make her one. As my wife."

Her eyebrows lifted in surprise, but she said nothing. I liked that about my housekeeper. Nothing shocked her, and she was always ready to aid me.

"It will happen quickly."

"I shall air out the marchioness's room in preparation."

"Please. I will let her change it in any fashion she wishes once we are wed. It requires some refurbishment, I believe."

"It was done over not long ago, but we can make any changes she wishes."

"And Mr. Warwick will be bringing a young lady who will be her lady's maid. And an older woman—is there a situation here you can fit her into? Something not too strenuous?"

"Of course."

"Miss Smythe has come from unusual and trying circumstances. She is easily spooked and is fearful of the world around her. I will endeavor to help ease her back into society, but we will be staying here for the foreseeable future."

She looked sympathetic. "How sad for her."

"Her life was frightful. She was forced to be a servant in her own home and mistreated. I could not leave her there."

"You are a good man, my lord."

"You have always been biased."

She shook her head, looking sad. "And you will reside in London?"

"No, I plan to make this our home."

Those words cheered her up. "You have always preferred your time at Wheaton."

"I have."

She hesitated. "My lord, the young lady informed me she would stay in her room unless you summoned her and she wouldn't require dinner."

I frowned. "Of course she needs dinner."

Mrs. Dougall met my confused gaze. "She stated she cannot attend your table dressed worse than a servant, my lord. That was what she said to me." Her eyes shone with sympathy. "She was so ashamed. It hurt my heart to hear her confession. And knowing some of what she has been through, I feel it even more deeply."

"She has nothing," I stated, thinking of the small case she had brought and hating the fact that Madeleine had been made to feel less. "I need to aid her but am unsure how."

"Perhaps, if you are amenable, I can go to the village and see if the dressmaker has anything suitable. A simple gown perhaps that would fit her."

"Yes," I agreed eagerly. "Anything you see that you feel would be appropriate. I will settle the account tomorrow when I am able to move a bit easier. Purchase whatever you think is best."

She stood. "I shall, my lord." She paused. "And I

believe you will be happy with your decision, if I might be so bold as to state my thoughts."

I chuckled at her directness. I had known her for most of my life, and she often stated her thoughts, whether or not I wished to hear them.

"One last thing—she may have questions. About me. Feel free to answer."

"My lord?"

"She knows nothing of me. The person I am. She will undoubtedly need some of her worries laid to rest. You would be the person she might ask. I give you leave to tell her your thoughts on my, ah, *character*," I said with a small smirk.

"I shall indeed," she replied with a lift of her eyebrow. "I shall tell her how you muck in the fields and track dirt across my freshly washed floors. That you roam around without a proper cravat." Her tone softened. "That you treat your servants and tenants with a respect and kindness that very few men of your station would ever think to do. I will tell her how respected and well thought of you are— despite these minor unconventional behaviors you have."

I chuckled at her speech. I was rather eccentric, but I believed life was short and should be enjoyed. And if one could not do so in their own home, where could they? Besides, she knew I was fond of her, and she felt the same of me. I had no qualms in letting her speak to Madeleine.

"Thank you, Mrs. Dougall."

She departed, and I leaned back in my chair. Once I convinced Madeleine to join me for dinner, I would have a greater task to convince her to marry me. I was only hoping that she, too, would be happy with my decision.

CHAPTER 9

MADELEINE

I stared at the note, reading and rereading the dark, masculine scrawl. The written words both thrilled me and filled me with dread.

Madeleine—

I request your presence in the library this evening for dinner.

Please know it matters not to me what you wear—a potato sack borrowed from the kitchen would be lovely if you donned it. But I believe a solution is at hand.

We shall eat later, as you may rest. Please join me at seven. We have much to discuss.

Yours,

Alexander

Much to discuss.

Yours, Alexander.

He believed himself to be mine? That I was his, then?

His announcement before his footman opened the door of the carriage drifted through my mind continuously. I could not stop thinking of it.

When he had simply informed me he wished to marry me, I was speechless. Certain it was but a cruel jest on his part.

Except the way he looked at me—his dark gaze all at once sincere and intense—I knew he was not jesting. I had never had a man stare at me the way he did. Bold. Decisive. In command.

Making me breathless and want things I did not comprehend nor was able to understand.

But I knew this. Lord Wheaton was not a cruel man. After the time we had spent in the carriage, I knew that with an absolute certainty. The way he had spoken of his estate, his regard for the land and his farmers. His worry over his horse. He never complained about how much pain he had to be in, only accepting my attempts to ease it with a warm, genuine smile of gratitude. He was polite and honest with his emotion when he thanked me for the small repast I had thought to bring him. Praised my talent for drawing. Asked me question after question about my life. His open disdain for my father made me want to laugh. He was amusing, and his unfiltered words were as accurate as they were scandalous.

Yet, they made me feel better on some level I could not identify. And he seemed to regard me with respect and perhaps a little admiration.

I knew I admired him. He was rakishly handsome. I loved the way he wore his hair—far too long to be fashionable, yet I sensed he cared not a whit for others' opinions. It suited him, and I wondered how he would look with it loose. I could see the waves in the thick brown strands, and I felt the urge to touch them and ascertain if they were as soft as they appeared to be. He smelled of fresh air and cut grass—rich and lush in the sun. I couldn't stop staring at his broad shoulders, the sheer size of him dwarfing me.

Yet I was not afraid to be alone with him.

But...*marriage*? To me?

Why would he desire such a thing? I was certain he could have any woman he set his eyes on.

I was nothing. A nobody. A discarded daughter of a baron who was cruel and unjust. Disliked and unrespected by many. I had heard the other servants talk. Caught whispers of the many rumors of his debts and dishonor. Deep in my own heart, I was embarrassed to be associated with him and grateful I was only thought of as a servant by most people.

Why would Lord Wheaton want me?

A knock brought me from my confused thoughts, and I crossed the room, opening the door. Mrs. Dougall bustled in, fabric draped over her arm, a small bundle clutched in the other.

She laid the fabric on the bed, and I gasped when I saw what it was.

A pretty gown. Not only one. Four of them that she spread out on the mattress, then stepped back with a satisfied smile and a nod. From the bundle, she produced a smart pair of nankeen walking boots, a night rail, and some underpinnings. A proper hairbrush and a set of lovely combs.

"I believe these will fit well enough for now," she informed me.

"I don't understand."

She patted the closest gown. "Lord Wheaton asked me to get you some proper-fitting clothing. The dressmaker in the village had a lady come through and order some pieces for her daughter but never returned for them. They looked to me as if they would suit for the time being."

I blinked, running my hand over the fabric. The gloves covering my skin prevented me from feeling the soft material, but I could see they were lovely pieces. Simple but well made, with beautiful stitching and lace. I caught sight of a soft pink walking gown trimmed with passementerie at the hem, complete with a matching spencer, and a pale-jonquil muslin day gown that was spare of trimmings and perfect for the country. There was even a riding habit in Pomona green. The last one was an evening gown of deep celestial blue, stunning in the vividness of the color. It was more elegant, yet still refined, the bodice ornamented with embroidered rosebuds. I loved every single one.

"I added these as well, child," she murmured, handing me a pair of the softest kid gloves I had ever beheld in an ivory color trimmed in a rich brown. "The master said you always wear gloves. These are lighter than what I think you have and would be more comfortable."

I stared down at the gifts laid out before me. I had been still a child the last time I was given a new dress to wear. My own boots. Fresh underpinnings.

I looked around the room, the rose-covered walls feminine and elegant. The comfortable bed and the large armchair where I could soak up the heat of the fire that was banked low at the moment. The long and beautifully scented bath I had been allowed to relax in at my leisure earlier. I could scarcely believe all this was happening.

"Am I dreaming?" I whispered.

Mrs. Dougall smiled. "I think perhaps, my dear, you are finally waking up from a long, bad dream."

I caught my lip in my teeth, worrying the flesh. I met her eyes, and she nodded slightly, seeing my question.

"Ask me," she instructed.

"Have you known Lord Wheaton a long time?"

"Yes. I came here as a maid in my young years. He was a lad. Eventually, he became the marquess and made me his housekeeper. My husband is the head gardener and keeps a small cottage on the property, and I join him there when I'm able. We are fortunate Lord Wheaton has made an exception for us."

I knew how rare it was for a housekeeper to marry, let alone live at the same estate as her husband. It was another example of the marquess's generosity of spirit, and I was heartened by Mrs. Dougall's revelations.

"Is he—is he a good man?" I asked, my heart thumping in my chest so loudly, I was certain she could hear it.

"He is. He is a kind and generous employer. Strict but fair." She smiled as she shook out a gown, holding it up to me with a satisfied look. "He has a reputation for being cold and aloof, but to those closest to him, he is not."

I recalled seeing him for the first time. The fear I felt at his regard. His stern expression and the way his lips turned down as he studied me.

"He has had a difficult life, but he has risen above it. He had to work very hard to bring this estate back to life, but he has never complained. He is honorable, and I am proud to work for him. But he is private and keeps his emotions private as well."

"I understand."

"He does not suffer fools easily and dislikes society as a whole. He trusts few and allows even fewer to be part of his life, but once you are within his world, he is a benevolent and compassionate gentleman."

I nodded at her words.

"Now, dinner is at seven. I shall return in a while to help you dress. You will join the master."

It wasn't a question. It was a statement, and her tone told me not to argue.

"Yes."

ALEXANDER

I paced the library, not understanding the anxiety that pulled on my nerves. I had no doubt that Madeleine would appear momentarily. We would dine together, and I would lay out my plans. The more I thought on my idea, the more I liked it. Marrying her was a good thing. She would make a fine wife and companion. And, I had no doubt, a good mother. I was certain she would agree. Surely marriage to me was a more pleasing situation than working as a servant elsewhere?

I was thought to be handsome. I was wealthy and could provide a good life for her. Children. Unfettered with worries and away from the dreary life she had been living, my offer had to be tempting at the very least.

I rubbed my temples, feeling doubt. She had admitted to wanting a husband and a happy life. Was she hoping for love? I was not known as an emotional man. In fact, I was certain my father had beaten that idea out of me. But I could care. Feel fondness. Desire.

She intrigued me—more than any other woman I had

ever met. There was an intelligence hidden under her fear. I found her charming, and when she forgot to be afraid, I could see a slight glint of mischief in her eyes. I liked her laughter and her sweet smile.

What I didn't like was the exhaustion etched into her skin. The apprehension she carried with her. The timidness she showed to the world. Her belief that she was nothing. Her worth was far greater than she realized, and I planned on proving it to her if she allowed me to do so.

A soft rustle made me turn to see Madeleine hesitating in the doorway. I smiled widely at the vision she presented. The dress she wore was simple, a soft pink color that looked pretty against her pale skin and dark hair. Gathered under her ample bosom, it showed off her figure far more than the dowdy gray hand-me-down frocks she had been forced to wear. Her hair was up, revealing her delicate neck. The only thing missing was some jewels to set off her eyes and skin, but I planned on changing that soon enough. For now, she looked sweet, lovely, and I realized, with a small smirk, decidedly nervous.

I held out my hand to her, and she entered the room. I lifted her gloved fingers to my mouth, kissing the soft leather that covered her skin. "How lovely you are, Madeleine."

She curtsied, a light pink flooding her cheeks. "I cannot thank you enough, my lord. I have not worn such a pretty gown since I was a child. I'm not sure I am worthy of such gifts."

"Nonsense. You are worth that and more. Now, come sit with me, and our dinner will be served shortly."

I escorted her to the table, inhaling her familiar scent. Lilacs, one of my favorite flowers, filled my nose. I had to stop myself from burying my nose into the juncture of her neck and inhaling. The knowledge the scent would be strongest there was tempting. The urge to hold her close surprised me.

Instead, I waited until she had sat down and seated myself across from her. She looked around in wonder at the shelves of books, craning her neck to peer at the items I had purchased on travels that sat on shelves and tabletops.

"You may explore to your heart's content," I assured her.

"It is so vast," she murmured. "Such treasures to be discovered!"

I met her eyes. "There is more than one treasure," I agreed, my stare frank.

She bit her bottom lip, bringing attention to her full mouth. I was drawn to it. To her. How, I wondered, would she taste under my lips? Would she be as sweet as I thought? Would she gasp softly as I slid my tongue in to taste her? Whimper as I dragged my mouth down her neck?

How silky would her skin be under my tongue?

Dinner arriving interrupted my passion-filled thoughts. I had to shake my head and shift in my chair to ease the growing ache in my cock. It seemed he was as on board with my ideas about Madeleine as my thoughts were.

But he and my brain needed to be patient. Madeleine was not only fearful of the world, she was innocent. It would take patience and time for her to trust me and for our physical relations to begin.

But I had a feeling she would be worth the wait.

We supped on my favorite—roasted beef with fresh vegetables. A rich sauce accompanied the meal, and I ate heartily, grateful to be home and eating from my own kitchen. My cook, Mrs. Dodd, was excellent and could as easily prepare a feast for twenty as a simple meal for two. Madeleine ate slowly, her portions far too small for my liking, but I knew she was nervous. She would relax eventually. She enjoyed her dessert, though, the rich bread pudding with a brown-sugar sauce sweet and indulgent. I would have to ask Mrs. Dodd to regularly make more desserts for Madeleine to enjoy.

After dinner, we strolled in the garden, and I was amazed at her knowledge of the various plants and flowers, once again surprising me with her intelligence. I had kept our conversation at dinner light and easy, answering her questions about the estate and the village.

I looked down at her, her small hand tucked into the crook of my arm. We paused, and she looked out at the well-laid property, inhaling the scent of the flowers and grass.

"Your estate is so lovely," she mused.

I turned to her. "I would like it to be our estate, Madeleine. I meant what I said in the carriage. I wish to marry you."

Her eyes were huge in her face, and her one-word response was shocked. "Why?"

I smiled and dared to tuck a lock of hair behind her ear, enjoying the feel of the silky curl against my skin.

"I require a wife. You require protection. I find you fascinating. Intriguing. Beautiful. I wish to give you the life I think you deserve. I believe we would suit."

She didn't respond, and I kept speaking.

"I am not a man of emotion, Madeleine. But I promise to be a good husband. I will care for you and make sure you want for nothing. We can have a family and reside here at Wheaton. Is that not your wish? A husband and children? A home in the country?"

"Yes," she whispered.

"But you are hesitating."

"I am in shock."

I laughed lightly. "I am as well, if I am being frank. I went to Cliffwood to best your father and win back a piece of land I coveted for years. I did not expect to return with a fiancée."

"Lydia? Geraldine?" she asked anxiously.

"Will stay on here, with you. Lydia will be your lady's maid. Mrs. Dougall will find a place for Geraldine. Something that will give her purpose but not be too taxing."

"She is a wonderful seamstress, and she loves to bake. Her pastries are decadent."

"Then I will instruct Mrs. Dougall to use her skills."

"Are you certain, my lord?"

"Quite." I paused, studying her face. "Do you fear me, Madeleine?"

She hesitated, and I took her hands in mine. I wanted to peel away the gloves, but I had a feeling she needed to trust me before she would show me what she was hiding under the leather. "I swear to you that you will not be mistreated here. You will have nothing to fear from the world—or from me. I will protect you, Madeleine. Your life will be vastly different from what you have known. You have only to say yes, and I will arrange it all."

To my horror, her chin began to quiver, and tears filled her eyes. "Madeleine?" I asked. "Is the idea of being married to me so repugnant?"

She turned away, covering her face. I moved behind her, gently holding her shaking shoulders. "Speak your thoughts out loud, my sweet. I shall not be angry."

She turned, her cheeks wet, her eyes bright in the waning light. "My lord, only days ago, I was cold, scared, and hungry. My life was nothing but pain and work. I felt only hatred and anger directed toward me. It was a continuous circle I thought would never be broken."

I wiped the tears from under her eyes. "And now?"

"You took me from that. I am in a stunning garden, wearing a dress that makes me feel beautiful. I soaked in a bath for the first time in years. I feel clean and rejuvenated. There is a bed to sleep in with blankets. A fire to warm me. A full belly." A sob escaped her lips. "And you are standing in front of me—a kind, wonderful man—asking me to marry you. Promising me I will never return to that place. Offering me the dream I kept hidden for so long. I am overwhelmed with gratitude and a feeling I had lost long ago."

"Which was?" I asked tenderly.

"Hope."

"Then you will agree?"

"Yes, my lord. I will marry you. I will strive to be the best wife I can be and make sure you never regret your decision. I would be proud to be your marchioness."

I smiled at her and ran my fingers down her cheek. "I shall not regret anything. And you are correct. You will make a wonderful marchioness."

Then I leaned forward and kissed her forehead.

I wanted her mouth, but for now, that would do.

We had a lifetime to explore the rest.

Another sob escaped her mouth, and she covered it. "Forgive my emotions, my lord. I should not bother you with such trivial feelings."

I shook my head and removed her hand. "No, Madeleine, as your betrothed, I expect you to bother me with everything. Because it is not a bother—it is my privilege."

Then I drew her into my arms, her head the perfect

height for me to rest my chin upon. She fit well into my embrace, her tiny figure molding to my much larger one perfectly. As if made for me.

It was the strangest thought, and yet I liked it.

And it gave me the same hope she had that one day we would fit together in an entirely different way.

CHAPTER 10

MADELEINE

I ran my gloved hand along the beautiful chestnut mare's muzzle. The air was cool and damp in the stables this morning. But the familiar scents of hay, horse, and saddle leather filled me with a sense of deep contentment, chasing any discomfort from the cold swirling about my new nankeen boots.

At Lord Wheaton's request, I was dressed in my Pomona green riding habit, a jaunty hat that had been procured from the village milliner upon my head. The hats had been sent up at Mrs. Dougall's request, and like the gowns she had managed to obtain on my behalf, I had fallen in love with each one. Choosing which to wear this morning had been its own gift in a sea of so many that I was beginning to become overwhelmed.

"Do you think she will suit as your mount?"

I turned to find the marquess looming over me, an expression of concern on his countenance that matched the fretting tone of his voice. He truly wanted to please me, and the knowledge never failed to astound me. No one had gone to such an effort on my behalf since my mother had been alive.

I had to blink at the stinging rush of tears, tamping down grief I had never truly allowed myself to feel as the young girl who had lost her only champion at such a tender age.

I forced a bright smile for his lordship's benefit, not wanting to explain the sudden rush of sadness. "She is gentle and calm, and yet I see a sparkle of mischief in her eyes. I think she and I shall get along nicely."

"I was hoping the two of you would make friends. Empress is just as you have described her. Capable, gentle, and calm. But she also has a bit of fire within her. She is soft and sweet when she wishes to be, but she has a will of steel. You are a well-matched pair, I think."

His words warmed me, as did the honest appreciation reflected in his dark gaze. But I couldn't shake the feeling that I wasn't worthy of his esteem. Despite his reassurance in the garden, I was terrified that Lord Wheaton would come to his senses and change his mind. That he would realize he didn't wish to marry a woman who was too far beneath him and send me to London as he had originally intended instead.

I averted my gaze back to Empress, who was looking at me trustingly as I continued to stroke her muzzle, wishing I might feel the velvet-smoothness of her coat beneath my fingertips.

"I'm afraid I haven't any fire in me, my lord, nor a will of steel. If I had, I would have burned Cliffwood to ash instead of meekly obeying my father."

Lord Wheaton stepped nearer, bringing his scent, familiar and tempting above the smells of the stables. "I saw it myself in the carriage," he said quietly, "when you were finally free to speak your mind. You are strong and determined, or else you could not have possibly endured. And you can neither blame nor judge yourself for the machinations of a cruel man. You were but a child when your father forced you into a life of servitude."

I shook my head. "You are far too intent upon seeing the best in me, and why, I cannot begin to fathom."

The mare nudged my palm gently.

"Because you deserve it, Madeline. Empress is an excellent judge of character, as am I." He moved forward until he stood at my side, his towering presence a source of comfort rather than intimidation.

I never felt the need to cower or fear for myself in his presence. His broad shoulders, impressive height, and strong form had only been used to protect me. To show me gentleness.

I slanted another glance in his direction. His long hair was pulled back into a queue at his nape, his head covered by a dashing hat. His riding breeches and boots showed off his muscular calves and horseman's thighs. Goodness, what was I doing, ogling his lordship? New heat crept up my throat, scalding my cheeks. I hoped he hadn't noticed.

"Thank you," I said simply, seeking to distract myself.

His eyebrows rose. "For being honest?"

"For inviting me to ride with you. I hadn't realized how much I missed riding until the opportunity was granted me once more."

"You needn't thank me, my dear. As my marchioness, you can have your choice of horses and ride as often or as little as you like."

I gave Empress another fond stroke. "You are far too generous, my lord."

"Let me be," he said, reaching for me and briefly caressing my cheek, the soft leather of his glove brushing against my heated skin for a fleeting instant.

"Why?" I whispered, afraid to ask the question, yet needing to know the answer.

"Because it makes me happy to do so." His hand fell away. "And because you deserve it."

He shifted again, putting a proper amount of distance between us just as the groom who had brought Empress to us returned. Lord Wheaton must have heard the young man approaching.

"Miss Smythe has settled upon Empress as her mount," the marquess announced to the groom. "Please have her saddled and brought to us, along with Lightning for myself."

The young man tugged at his forelock. "Yes, my lord."

I still felt woefully inadequate, and yet as the marquess led me from the stables where we could wait for our mounts to be brought to us, for the first time, the life he promised me felt within my reach. Everything I wore was new and fine. I was betrothed to a marquess. I was no longer a servant in my father's household, forced to bend to his every whim.

The sun was even emerging from the clouds overhead, and birds were calling. The fresh scent of mown grass and turned earth greeted me. The day seemed alive with possibility. It had been so long since I had last sat upon a horse that I wasn't certain I could ride with the poise I had once possessed. But I yearned to try.

"You are quiet," Lord Wheaton observed at my side. "Tell me, what are you thinking?"

I met and held his probing gaze. "That I am thrilled for the chance to ride, my lord."

He smiled, and my breath caught. "Hearing so pleases me more than I can say. I want to show you more of my estate and what it has to offer. Fortunately, the weather looks as if it shall hold for us."

"There's no need for that."

Good heavens, he was already giving me more than I had dreamed possible for myself—a home, a husband, a family of my own.

He frowned. "A groom will accompany us at a proper distance for propriety's sake, if that is what concerns you. Although the nature of our engagement is rather unusual, I'll not have a word of scandal breathed about you."

His words sent a trickle of some indefinable emotion through me. "I thank you for that, but what I meant was that you hardly need to persuade me to marry you by showing me your estate. I've already agreed to become your wife."

"Of course you have," he agreed smoothly, "but won't you allow me an excuse to spend more time in your delightful company?"

"Is that what you are truly about, my lord?"

"Without question."

A smile twitched at my own lips, and my heart felt lighter than it had in as long as I could remember. "Then I suppose I must allow it as your future marchioness."

"Indeed," he said with mock sternness, "you really must. In fact, as your future husband, I insist upon it."

Another flutter of something wonderful and terrifying went through me. The Marquess of Wheaton could be quite charming when he wished to be. How easy it would be to fall in love with him.

The grooms emerged from the stables before either of us could say another word, and we spent the next few hours riding across the farms, fields, and woods of his estate. By the time we returned, I was sore and tired and a trifle chilled, but my heart had never been happier.

ALEXANDER

Two days later, Edward strode into my study, his coat swinging behind him. I stood to greet him, surprised and pleased to see him so soon.

"Edward." I clasped his hand and shook it firmly. "How fare you?"

"Excellent, my lord."

"And what of Knight?"

"He is in the stable being rubbed down and his own groom attending him."

"I did not yet expect to see you so soon." I indicated the chair in front of my desk. "Sit and tell me all."

"Knight's leg healed well enough to travel slowly. Lydia and I started out very early and arrived a short time ago. She handled Knight well."

My eyebrows rose in surprise. "Lydia?"

"She grew up on a farm and is an excellent horsewoman. We went slowly, and her weight is so slight it was as if Knight was carrying nothing at all. He liked her."

"Ah. And Geraldine?"

"Is being driven by the groom. They will arrive later, and he will spend the night and return tomorrow. I knew you would prefer to get Knight here as quickly as possible."

"Excellent decision."

"I also assumed you would be wanting to take Miss Smythe on to London. Have you received word from Beckett?"

"Ah." I rose and poured us each a measure of scotch. I

handed him a glass and perched on the edge of the desk. "There has been a change of plans. I have written to Beckett, but she will not be going to London."

"She is to stay here, then? As a maid?"

I cleared my throat, took a sip of my scotch, and met his eyes. "As my wife."

For a moment, there was silence. He blinked, looked around, then met my gaze, his confused. "I beg your pardon, my lord. I thought you said you were marrying the chit."

"That chit is about to be my marchioness, so watch your tongue," I rebuked him mildly. I knew he was confused. Hell, it was my idea, and *I* was still confused.

"Forgive me."

"Of course. I know it was surprise that colored your words."

"Marry her?"

"I met with the parish bishop earlier today and obtained a common license. We'll be marrying in the parish church seven days from now."

"My lord, I have no doubt she is lovely, but marriage? So quickly?"

I sighed and sat back down in my chair. I told him of our conversations. How she tended to me. How fascinated I found myself with her.

"It solves so many issues. I like her, Edward. I find her interesting and highly intelligent. I believe she will be a good wife and an excellent marchioness. Despite everything, she is kind and thoughtful. Gentle. She reminds me in some ways of my mother. She will stand by my side. Bear my children." I shook my head. "I cannot abide the thought of spending time with the empty-headed chits in London. Listen as their mamas push them in my direction, citing their talents like virtues as they scheme to outdo another interested party. Dream of my money and name." I shuddered. "Last season was almost my undoing."

"You lasted three days, my lord, and left town. The ladies of the *ton* were most aggrieved."

"I was most relieved."

He chuckled.

"Miss Smythe is different from them all. I enjoy conversing with her. The servants already love her and are anxious to welcome her as their mistress. As am I."

He looked thoughtful then nodded. "Then let me be the first to offer congratulations. I wish you all the best."

"Thank you." I tapped my thumb on the desktop as I gathered my thoughts.

"She is still fearful and wary. I hope now that Lydia is here, she will settle. I think when Geraldine arrives, the familiarity of a beloved face will help soothe her nerves as well."

"You will be a good husband, my lord."

"I intend to be. In that vein, I have written Beckett, requesting his wife's help with a wardrobe for Madeleine. I explained we are to be married and require her help. I expect a swift reply."

"She would need direction, I should presume. Measurements?" he asked, his brow furrowed. "Lydia would be able to do that."

"I described her well, I think. Enough that Constance should be able to begin the preparations. I am not concerned."

"You've thought of everything, it would seem."

"I believe I have."

"And this has all transpired in a matter of mere days," Edward added. "You're certain you wish to marry her?"

I could not find fault with my friend for his concern. I'd had no intention of marrying any time soon when we parted during the journey back to Wheaton. It was not like me, but I also couldn't deny the rightness that existed between Madeleine and myself.

"I can see what you're thinking, and let me reassure you that I've never been more certain of anything in my life."

CHAPTER 11

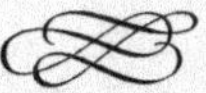

MADELEINE

"You look so lovely in this blue evening gown," Lydia told me as I stood before a looking glass, sure that the young lady staring back at me was someone else.

Anyone but me.

The gown had been a bit too large for my smaller form, but Lydia was a deft hand with sewing, and with a few alterations, it now looked as if it had been commissioned for me alone. Lydia had expertly plaited my hair into a circular braid, leaving a few curls free to frame my face. I wore a new pair of slippers that were so fine they felt as if they were fashioned of clouds. I had dabbed some lilac scent I had made myself and brought with me from Cliffwood on my wrists and throat.

"I don't look like myself," I said, still awed by the transformation that had occurred ever since I had arrived at Wheaton.

Having Lydia and Geraldine here pleased me greatly. Over the course of the last few days, I had settled into a comfortable, familiar routine. I no longer felt quite as much like a stranger or a usurper at Wheaton. I no longer woke each morning thinking I was in a dream.

It was real, as real as my reflection staring back at me was.

I wasn't a maid, beneath my father's thumb, forced to do his bidding. Instead, I was the next Marchioness of Wheaton.

"You look as you were always meant to look," Lydia corrected me gently. "You are a lady, Maddie. You were born a lady, and Lord Barnett stole that from you when he forced you to serve as a maid. Soon, I shall be calling you Lady Wheaton."

I spun away from my reflection. "You'll do no such thing. You are to call me Maddie always. We are friends."

"I am your lady's maid."

"You are like a sister to me."

Lydia smiled, shaking her head. "You've a heart of pure gold, Maddie, that you do. I'm just thankful that his lordship is willing to offer me this situation. It's far more than I could have hoped for at Cliffwood."

"The marquess is a kind and generous man," I said, feeling my cheeks go warm as I thought of the man I would soon be marrying.

Our days had been filled with getting to know each other. The more I learned, the more I respected and admired him. He was everything I had supposed him to be —and more.

"Edward tells me that the marquess is a fine and honorable gentleman, that you could not hope for a better husband."

I took note of the familiar way Lydia spoke of the marquess's steward at once.

"Edward?"

A pink flush tinged Lydia's cheeks. "Mr. Warwick, that is. Forgive me. I should not have been so bold."

I wondered if I would be losing my friend as my lady's maid so soon after she had been granted the position. Selfishly, I hoped not. Having Lydia at my side had been a much-needed reassurance. I missed our time in the garret room, though not the inferior lack of comfort. Still, I would never stand in the way of my dear friend's happiness.

A sudden, unpleasant thought occurred to me then. While I had begun to trust the marquess, I knew almost nothing of his steward.

"Lydia, Mr. Warwick was not unseemly, was he? He didn't behave in an improper manner toward you when you were at the coaching inn, did he?"

"Of course not," she reassured me. "Mr. Warwick has been a true gentleman to Geraldine and myself both. We were grateful for his escort. You mustn't think ill of him because of my own mistake."

There was a protectiveness in her voice that I had only heard previously when she had been taking my side in battles with Mrs. Wells back at Cliffwood. I stared at my friend, thinking that this was an interesting development indeed. It was plain to see that she had burgeoning feelings for Mr. Warwick. But I wouldn't poke my nose into the matter further for now. There would be time aplenty for that later.

I had a dinner to attend.

"I don't think ill of him," I promised. "Now tell me, have you finished turning this sow's ear into a silk purse? I should hate to be late for dinner, what with his lordship's guests in attendance."

"You are not, nor have you ever resembled, anything

close to a sow's ear," Lydia told me, smiling. "You're beautiful, Maddie."

"You flatter me because you are my friend."

"No, I tell you the truth because I am your friend." Her smile deepened. "Moreover, have you ever smelled a sow's ear? I can assure you that you smell nothing like one."

I laughed, grateful for the levity. "I should hope not."

Lydia chuckled. "I'll just tend to a few things here. Go on. Off to dinner with you."

I hesitated, smoothing an imaginary wrinkle from my skirts. "What if the marquess's friends disapprove of me?"

Earlier this afternoon, the house had been abuzz with the unexpected arrival of Lord and Lady Beckett, good friends of his lordship. I had only briefly made their acquaintances, for the efficient Mrs. Dougall had instantly sent the viscount and viscountess off to their chambers after their arduous day of travel from London. I was nervous to be seated with them at dinner. What would I have in common with an accomplished lady who was accustomed to the *haut ton*?

"Why should they disapprove?" Lydia asked, frowning. "You are a credit to his lordship in every way—lovely, intelligent, kindhearted, considerate."

"I have none of the polish expected of a genteel lady," I fretted, giving voice to the worries that had been assailing me ever since I had curtsied to Lord and Lady Beckett.

What a handsome pair they had made, both undoubtedly dressed in the height of fashion. Even in their travel garments, they had been elegant and refined.

"And what is the polish that's expected? I confess, I wouldn't know, and I'm likely the better for it."

"I'm not sure I know either. Dancing, watercolors, playing the pianoforte…"

"None of which you will be asked to do at dinner," Lydia pointed out. "Lord and Lady Beckett are friends of the marquess. I cannot imagine he would keep company with anyone who is uncharitable enough to judge you for lacking the refinement your father denied you."

Lydia was right, and I had been telling myself the same. But somehow, hearing her affirmation quelled my concerns in a way that nothing else could.

"You are right, of course, my dear friend. I am sure they will be most kind."

"Of course they will, and if they aren't, I'll sneak into their chambers and hide frogs under their beds," Lydia teased.

I laughed and impulsively reached for my friend, taking her hands in mine. I wore my customary kid gloves, and I had not as yet determined how I would avoid removing them at the table. I would somehow muddle through.

"I am so happy you are here with me, Lydia," I told her. "I couldn't do this without you."

Lydia gave my fingers a reassuring squeeze. "Of course you could. But I am glad to be here with you too, and far from the reach of the odious Mrs. Wells."

"As am I." I took a deep breath. "I suppose it's off to dinner with me."

"Just be yourself, Maddie. They'll love you just like everyone who has come to know you does."

I took my leave of the chamber, Lydia's words echoing in my mind with each step. Not everyone loved me, but I had left my father and Cliffwood behind forever. It was time to turn my mind toward the future awaiting me, a future that was filled with more hope than I ever could have fathomed not long ago.

"I hope you don't mind a few unexpected guests for your wedding," Lady Beckett told me in conspiratorial fashion in the drawing room after we left the marquess and viscount to their port following dinner.

Thanks to my tête-à-tête with Lydia earlier, I had entered the dining room with tentative confidence that had bloomed over the course of the meal.

"Of course not, my lady," I reassured her. "You honor us with your presence."

The viscountess beamed back at me. "Please, you must call me Constance. We are to be dear friends, I can already tell, and I refuse to stand on ceremony."

"Then you must also call me Maddie," I invited, still feeling a bit shy.

Our shared meal had gone a long way to ease my concerns. It had been clear that Lord Beckett held the marquess in high regard and that the feeling was mutual. Lady Beckett—Constance—had been welcoming and warm. The four of us had fallen into an easy pattern of conversation, discussing everything from London to the weather to Lord Wheaton's latest property acquisition.

"It would please me greatly to do so," the viscountess said. "You are a dear heart to be so understanding about our arrival. When Wheaton wrote to my husband with news of your impending nuptials, I decided that we simply had to be here to join you."

"I hadn't realized he wrote you."

What had he said about me? Had he mentioned the unusual circumstances surrounding our betrothal? I rather hoped he hadn't.

"You mustn't be cross with Wheaton for doing so," Constance said. "He wrote to ask for my aid in sending a gown from London that you might wear on your wedding day. My modiste is a godsend, and she offered up a gown that I hope you will find more than suitable. I didn't dare entrust it to a servant, however. What if it were to become lost or dirtied? No, I knew that I needed to deliver the gown myself."

"You needn't have gone to such efforts on my behalf. Mrs. Dougall was able to secure a handful of dresses from the village that would have served me."

The moment the words left me, I realized that I had revealed too much. No ordinary lady would require a housekeeper to find gowns for her in the village. She would already have a wardrobe of her own. Embarrassed heat scalded my cheeks.

But if she took note of my error, the viscountess graciously chose not to comment upon it.

"It is no trouble at all, I assure you. Beckett considers Lord Wheaton a brother, and neither of us could countenance the notion of the two of you marrying without our being in attendance. It pleased me to think that I might be of assistance in some small way with the dress. I directed my lady's maid to take it to your chamber whilst we were at dinner, so it ought to be awaiting you when you retire. I do hope you will find it suitable."

"I am certain I shall," I managed, overwhelmed by this woman's generosity and my sudden change in circumstances.

The luxury of a wardrobe all to myself was naught but a distant memory. My mother had always seen to such matters. I had vague recollections of being measured, selecting fabrics, of paging through engravings from *Gallery of Fashion*. I had been but a girl dreaming of her debut then, and my mother had been gone before any of those hopes had a chance to materialize. When she died, so had my future, along with any love I had known.

How I wished my mother could have been here with me now.

"You will need to try it on before the wedding," Constance continued, eyeing me as she warmed to her task. "I do think the gown shall fit, though we may need to make some alterations to the bodice, perhaps let out a few seams."

My cheeks warmed again at the viscountess's tactful reference to my breasts, which were far too large for a woman of my diminutive size. To accommodate them, I was accustomed to hiding my body in overly big gowns. The fitted nature of my new dresses had been yet another surprise to me, though the décolletage of my evening gown was the most daring of all.

"We have tomorrow to make adjustments," she added, nodding to herself. "After breakfast, we can convene. Do you have any jewelry you might wish to wear, my dear?"

I thought of my mother's lovely collection of jewels, the necklace she had oft worn. Likely, the baron had long ago sold off anything of value belonging to her.

I shook my head sadly. "I have nothing, I'm afraid."

"I have a parure that will do," the viscountess told me. "Only if you wish it, of course."

My throat constricted as emotion overwhelmed me. "I would be honored. Thank you."

Before anything else could be said, Wheaton and Beckett arrived in the drawing room. The marquess's warm, dark gaze found mine, and a frisson of awareness went through me. He was so very handsome, so large and powerful and imposing standing next to the viscount. Lord Beckett was a pleasant-looking man with his golden hair and lively green eyes, but Wheaton alone commanded my attention.

Soon, he would be my husband.

Something fluttered low within me. My gaze dipped for a moment to the stern set of his jaw, to his mouth. What would it be like to feel those lips on mine? To be free to touch him, to embrace him…to lie with him?

Good heavens, what a wicked thought to have in the midst of a drawing room.

Sure that my face was flaming, I jerked my eyes back up to his, just in time to catch the slight upturn of the corners of his mouth. Did he sense the nature of my thoughts? Good heavens, I hoped not. I was shocking myself with my newfound desires. It was as if my body had come to life. I felt like a butterfly, stripped from her cocoon, flitting about in the world for the first time.

It was intoxicating and terrifying. I wasn't even sure I knew who I was now, but I was also eager to discover this new part of myself.

"Have we interrupted?" Beckett asked lightly, sending a fond glance in his wife's direction.

It was plain to see that the two of them were a love match. They had shared longing looks over dinner and spoke of each other with undisguised fondness. My mother and father had never been overtly affectionate; indeed, their relations had been cool and polite. I wondered now if they had ever loved each other.

"Of course not," Constance said to her husband. "We are happy to have the two of you join us."

The gentlemen seated themselves, the viscount joining his wife on a settee and Lord Wheaton folding his large frame into a chair near me that looked almost comically delicate with his powerful body dominating it.

I caught a hint of his intoxicating scent, his proximity

having a wholly new effect upon my senses. Was it because we were betrothed? Or was it because I was already developing feelings for the marquess?

He sent me an encouraging smile, and my breath quickened.

"What have the two of you been discussing in our absence?" he asked. "Lady Beckett, I sincerely hope you weren't relaying all my dreadful habits."

His teasing tone had me smiling. I wasn't accustomed to such unrestricted cheer. My father's moods had been mercurial and unforgiving.

"I'm reasonably sure you haven't any, my lord," Constance returned with a similarly mischievous air before turning an arch look in her husband's direction. "No, I daresay you are perfection personified, quite unlike my own husband. My dear Maddie, be forewarned that you are marrying a paragon."

Lord Beckett pressed a hand over his heart in mock outrage. "My beloved lady wife, I am deeply wounded that you find me anything less than flawless."

The viscountess grinned. "Perhaps if you did not insist upon interrupting my reading."

"But you know I cannot resist when you look like a cat, curled up in a chair by the fire," Lord Beckett rejoined before turning to the marquess. "Some husbandly advice— never interrupt your wife's reading."

"I shall endeavor never to do so," Wheaton said with a chuckle. "She will have *carte blanche* to fill my library as she wishes, and if I should find her with a book in hand, I shall keep my distance."

I hadn't read a book in years. They were yet another luxury I wasn't afforded. But even if my father had permitted me to take a book from his depleted library, I wouldn't have had time to read it.

"Wise man," Beckett said, then turned to me. "Tell me, Miss Smythe, do you prefer poetry or prose?"

"I don't think I can choose between the two," I told him carefully for, in truth, I hadn't had occasion to compare, having been kept from reading for so long. "They are equally lovely in their own ways."

"A politic response," the viscount said. "My wife prefers poetry, particularly when I read the verses aloud to her. Do you not, my dear?"

"Of course I do," Constance drawled, her countenance suggesting the opposite. "Pray don't allow my husband to fool you," she added to me in an aside, "he hasn't read me poetry since we were courting."

"An egregious error I would be more than happy to rectify," Lord Beckett said with a roguish grin. "Only tell me which poem you would like to hear."

"I'm so pleased you asked. I would dearly love to hear 'The Rime of the Ancient Mariner' spoken aloud," the viscountess countered.

"Whatever my dear wife commands of me," her husband returned with a grimace that made it apparent he had no wish to recite the poem in question.

At my side, Wheaton chuckled. "Perhaps you ought to read it to us all now, Beckett. I'm certain I must have a volume of *Lyrical Ballads* about somewhere. I shall go and fetch it."

Beckett shook his head. "Ha! Do not, I beg, go looking for it on my account."

I watched the lively interactions between the three in the room with great interest. They were clearly at ease with one another, and the friendship between Wheaton and Beckett was an old and solid one. I felt at once quite fortunate to be included in this charmed little circle. To feel, for the first time, as if there were truly a place where I *belonged*.

"What do you say, Miss Smythe?" Wheaton asked, his keen, intelligent eyes upon me once more. "Shall I go on a quest to find the Coleridge and Wordsworth book? Do you also harbor a yearning to hear Lord Beckett regale us with verse?"

His regard sent a new wave of heat over me. I liked the way he looked at me, the way he spoke to me, with reverence and respect.

I smiled. "Perhaps his lordship might be spared this evening."

"My dear Miss Smythe, I am forever indebted to you," Beckett said with a dramatic flourish. "Only see how quick these two were to make a minstrel of me."

I couldn't contain my laughter. The other three joined in, and we spent the rest of the evening in pleasant banter until we at last retired. As I made my way to my bedchamber, my spirits were lighter than they had been in as long as I could recall.

I had begun to feel as if I had truly escaped my father.

Forever.

CHAPTER 12

MADELEINE

"How does it feel to be the Marchioness of Wheaton?" Lydia asked me as she pulled the pins from my hair, preparing me for my wedding night.

"Exhausting," I answered honestly.

The last two days had been a whirlwind. This morning, Lord and Lady Beckett, along with Mr. Warwick, had been witnesses in the parish church as the marquess and I married. Afterward, we had returned to Wheaton for an extravagant wedding breakfast I had scarcely been able to consume.

"I expect it was a rather long day for you," Lydia commented, unwinding a plait with gentle, efficient motions. "First your wedding, then the wedding breakfast, and of course, seeing Lord and Lady Beckett off this afternoon."

The viscount and his wife had taken their leave, having had plans to visit friends several hours north. I had enjoyed their company thoroughly, and I was especially grateful for the new friendship I had forged with Lady Beckett. I would miss them, but they had been insistent upon the need to allow Lord Wheaton and me to have some time to grow accustomed to married life.

As Constance had said when she embraced me, "We shall leave the two of you to enjoy your wedded bliss."

I hadn't been sure what she meant, though I had flushed as red as an apple, I was sure of it. I still wasn't entirely certain, although I had a suspicion.

"It has been a great deal of change in a short time," I agreed, meeting Lydia's gaze in the looking glass. "I do so wish you would have joined us at the wedding breakfast, if not the church, however."

"Your situation has changed greatly, and whilst mine has as well, I am still a humble lady's maid," Lydia said, plucking the last of the pins free and allowing my hair to fall in heavy waves down my back. "I must remember my position here at Wheaton and not reach above myself."

"It isn't reaching when you are invited to do so," I pointed out. "You are my oldest, dearest friend, Lydia."

"And you are mine, but you are also my employer now. We aren't chambermaids sleeping in a dreary attic garret any longer." Lydia had taken up a comb and was working it through the ends of my hair.

"I am your friend above all else," I countered sternly. "Perhaps if you would allow me to speak with Lord Wheaton on your behalf, we could arrange for you to find a husband of your own. I could find a different lady's maid to assist me."

"You'll do nothing of the sort." Lydia laid down the comb, frowning at me. "His lordship has already been far too generous, taking me into his household and giving me this situation after I stole away from Cliffwood."

She was not wrong; the marquess had exhibited a munificence that I was certain no lord would show a mere maid. But he had done so because of my affection for

Lydia and because he was an honorable man who genuinely cared in a way that few others did.

Still, though I was more than familiar with the fierce boundaries of our world, I couldn't help but to find it unjust that my dear friend should be my lady's maid while I became a marchioness. During our many nights in the garret room, Lydia and I had shared our hopes and wishes for our futures. I knew she wished for a husband and family of her own just as I had, and I also understood how impossible it would be for her to achieve if she remained my lady's maid.

I sighed. "I don't like it, Lydia. Why should I be a marchioness whilst you remain a servant?"

"Because you have always been a lady," Lydia told me gently. "You're the daughter of a baron. I was born to this life. You weren't. You mustn't think that I am unhappy with my lot. I am more than contented to be your lady's maid. Wheaton is a wonderful place, and everyone here is happy and treated well, the opposite of Cliffwood."

She finished with my hair and began tidying up the hairpins and combs. "Now, no more fretting about me on your own wedding day."

Her words were just the reminder I needed of what this day truly meant. I was a wife now. But in name only. Perhaps that would change soon.

I was already dressed for bed, wearing a fine night rail that Constance had gifted me, along with the beautiful gown I had worn for the wedding earlier that morning. My stomach quickened as I thought of what was to come.

Would Wheaton visit me after Lydia left me for the evening? Did I want him to?

The answer to the latter question was—to my shame— a resounding yes. I was more attracted to the marquess than ever.

I bit my lip as I watched my friend finishing her duties. "Do you think his lordship will regret marrying me, Lydia?"

"Not for a moment," my friend hastened to reassure me. "Now, if there isn't anything else you need, I ought to leave you to your time with his lordship."

I swallowed hard. "There's nothing else. Thank you, my dear friend."

Lydia bustled about and then took her leave from the chamber I had been moved to, which adjoined the marquess's. The marchioness's room, as Mrs. Dougall had informed me this afternoon, telling me that his lordship had given me leave to decorate it as I liked. The room was already fine, and I was so overwhelmed as I first entered it that I hadn't been capable of thinking of one thing I would alter.

I paced the thick Axminster now, aware of every sound, from the crackle of the low fire banked in the hearth to the light lashing of rain on the windowpanes beyond. I didn't have long to wait. A firm knock on the shared door between our chambers told me that the marquess had arrived.

"Come," I called, relieved when my voice emerged with far more confidence than I felt.

The door opened, and there on the threshold, clad in a dark, billowing banyan, was the man I had married that morning.

My *husband.*

ALEXANDER

I regarded Madeleine—my wife—from the doorway. She was a vision, her night rail a gossamer wisp of silk surrounding her, fine embroidery decorating the soft fabric. Her glorious hair was unbound, hanging in ribbons of dark waves down her back. I felt my body stir and my cock thicken at the mere sight of her. I wanted to take, to claim. To make her mine.

But it was the way her small glove-covered hand fisted the fabric of the chair she stood beside, the distress she tried to conceal, that brought me under control. I smiled at her as I approached. "Are you well, Madeleine?"

"Of course, my lord."

I shook my head in mild rebuke. "I am Alexander to you."

She colored prettily, the rose color blooming under her skin emphasizing her delicate features. I dropped my gaze to her hands, wondering once again about the gloves. I had never seen them off—even at dinner. She had offered an excuse about painful joints and requiring them on at all times, but I already knew her well enough to know she was lying. I wanted to know the truth, but I also knew she had to trust me in order to get her to be honest. I could demand her to remove them, but I feared pushing her away. I wanted her to know she was safe to tell me anything, and I needed to be patient in order for that trust to build.

"Alexander," she repeated.

"I like how that sounds when you say it," I murmured.

Her smile was that of the sun on a summer's day. Bright and warm. It brought forth unfamiliar feelings. The urge to be close. To touch her. Protect her from anything unpleasant and frightful. I had never known such intense emotions. The need to protect, to cherish.

To love, perhaps?

The past days spent with Beckett and his viscountess had shown more of her sweet personality. I found myself drawn to her over and again. Wanting to be close. To hear her laughter. Watch her discover something new and revel in the knowledge I had given that to her. I found her in the library on more than one occasion, peering at the shelves, a small pile of books set to one side, or curled into the large chair in the corner, reading, lost to a world I could not enter. I enjoyed watching her, often doing so quietly as not to disturb. Her expressions fascinated me. Happiness, confusion, sadness, excitement, all showed plainly on her countenance as she read the words in front of her, her lips silently forming the sentences and scenes the books painted for her. My chest warmed at the thought I could bring her joy.

The same joy she had unknowingly given to me by simply observing her.

She shifted on her feet, bringing me back to the present. "Sit, my wife," I urged her, the words sounding pleasant on my tongue. "You must be tired from today."

She did as I asked, a small frown on her face. "As you must be too, my—ah, husband."

I beamed at her, liking how it sounded to be called her husband.

"Perhaps a sherry?" I questioned. "I prefer a brandy, but that might be too much for you."

"I have never had either," she confessed.

I headed to my chamber, then returned to her and handed her a small glass. "Sip it slowly," I instructed. "It is sweet, and I think you will like it."

She sipped it, and I watched as a pleased smile pulled at her lips. "It is delicious."

I swirled my brandy glass in my hand, warming it, then taking an appreciative mouthful, the decadent liquor flowing down my throat. Madeleine observed me, looking curious. I offered her the glass. "Try it, but only a small taste. It is very strong."

She accepted the glass and sniffed it, then tilted it back, barely wetting her lips. I discerned a small grimace on her face as she handed me back the glass. "I believe I will keep the sherry," she informed me with a small cough.

I chuckled at her politeness. "Excellent choice."

As we sat in silence, I shifted, trying to get comfortable. The chair was smaller than those in my chambers and more delicate in form. The fire in Madeleine's room was banked low, the servants no doubt thinking she would be joining me in my chambers, where the logs burned bright and warm. Madeleine studied me with concern.

"Are you unsettled, my lord?"

I nodded and stood. "The furniture here is made for someone much smaller than I. I would like to sit in my chamber if you would be agreeable."

I saw the tremor that went through her body, the flare of fear that flickered in her eyes before she lowered them. "Of course. Whatever you desire."

In an instant, I sank to my knees in front of her, setting aside our glasses and taking her hands in mine. "Look at me, Madeleine."

She hesitated, another tremor shaking her body, then looked up, meeting my gaze.

"Do not fear me, my wife. I know you are innocent and worried of what comes next in our marriage. But this evening is not what you are frightened it will be."

"My lord?" she whispered.

I drew a finger down her cheek, the softness of her skin pleasing. "I wish for you to be comfortable with me. For us to know each other more before we begin our, ah, relations."

"I do not understand. It is my duty—"

I stopped her with a shake of my head. "I do not wish for you to lay with me as a duty. I want for you to desire it as well. I want you to come to me of your own free will, not because you feel it is a duty you must perform."

Her eyes glimmered in the low firelight. "Will I not have failed you, then?"

"No," I responded with a firm shake of my head. "It is what I wish for. I only planned on celebrating our union by spending time with you this evening. Conversing. Reading to you a little. It is my greatest joy to watch you smile, to hear your laughter. To perhaps hold your hand or stroke your cheek. For now, that is enough."

"And when it is not?" she asked, her question bold despite the worry lingering in her gaze.

"I pray you will want more as much as I do. But I will not force you, my wife. You are safe."

Her shoulders relaxed, the anxiety leaching from her eyes.

"Will you come with me and sit in my chamber? Allow me to read to you and let us enjoy the warmth of our shared company?"

"Yes."

I stood and offered my hand, and she allowed me to tug her from her chair. She followed me to my chamber, and I indicated the chair by the fire as I prepared fresh glasses. "Sit."

"But where will you sit?"

"I can sit on the footstool."

"No, you must sit in your chair. It is only proper. I am

much smaller, and the footstool will be fine for me," she stated and sat down, tucking her night rail around her.

I sat with a frown, then stood, crossed the room, pulled the coverlet from the bed, and sat down again. I patted my lap. "Sit with me, my wife."

Her eyes widened.

"This chair is large enough for two. The covering will keep you warm. I would enjoy having you close."

She hesitated, and I held out my hand again, waiting for her to take it. She did, and I pulled her to my lap, wrapping the coverlet around her. She was stiff and uncertain, but I picked up the book I had selected. It was one I had seen her peruse more than once, so I knew it was a favorite of hers.

"Shall I read?"

"Please," she murmured.

I handed her the sherry, took a sip of brandy, and opened the book. I began to read, and after a few moments, I felt her relax, her body molding to mine as I kept my voice low and soothing. When her glass of sherry was empty, I slipped it from her hand, placing it on the table. I gently cupped her head, tucking it to my shoulder and pressing a lingering kiss to her thick hair. "You smell so delightful," I murmured. "Lilacs."

"I make the scent myself," she replied, her voice low and sweet. "The lilac trees were abundant around Cliffwood. They grew wild everywhere, and no one cared if I picked them. It was something my mother taught me."

"I like it."

"I like this," she murmured.

She nestled into me, as if seeking my warmth. I adjusted my body, leaning back slightly so I could take more of her slight weight. I liked how she felt on my lap. Small and delicate. Needful of care. Seeking my touch.

Unable to resist, I ran my hand over her tresses as I continued to read. She sighed in contentment, and I glanced down, seeing her eyes shut and a smile playing on her lips. She was fully relaxed, and I knew she would be asleep within moments. Resting in my arms as she ought to this night. Surrounded by me. Safe and peaceful.

That was the way I planned on her staying for the rest of our lives.

CHAPTER 13

MADELEINE

I woke the next morning, tucked into the bed of my new chamber. The room was lovely, facing the front garden, but days previous, I'd had a glimpse of the view from Alexander's window. It was spectacular, looking out over lush fields and trees as far as my eyes could see. The scope of beauty here took my breath away. Last night, I had asked him if he ever thought to leave the heavy draperies open and gaze at the stars or watch the sunrise. He had studied me for a moment before shaking his head.

"I confess, I have not. Perhaps it is something we could do together."

I had tried not to blush at his words. It was subtle, but I heard the innuendo behind his utterance. Once we laid together, I would be in his chamber—in his bed. The view would be mine.

And I would be his.

His statement he was not rushing our relations had been both a blessing and a curse. I was sheltered and innocent, although I saw the coupling of animals often in the barn. Still, I was not innocent enough to think that Alexander was without a past. He was too handsome and virile not to have had many interludes. I worried he would be bored with me and lose interest quickly at my lack of knowledge.

Aside from the occasional brush of his finger along my cheek or the press of his lips to my head or high on my cheek, he had not touched me. Yet every time he was close, every time our eyes met and he stared at me, I felt his desire. Last night was the closest I had ever been to another person. Wrapped in his embrace, his voice murmuring my favorite passages in my ear, I felt nothing but peace. Affection. Adoration perhaps.

And I wanted more.

The very sight of him caused flutters within my stomach. Watching him laugh made me want to smile. When he threw back his head, the corded muscles of his neck made me swallow, my own throat dry. I had never seen a man with such wide shoulders and long legs. Recalling how the heavy muscles felt under my touch when he had injured his foot made me wonder how all his muscles would feel. I yearned to touch him.

His hands fascinated me. Strong and capable with long, thick fingers, elegant, yet not only used to pen correspondence. He worked his own land. Tilled the soil and hammered in posts for fencing and even fed the animals.

There was nothing he could not do.

My favorite moments were when he would look at me. Speak to me in his low, modulated voice. Offer me his arm as we were walking. Tuck a stray curl behind my ear. Tease me. It made me feel giddy. The touch of his hand made me want more. I found myself staring at his mouth when he spoke, wondering how it would feel if he kissed me.

I had thought I would know this morning, but he had been a perfect gentleman.

He was right to decide we should be patient. Despite all the wonderful things I knew about him, at times, I was still frightened. I recalled hearing whispers of women who visited my father's estate years prior, of how men acted one way to some people and mistreated their wives, believing them to be their property and theirs to do with as they pleased. I knew from experience how my father mistreated me, although he chose not to hide it.

I prayed Alexander was not that type of man. That the gentle soul I was beginning to know was the only side to him.

I could only wait to find out.

ALEXANDER

I walked into the study, tugging on my cravat. It had been a vexing morning, and I was tired of dealing with difficult servants, all the issues of the farms, and the vast amount of correspondence that kept flowing across my desk. All of it kept me from enjoying my new wife and getting to know her more. I was finding it quite frustrating only seeing her at dinner the past two nights. I headed toward the corner, intent on a tumbler of scotch, some peace and quiet, and a good luncheon. I poured the scotch and took a large mouthful, enjoying the taste of the rich amber liquid. The Scots could certainly brew a fine liquor.

A noise startled me, and I turned, seeing Madeleine,

hovering beside the mantel. I frowned at her unexpected appearance.

"Madeleine?"

She bobbed an awkward curtsy, and I had to resist rolling my eyes at her unneeded gesture. She was my wife, not my servant.

"Forgive me, my lord, for the intrusion."

"What are you doing in my study?"

Her eyes widened and terror laced her voice. "I was not doing anything dishonest, my lord. I was trying to bring a little sunshine into the room." She indicated the vase of flowers on the mantel.

I stared at them, blinking. No one had ever brought flowers into my study. Under my strict instructions, unless it was to clean the room under Edward's watchful eyes, no one ventured in here.

"Who let you in?"

Her hands fluttered. "The door was unlocked."

I scowled in frustration. Had I not locked it?

Her hands moved to her throat. "I have angered you. Displeased you, my lord?"

I looked at the mantel, unsure how to answer. Her offering was sweet, and I wasn't used to gestures of that sort.

With a grimace, I turned back to the liquor, picking up my glass and downing the remaining contents. I supposed, as my wife, she would be allowed to go anywhere in the house, without question. I needed to remember that. A smile tugged on my lips.

I wasn't used to having a wife either. I had just been bemoaning the fact that I hadn't seen enough of her and there she was, and I was acting like an arse.

I spun around to assure her all was well, but she had

disappeared. No doubt hurried away, upset by my silence. Thinking I was displeased, as she put it.

The flowers looked…nice on the mantel, the bright colors standing out in the otherwise masculine room.

I would seek out Madeleine and escort her to lunch. Assure her I was not angry. Otherwise, she wouldn't eat, and I wanted her to get healthy. I withheld a sigh. I wanted her to stop cowering in alarm as well, but I knew it would all take time.

I WAS SITTING at the desk, reading some correspondence, when Madeleine entered the room again. She shut the door behind her and approached the desk. Confused, I watched as she placed a small bundle of reeds on my desk along with a rose. Her words send shards of ice down my spine.

"I am ready for my punishment, my lord."

For a moment, I was numb with shock.

Punishment. She thought I meant to mete out punishment on her for the infraction of placing flowers in my study. For attempting to add a little color in a place she did not yet consider to be her home.

I had to shut my eyes and count to ten. I unfurled myself from the chair and rounded the desk.

She stood, her head bowed, hands clasped, as always, in tight fists. I noticed for the first time ever, her gloves were not voluntarily on her hands. Her shaking fingers were even more delicate than I recalled from the brief glimpse I'd had on the day of our wedding.

"And what, pray tell, is your punishment?" I asked

mildly. "I confess, I have little experience with matters such as this."

A long, furious shiver ran through her body. She held out her trembling bare hands, opened her fists, displaying them palm side up. Her eyes were downcast, but I knew if I saw them, they would be petrified yet resigned.

"To be taught a lesson, sir. Not to overstep my bounds."

I caught one hand in mine, lifting it closer for inspection. Thin white scars, multitudes of them, showed on her skin. Small puncture marks dotted the thin flesh. All healed over, yet telling a story so ugly, it made my stomach roll. I stroked the palm, feeling the thickness of the scars she carried, wondering how much deeper the scars in her mind were.

"Your father beat you with reeds," I stated, keeping the fury from my voice.

"Yes."

"And the rose?"

"I held the stem in my other hand and presented it to him when he was done as a gift."

"Your blood to soothe his anger?"

"Yes."

I released her hand and picked up the other. It was similar, but it bore more scars. He had purposefully beaten her weaker side with additional strokes so as not to render her useless. She could still perform her chores.

I dropped her hand and picked up a reed, swishing it in the air. It made a low, hissing sound before hitting the wood. Madeleine flinched at the noise.

"Why have you brought me so many reeds?"

"So you could choose which one to use, as my father did. I followed my usual instructions, my lord. Have I displeased you again?"

I had to clear my throat before speaking. Rage coursed through my veins, but I did not wish to frighten her more. The fury was not directed at her, but I suddenly understood her fear more than I had before, and the reason for it sickened me. "Madeleine, look at me. Now."

She lifted those glorious eyes, all that much brighter with the tears she was seeking to hide and the terror that lay within them. Her skin was whiter than snow.

"Pick up the reeds and the rose."

Shaking, she did as I asked.

"Hand them to me."

Her breathing was picking up, and I knew she was imagining the horror of the punishment that lay ahead.

"Watch me carefully."

I strode to the fireplace, snapping the reeds in half and flinging them into the flames. I stripped away the thorns on the rose and added those to the rapidly burning strips of wood. I returned to her side, lifting her hand and placing the rose within her palm. I closed her tiny fingers around the stem.

"The only roses you shall ever hold from this day forward will cause you no pain. You will never again know the sting of a reed on your palm—or anywhere else."

I stepped closer, cupping her face, meeting her bewildered and increasingly watery gaze.

"I promised you that you would never come to harm under my protection. Not from anyone, but especially from me."

"But I—"

I interrupted her. "You did nothing wrong. Your act of kindness caught me off guard. The flowers are as lovely as you are. I thank you for the gesture." I lifted her hand to my mouth and kissed the soft skin.

"Do not fear me, my wife. I swear to you, nothing shall hurt you under this roof. Ever. I will not allow it."

An agonized sound escaped her mouth. Without a thought, I drew her close, encasing her in my embrace. "Show me your pain," I urged her. "Allow me to comfort you."

She began to sob, the sound muffled as she hid her face into my chest. I lifted her off her feet and sat in the great chair with her on my lap, allowing her to cry. I stroked her back, making small noises in my throat as I held her close. At one point, Edward walked in, stopping short at the tableau in front of him. I shook my head in warning, and with a bow, he stepped out, drawing the door closed once again. I knew he would ensure we were not disturbed.

Aside from her, I had never held a woman this way before. Offering the shelter of my arms for something other than pleasure. Madeleine was a warm weight on my lap, still far too thin, but she fit against me well. The soft scent of lilacs I had come to associate with her was stronger with her so close, the smell alluring and warm.

Finally, her cries stopped. I slipped a square of linen into her fist, soothing my hand over her hair one last time. She sighed, blew her nose in a dainty fashion that made me smile, and wiped her eyes.

Silence hung between us.

"Are you well now, Maddie?"

She lifted her head, surprise on her face at the shortened version of her name. "My lord?" she whispered.

"I heard your servants call you that name. I like it, and it suits you."

"My—my mother called me Maddie when I was a little girl."

"Then Maddie it shall be. And I should like for you to call me Alexander. I am, after all, your husband." I touched her cheek. "And this is your home. If you wish to put vases of flowers in every room, then do so."

She didn't say anything for a moment, her gaze flitting around the room. I felt her desire to say something, and I drew a finger down her pale cheek. "Speak."

"You will not punish me if I make you angry?"

"No. You need to stop living in the shadows of the past. No harm will come to you here. On my honor, I swear it."

I gathered her hands, holding them tight. "You can trust me, my wife. I promise your life will be different from now on. Let go of your fear and worry."

She blinked. "I will try."

"I am your husband. You can discuss anything with me. I wish only to help you adjust and find your happiness."

She simply nodded, her eyes wide in her face.

"How often did you make your father angry?" I asked.

"He was angry at me all the time. He punished me every fortnight or so."

"Your father," I spat, "is a monster. A fucking bastard."

At her shocked gaze, I smiled. "I apologize for my rudeness. I realize your tender ears are not used to such vulgarities."

She swallowed. "I have heard that and much worse, my, ah, Alexander."

The simple joy of hearing her say my name made me smile. "I imagine you have."

Her voice became a whisper. "There are times I uttered those words myself."

I had to laugh at her confession. "They were well deserved."

She offered me a smile. It was timid and tremulous, but it was there. It changed her expression, and I could see the beautiful woman under the mask she'd worn for so long.

I decided I wanted to see more of that woman. I felt as if we had turned a corner, and if I allowed her to walk away, her doubts would creep back in and she would become fearful again.

"It is a lovely day. Why don't I ask Cook to pack a lunch, and we will walk to the woods and have a picnic. I can show you more of the estate." Teasingly, I lifted my knee, making her bounce. "Would you enjoy a stroll with me, Maddie mine?"

Her eyes widened at my term of endearment, but she looked pleased.

"Yes."

"Then allow me an hour. You prepare yourself, and I will instruct the kitchen to fill a basket with all varieties of delicious morsels."

She slid from my lap. "Thank you."

I kissed her hand. "Thank you, Maddie."

She departed, leaving a trail of her soft scent behind.

What, I wondered, had just begun?

Something wonderful, I hoped.

I strode to the door and called for Mrs. Dougall. I instructed her to have the kitchen prepare a feast and to procure a soft blanket on which Maddie could sit outside.

When she departed, I rode the short distance to the steward's house I had granted Edward, hoping I would find him at home. Thankfully, he was there to greet me as I rapped at his door.

"Is something amiss?" he asked, concern lacing his voice. "Is Lady Wheaton well?"

"She is," I reassured him. "However, I need your expertise again."

He nodded, waiting for my instructions.

"I wish to know everything there is to know about Barnett. Dig deeper than before. His past, now. Finances, holdings, consorts." I paused. "His dead wife."

"I shall begin immediately."

"Use great discretion. I do not wish for him to catch wind of this."

"Of course." He regarded me. "What will you do with this information?"

I smiled without warmth. "Ruin him. Completely. He will pay for the transgressions against my wife."

He looked pleased. "Consider it done."

I pulled down my sleeves and adjusted my collar, wanting, for some reason, to look nice for my wife.

"I am taking Maddie for a picnic," I announced.

Edward startled. "A picnic? Alexander, I have never known you to have a picnic."

"You have never known me to have a wife either."

His countenance changed. He almost beamed at me.

"Enjoy yourself, my lord."

"I plan to."

MADDIE HAD CHANGED into a linen dress, the soft yellow of the gown complementing her dark hair and lovely eyes. She wore a bonnet perched on her head at an angle that covered her face unless she lifted it to me. I frowned at it, and she paused.

"My lord?"

I tutted, and she smiled hesitantly.

"Alexander," she corrected herself. "Is something amiss? My gown displeases you?"

"Your gown pleases me very much, but that hat hides your face. I like to gaze on your loveliness. It brings me pleasure."

She blinked, appearing shocked at my words.

"It is to protect my skin," she explained.

"If we sit in shade, then you will remove it for me?"

"Yes."

I crooked my arm. "Let us be off, then. I am suddenly anxious to venture into the dimness of the forest."

Her pleasant laugh was an ample reward.

So was the feeling of her arm crossed with mine. I liked how it felt. How she felt.

We strolled toward the forest, the perfect destination already in my mind. A small brook was nestled not far into the trees, surrounded by flat boulders and grasses. I had spent many an hour there as a child and after returning here later in life. It was one of my favorite places on the estate.

The basket I carried was heavy, and I hoped the cook had included items Maddie liked. I was still concerned with how thin she was and how little she seemed to eat. I wanted to tempt her appetite, make her comfortable enough to express her desires and wishes.

To my satisfaction, Maddie removed her hat quickly, staring around in obvious fascination and delight. She reached out to touch the leaves on the bushes and trees, stopping once to bend at a flowering shrub, remarking on its loveliness.

"You have such beauty here," she breathed out.

"It is yours now too, Maddie."

She glanced up at me, her eyes wide and filled with emotion.

"It is still a dream."

"A good one?" I questioned.

"Yes," she replied with an emphatic nod. "Very good."

We came to the brook, and her glee could not be contained. "Alexander!" she gasped, running ahead like a child. "How wonderful!"

I felt a warmth to my chest as I watched her. Such a simple thing. A spot to sit and enjoy the early summer warmth. The sound of water rushing over stones was nice, but to her, it seemed more so.

I felt the swell of sadness, knowing something as easy as a picnic or time spent enjoying a simple pleasure such as this had no doubt been denied to her. I was determined to give her as many of these small gestures of happiness as I could offer.

I set down the basket, spreading out the blanket close to a spot I liked the best. The flat boulders could be leaned against or sat upon, the shade was welcome, and the water was easily seen. All of which I knew would please Maddie.

I strode toward her, wrapping my arm around her waist and drawing her back to my torso. It pleased me greatly when she didn't startle, but instead laid her hand on my forearm, patting it in a fond gesture.

"Such a treasure," she murmured.

Unable to resist, I bent and pressed a gentle kiss to her neck, smiling at her shiver. "It is," I murmured, not even looking at the brook, but instead at her. "A king's ransom."

For a moment, I stood behind her, feeling as if I were seeing the vista with different eyes. The way the branches bent in the breeze. How the water skipped and danced over the rocks. The feel of the wind on my face and the sound of the birds chirping happily in the trees.

It felt like a gift. And the gift was because of her.

"Come, Maddie mine. Let us see what the cook has sent us."

MADDIE EXCLAIMED in happiness over the array of foods the basket contained. Small pork pies and cold chicken and beef. Cheese and bread. Jam puffs and biscuits. Fresh fruit. A container of lemonade—something I knew Maddie enjoyed. I spread out the food, offering her a plate I filled with her favorites. She accepted it, spreading the linen napkin over her lap and waiting until I filled my plate before starting to eat. She picked delicately, observing her plate with almost confusion on her face.

"Maddie," I began as I watched her nibble.

"My—I mean Alexander?"

I smiled at her. "Why do you eat so little? Are you still uncomfortable with me?"

She sighed. "I wasn't allowed much to eat. He—Father —had strict instructions as to what I was allowed and how much. It was always the end bits, the slightly burnt, or the leftovers."

"You will have only the best. Always. I want you to eat until you are satisfied. And anytime you want something, ask for it," I said earnestly, leaning toward her. "I never want you hungry. And if there is something you desire, make it known. The servants want to make you happy. I want you to be happy."

She blinked, turning her head so I would not see the tears in her eyes.

"Your life is different now. You must cease being afraid, for nothing will harm you. I will not allow it. Do you understand?"

She lifted her glorious gaze to mine. "I do. I will try. I wish to please you."

"Then eat." I paused. "And remove your gloves."

"But people will see. I was never allowed to remove my gloves. Father forbade it."

"Your father is no longer here and never will be. And if they see, let them. Your scars show you survived something. Do not allow your father's warped transgressions against you to color your decisions going forward. Besides, I have an idea."

"An idea?"

"There is a healer in the village. She makes things—potions, ointments—like your friend's mother did. When I burned my hand last year, it was her salve that gave me relief. Even my physician agrees with her methods. I will take you to see her. Perhaps she can help diminish the scars and dull some of the stiffness they cause."

I had noticed her grimace a few times when using her hands, and I didn't like it.

"We will go see her tomorrow. But I would like you to try no gloves in my presence. They do not offend me except that the person who inflicted the wounds should be punished. But not you."

She hesitated, meeting my eyes in a silent plea. I nodded in encouragement. "Trust me, my wife."

I waited until she peeled off her gloves, shutting her eyes as the warm air drifted over them. She lifted her hands, rolling them gracefully, allowing them to feel the sun and breeze for the first time in what I imagined was a long while. I smiled at the innocent tableau in front of me and marveled at her bravery in doing what I asked.

Then she picked up a jam puff and ate it, allowing herself to enjoy it. A hum of pleasure escaped her mouth, and I wondered what noise she would make when I kissed her.

I wanted to find out.

I moved closer, still holding her hands. "Will you tell me, Maddie? Why your father treated you as he did?"

She lifted her shoulders. "I do not know. He was never a warm or affectionate father. He never spent much time with me except to show me off at gatherings. I spent most of my time with my momma. But I didn't fear him. They met when she was staying here, having fled Paris. From what she always said, he swept her off her feet, married her, and she stayed here in England. I thought they were happy. I remember balls and parties and Momma looking beautiful." She paused, as if in thought. "About two weeks after she passed, I was pulled from my room and taken to the servants' quarters. My clothes were changed, my life thrown into chaos. I was informed I was no longer the daughter of the house. I was a servant and would be treated as such." She paused, a faraway look in her eyes. "My father punished anyone who tried to help or protect me. The servants did what they could, making sure to teach me everything I needed to know. Shielded me from some of the more difficult tasks when my father wasn't around. When he was, he was the hardest on me. Any infraction was noted. I was punished often. My rations were always smaller than anyone else's. At first, they all tried to give me more, but as time wore on and the servants changed, I simply became what he wanted. A servant with no name or dowry. No hope of a better life." She slipped her hand into mine, the shock of her touch surprising me. "Until you, Alexander."

I stroked her skin, feeling the scars on her flesh as if they were mine. Hating her story and knowing she wasn't telling the entire truth. She was still afraid—or perhaps too traumatized by the past.

"Thank you for telling me," I murmured, touching her cheek. "For trusting me."

She smiled, the hesitancy of it once again bothering me. I wanted her to be free and open with me. I wanted her smiles, her laughter. With a start, I realized I wanted to give her mine.

She leaned into my hand, and I cupped her cheek.

"You are so beautiful, Maddie."

"Father told me I was ugly."

"Your father, as we determined earlier, is a cad and a bastard."

Her giggle made me smile.

"Tomorrow, we shall go into the village and see the healer. And the dressmaker."

"But I have new frocks," she protested. "You purchased them for me when we were married. And you ordered Constance to procure some from London."

I shook my head. "I did, but Constance convinced me to purchase only a few and that we should venture to London in the future and you will have a complete new wardrobe from the best modiste in the city. But I wish you to have everything you desire or need right now as well. I want you to have all of it. I want you to eat. Sleep. Relax. I want your body strong and healthy." I paused. "Not right away, but we will want to entertain. When word reaches the ears of those in London that I have married, we will have guests. Perhaps a ball." I smiled at her. "I will dance with my wife wearing a beautiful gown, only outshone by her own loveliness."

She blinked and looked down. Then she raised her eyes to mine and studied me as if she was unsure how to take me. "You are a gift, sir," she whispered. "One I am not sure I deserve."

"You do," I assured her. "And I am happy you are here with me."

"Thank you."

The air around us changed, grew warmer. My gaze dropped to her mouth. Her full lips I wanted to kiss.

Her breath caught as our eyes met and locked. Her mouth opened slightly, and I lowered my head, giving her the chance to move or protest.

She did not.

I pressed my mouth to hers, feeling the softness of her lips underneath mine.

She gasped softly as I wound my arm around her waist, pulling her to my lap and cupping her head. I kissed her again, tracing the seam of her lips with my tongue and sliding inside as she opened for me.

I teased her tongue, coaxing her to kiss me back. I felt a tremor go through her, and I held her, exploring her thoroughly. Licking deep into her mouth, smiling as she kissed me back, tentative and soft, then slowly responding to my ardor. She was sweet and perfect. She tasted of lemonade, jam, and pure Madeleine. She grew bolder, sliding a hand around my neck and playing with the hair on my nape. Her full breasts pressed into my chest, and I longed to lay her on the blanket and undress her, expose her to the fresh air and my mouth. But I knew it was too soon and it would overwhelm her. Frighten her. I had no wish for that to happen, so I slowed my kisses until I drew back, staring down at her, liking what I saw.

Her cheeks were flushed, the pink spreading down her neck and chest. Her breathing was rapid, her eyes shut. One hand fisted my shirt, the linen crushed in her fingers. She opened her eyes, the bottomless pools of blue filled with wonder and what I hoped was passion.

"You stopped," she whispered.

"I had to, Maddie mine."

She frowned.

"I do not wish to frighten you."

"You did not. I liked it."

I smiled, running my hand along her cheek. "As did I. What I want to do to you would frighten you very much, I fear. But we will take our time. Get to know each other. And I will teach you everything."

"There is more?" she whispered.

"So much more, my darling girl. And I will show you everything. And you will tell me what you like and what you don't."

"And you will do the same?"

I laughed quietly. "I doubt there is anything you can do I will not enjoy, but yes, my love. I will tell you too."

I pressed another kiss to her tempting mouth. "But for now, we will enjoy the day and our new closeness, yes?"

She nodded.

"Let us take a walk. Maybe we can find more flowers for my mantel."

"You like them?"

"I do. In fact, I expect fresh ones all the time now."

She smiled eagerly. "I can do that. I love to work in the gardens. Father thought I hated it, so it became one of the tasks I had to do every day. But I loved being out and away from his sight. And I loved to grow things."

"Then we will get the gardener to give you a plot and help you."

She threw her arms around my neck, holding me, her emotions getting the better of her. I hugged her back, loving her affectionate nature.

She drew back, smiling at me. "Thank you."

I pressed her hand to my lips, turning and kissing her scarred palm.

"You are welcome, my wife."

WE STROLLED, coming to the edge of the property. I stared across the barren land, shaking my head.

"It is so overgrown," she said with a frown. "Your land puts it to shame. Who does it belong to?"

I sat on a large rock, drawing her beside me. "Me now. I won it back from your father."

She turned to me. "Oh?"

I sighed, unsure how to explain. "That part of the land was my mother's favorite spot. We would ride and play there. I loved her dearly. She was an incredible mother. Warm and loving. She even made my father smile."

"What happened?"

"She held such affection for that piece of earth that my father purchased and gifted it to her from the original owner of Milton Manor. It was quite barren aside from the orchard. She added gardens, trees, and she planted and shared her crops with the village. She was so loved by so many," I explained.

Maddie slipped her hand into mine, and I held it to my chest.

"One day we were there—over in the orchard." I indicated the remains of what had once been a large planting of trees. "She climbed too high, trying to get the apples she saw. She fell out of the tree and broke her neck."

"Alexander!" she gasped. "How horrible!"

"My father went wild. Burned down the orchard and crops. Built a fence that has long since fallen over. Gave the land to your father over a card game." I lifted her hand to my mouth and kissed it. "He never got over her death. He stopped living. Stopped being my father. He drank and gambled. Put us in debt. Sold pieces of this estate that were not entailed and other land he had purchased himself. Then he died, and I inherited the mess he left."

"And you won the land back."

I nodded. "I had a head for figures and farming. I always loved the endeavors. Both of them. I worked and toiled along with my tenants. Slowly made back the monies he lost. Bought back the missing land, piece by piece. I couldn't care less about the town house in the city, but I have had it refurbished, although I spend little time there. I prefer it here."

"Your other land?"

"I sold some of the unentailed. Bought back others. Gave my farmers a chance for a good life. This estate brings in a tidy sum monthly. Others do as well. I have invested in the future. No son of ours will have to toil to get back what he inherits."

There was silence, and I realized what I had said.

"Does that shock you, Maddie? Thinking of children with me?"

"It fills me with joy," she stated quietly. "I have little knowledge of the workings of such things…" She trailed off, only to speak again. "I know of animals."

I smiled at her hesitant confession. "I will teach you, Maddie. We will do this slowly, and you will learn. I do promise you it is far more enjoyable than…animals," I teased.

I was rewarded with her blush.

"What is it you wish to do with the land?" she asked, refusing to meet my eyes.

"Bring it back the way my mother loved. Your father ignored it. Refused to sell it to me. It was only through the card game I was able to get it back."

"What if you did not win?" she asked, her eyes wide. "He cheats! I know this for a fact."

I laughed at her candor. "I was aware. We had someone in his house who told us how. We fixed it."

"So you cheated as well?"

I shrugged. "I did. Once he informed me he wanted me to take you, I knew I had to win. I wanted you out of there."

"Why?"

Her question caught me off guard. "I do not know," I admitted. "I kept catching sight of you, and I was intrigued. When I saw you fully, I was shocked. Horrified. Intrigued."

"Because I was ugly?"

I shook my head. "No. Because you were the most beautiful, sad thing I had ever seen. I had to act uninterested because of your father. But I was desperate to help you. The distress in your eyes reminded me of someone I knew when I was younger, and I wanted to stop that fear."

"He thought to complete his vendetta against me—for whatever it was. To have you ruin me."

"I know. I have—" I drew in a deep breath. "I have a reputation as a cold, unfeeling man. A rake, if you will. But as soon as I saw you, I could not do that."

"Why?" she asked again.

"Because somewhere deep inside, I knew instinctively you needed me. And perhaps I needed you as well."

"Thank you."

I bent low and kissed her, pleased when she kissed me back with no hesitation.

"Thank *you*," I murmured against her lips.

CHAPTER 14

ALEXANDER

I climbed the steps, feeling tired. Another problem had pulled me from Maddie, and I had missed dinner. Mrs. Dougall informed me Maddie had taken a tray in her room and offered to send up one for me, but I refused. The hour was late, and I wanted only to see my wife's face and hear her voice. The day had been an emotional one for her, and I was worried.

I was also furious, the hatred I was feeling for her father a living, crackling flame in my chest. Hearing how he mistreated her, seeing the scars he left behind—both those that I could see with my eyes and the ones Maddie kept hidden deep within—would keep that hatred and need for revenge burning until he himself was extinguished.

I had gone to Cliffwood to win back the land my mother loved so much, but the truth was, saving Maddie was more important.

And I knew my mother would approve of those feelings.

In my chamber, I dismissed my valet after having him

draw a bath. I slipped into Maddie's room, but she was asleep under the coverlet, her hands clutching the edge of the heavy fabric as if not finding the rest she sought in sleep. Even after the pleasant hours we had spent together in the afternoon, no doubt her emotions were still raw.

I left her, sliding into the bath and sighing in relief. My shoulders ached from the work, and I was weary. For someone who remained aloof of others' problems, seeing my wife so vulnerable this morning had done something to me. Broken something within that made me *feel*.

I wanted to fix it. Fix her. Heal her in any way she needed. Be the haven from whatever storm she faced and protect her at all costs.

I shook my head, realizing that my father had not accomplished what he had set out to do all those years ago. With her sweet ways and loving heart, Maddie showed me I was capable of feeling more than I thought possible.

More than I was able to grasp—even now.

I rose from the warm water, patting myself dry and donning a banyan. Although expensive and deemed excessive by many, plumbed heated water within the house was an addition I wished never to be without again. My kitchen ran smoother, the house was cleaner, and the water closet and bath a luxury I did not regret. In fact, I wished to add to the plumbing, and I had meetings coming up soon with a planner to do so. It was worth the chaos, expense, and repairs that followed.

I had just stepped into my chamber when I heard it. A low, keening sound. I stopped to listen, frowning when I realized it came from Maddie's room. I heard another noise and the sound of a muffled sob.

Instantly, I was in her room, hurrying to her bedside. Her cheeks were wet with tears, one hand clutching the coverlet, the other reaching out beseechingly.

"Please, Father, no. I beg of you. I will do better. *Please!*"

She winced as if feeling the sting of a reed or the slap of a hand. I slipped my hands under her shoulders, shaking her gently.

"Maddie, darling, wake up. It is only a dream, my love."

Her eyes snapped open, meeting mine. The terror I saw wrecked me.

"You are safe, Maddie mine. I am here."

"Alexander," she sobbed, flinging her arms around my neck. "I was there, back there…"

"Hush," I soothed, rocking her. "It was but a bad dream. You are safe here with me, and nothing shall harm you. You will never be anywhere but here with me."

She gripped me tighter, and I stood, taking her with me. In my chamber, I slid her onto the bed, keeping her close as I followed, pulling the thick counterpane over us and holding her tight.

"I am here," I crooned. "Nothing shall harm you."

I ran my hands along her spine, feeling the delicate ridges of the bones under my fingers. I soothed her with my voice and touch, sifting my fingers through her hair that felt like silk. Slowly, she calmed, and I pressed a kiss to her forehead. "I have you."

"Safe," she whispered. "With you."

"Always."

"Must I leave?"

"No, stay here with me. I will open the curtains in the morning, and you can see the sunrise with me. I will watch over you tonight."

"I should like that."

"Then so be it." I bent and pressed a gentle kiss to her mouth. "This is where you belong. With me."

Her eyes drifted shut, and she sighed. "I like belonging with you."

I liked it too.

MADELEINE

My father raged at me, spittle flying from his lips.

"What a worthless girl you are. Slothful and stupid. A waste of flesh."

I bowed my head, knowing it was best to accept his insults rather than defend myself. "Yes, Father."

"Did I give you leave to speak?" he snarled.

I shook my head, knowing his ire would only grow. He hadn't. I had only meant to show that I would obey, but nothing I did was ever enough.

"Time for your punishment," he announced. "Hold out your hands."

I did as he asked, hating to, knowing what was coming, trying not to whimper. It didn't matter that my skin was toughened from the harsh work of being a housemaid or the layers of scarring. The pain was always as sharp as a blade, and I had to bite my lip to keep from crying out. Sometimes until the coppery tang of blood invaded my mouth.

Strike went the reed, that same old pain surging through me.

I cried out, twisting, trying to get away from him. I wouldn't let him strike me this time. Why was he here? I was married now. Alexander would protect me.

"Alexander," I tried to call out, struggling to escape my

father, but my voice ceased to work. I couldn't seem to make a sound, no matter how hard I tried.

My father's fury only grew. He swung the reed harder, striking my wrist.

"No!" Hands were on me now, seizing me, gripping hard.

Pain streaked through me. He was angrier, his eyes blazing with fury. I had to escape. I had to—

"Maddie, it's me." The grasp was gentle, tender. Not like my father's.

I awoke with a jolt, aware of the darkness surrounding me, the faint ethereal glow of the moon on the ceiling. The heat and strength of a comforting, familiar body.

"Alexander," I murmured, my voice returning to me along with wakefulness.

"Hush, my darling." He pulled me into his protective embrace, tucking me against him and kissing my crown. "You're not in danger. You're here with me. You were having another dream."

It hadn't been real. Relief washed over me. I wasn't with my father. I was forever beyond his reach. I was safe. Alexander had me in his arms, the steady and reassuring thud of his heart beating against my ear.

His hands traveled in smooth, steady caresses up and down my spine, soothing the panic from me with each pass. My own pounding heart slowed. The fear was gone. My father couldn't hurt me here. I was the Marchioness of Wheaton. The title, though it belonged to me, still felt somehow as if it would have better served another. There was only one title of import to me, and that was being this man's wife.

I shivered, but it had naught to do with being cold.

"Are you chilled?" Alexander asked, his tone solicitous. "I can fetch another counterpane."

I shook my head. "I am perfectly well. Don't go. Please."

I couldn't bear the thought of him leaving me alone in the bed, of returning to those bad dreams. Already, I had come to rely on Alexander, but this sensation inside me was different now, twisting, almost desperate. He couldn't leave my side. I needed him here.

"You needn't worry, darling. I'll stay with you." His voice was soothing.

My frantic heartbeats calmed. Gratitude filled me. How many cold, dark nights had I risen in my little attic garret at Cliffwood, wishing myself somewhere else, starved for compassion, for someone who cared? More times than I could count. But never could I have imagined someone like Alexander.

His familiar scent curled around me, shaving soap and lemon with a hint of leather. I burrowed closer into his chest, seeking the comfort I knew I'd find there. He held me. He *had* me. The tension filling my body ebbed. I was safe. I was in his arms.

"Thank you," I murmured through the thick silence hanging between us as the air began to shift.

I became intensely aware of our bodies intertwined. Although he was wearing a banyan and I had on my night rail, there was an intimacy in the way my softness melded into his hard, stern angles and planes. He made me feel more than safe and protected. He made me feel cared for.

But he made me feel other things too. He made me aware of my breasts crushing into him, the way one of his long legs had come to tangle with mine. The differences between us. The warmth.

A liquid jolt of yearning flared to life deep within me, blossoming outward. A new but not unfamiliar desire.

I wanted this man, my husband. I wanted him to claim

me as his wife. Not just in word, in vows we had recited on our wedding day, but in deed as well.

Slowly, gathering my courage, I tilted my head back to drink in the sight of him, his cheekbones bathed in silver moonlight, his dark hair unbound and falling freely around his face. The light played over his stern nose and compressed lips, lips I had felt against mine and very much wanted to feel again.

"You saved me from him," I whispered, running my foot along his calf beneath the smooth weight of his banyan.

I heard his sharp inhalation of breath and felt the way his body stiffened against mine. Was it shock? Had I been too forward, touching his limb with my foot? I was yet new to being married. To yearning for a man's touch, to the marriage bed. I hoped I wasn't shocking or displeasing my husband.

"I woke you from a bad dream," he countered softly, still sweeping his palms up and down my spine, from the small of my back to the place between my shoulders where I carried so much tautness from years of laboring. Without saying a word, his knowing fingers found those sore muscles, massaging them and helping to quell the lingering strain. "That was all."

"My life without you was the true bad dream," I told him, meaning those words and needing to tell him.

He nuzzled my temple. "We found each other at the right time, Maddie mine."

I leaned into him like a cat seeking to be petted. "Alexander?"

He stilled, as if he sensed the importance of the words I struggled to find. "Yes, my wife?"

My wife.

Oh, I liked how he called me that. I stroked his calf

with my foot again, while my hands remained curled against his chest, the banyan keeping my curiosity contained for now. Who would have thought that a mere foot could be so alive with feeling? Everywhere I touched Alexander, potent desire followed.

I kept my gaze lowered to his throat so that I wouldn't have to meet his eyes through the shadows if he rejected me. "You said you would teach me, husband."

"Teach you." His voice was laden with sensual promise.

But still, he made no move to either accept my invitation or withdraw from me. I held my breath, wondering which one it would be.

"Are you speaking of…"

His words trailed away, his voice thick.

I ventured a glance back up at his face. He watched me with an intensity that threatened to set me aflame.

"The wedding night, husband," I explained. "The consummation. The mounting—"

"Enough," he interrupted, pressing a finger to my lips to keep me from saying more. "I've already told you, darling, it's nothing like animals." His head dipped, and he pressed a kiss to my throat.

I was on fire where his lips touched, my heart pounding faster and harder than a blacksmith on an anvil. Not from fear, but anticipation. I felt as if I were coming to life for the first time, every part of me burning with heightened awareness.

"Then show me," I begged with great feeling, pressing a kiss of my own to his throat, just above where his pulse pounded. "Please."

"Maddie." His groan told me everything I needed to know. He was every bit as moved by our proximity.

Like the gentleman he was, Alexander was trying to go

slowly. To grant me the time he believed I required. But I was tired of waiting. All I wanted, all I needed, was *him*. He had to know it too.

Growing bolder, I kissed a path up his neck to his clenched jaw. The prickle of his neatly shaved whiskers there teased my lips. "Alexander."

"You are likely half asleep and still unsettled from the dream that was haunting you," he said gruffly.

But tellingly, he didn't move away from me. Nor did he protest when I kissed the corner of his mouth. "I'm perfectly awake, I assure you."

Another groan. "Maddie, what you do to me."

I liked the helplessness in his baritone, as if he wanted to be noble but was waging an inner war with himself and was in desperate danger of defeat. I wanted that defeat. His surrender. I wanted him to give in.

"What do I do to you?" I asked innocently, fluttering a chaste kiss over his lips, as he had given me so many times. "Tell me, please. I must know."

He nudged my mouth with his. "You make me want to lose control. To make you mine. To take my cock and fill you with it."

A gasp left me at the word he had used, one I recognized from overhearing desperately vulgar and crude speech among the grooms and the footmen at Cliffwood. I had been shocked then. But hearing my husband speak such words, knowing the intent behind them, filled me with yearning.

"Forgive me. I shouldn't have used such a coarse word with you, nor to have been so blunt." He kissed me again, as if he couldn't resist, and I kissed him back, my lips chasing his, opening for his tongue.

I would have told him I liked his coarse word, this part of himself he had revealed to me—the part of the elegant, icy lord who lost control. But he was kissing me as if I were the very air he required for his lungs. And I clung to him, kissing him the same way.

When his lips left mine again, I caressed his cheek, a rush of tenderness for him bursting open inside me.

"Don't apologize," I rasped. "Just make me your wife in truth. It's time."

He stared down at me in unguarded wonder. "There's no rush, Maddie mine. I want to wait until you're ready."

His endless concern for me touched places in my heart that I had locked away years ago. I didn't need another moment to think about what I wanted, what I needed. It was this wonderful man.

I cupped his cheek. "I am more than ready for you, Alexander. Please."

With a shuddering breath, he took my lips again. We kissed hungrily, and I surrendered myself to these new feelings, to the sensations stealing over me. Not languid as it had been on the past occasions when he had kissed me, not slow and steady and burgeoning, like a new bud slowly unfurling its petals. But raw and aching and desperate. I was a flower in full bloom.

His mouth moved over mine, lingering and slow, as if he were as overwhelmed as I was. My confidence grew as I touched him, tentatively at first, and then with greater purpose. The strong breadth of his shoulders, the wall of his chest. He was warm, so warm, the heat from his body searing me through the fabric of his banyan. I was suddenly curious to know what his bare skin might feel like.

Would it be rough or soft? Would he like my touch, welcome it? Was I even permitted such boldness? I was a novice, a virgin. I knew little of the passion between a man and a woman. Whereas Alexander was older than I was, more experienced. What if I didn't please him?

As if he sensed my swirling thoughts, he lifted his head, tracing my cheekbone with the pad of his thumb. "Have you changed your mind?"

"No," I hastened to reassure him. "Not that."

Never that. I was firm in my decision, the rightness of it falling over me like the comfort of a blanket.

"I felt you tense." He swept his thumb back and forth. "We have the rest of our lives."

"I don't want to wait. I just want…" I hesitated, feeling my cheeks burn. "I just want to touch you, but I don't want to be too familiar."

He groaned, dipping his head as he buried his face in my throat.

"I am yours," he murmured against my pounding pulse. "Touch me all you like."

The invitation was exactly what I needed. I slid my hand over his collarbone, feeling the prominent ridge and tracing it to the collar of his banyan. There, my fingertips felt *him*. His skin was soft and yet sprinkled with hair in a delicious contrast to mine. I stopped over his heart, my palm flattened against the fast, steady beats.

He made a low sound of approval and kissed my throat.

With my other hand, I explored more of him, finding buttons and pulling them free of their moorings. Alexander kissed my ear, my temple. As he moved, I absorbed the flexing of his muscles. Such strength, his body no doubt honed from all his endeavors on his estate.

He cupped my breast through the fine cotton of my night rail, gently kneading, his thumb rubbing over the sensitive peak. I arched my back, seeking more. His lips returned to mine, and I opened for his tongue. We remained that way, wrapped together in the shadows and the silvery moonlight, kissing and touching until we were both breathless. Until a restless ache grew deep within me. My nipples were aching and hard, met by an answering pulse between my thighs.

I broke the kiss, my fingers returning to the remaining buttons on his banyan and opening them, one by one. He rubbed his cheek against mine, the rasp of his whiskers sending a jolt of awareness through me.

"I want to touch more of you," I told him, curious about his body.

This was a benefit to marriage I had never imagined. I hadn't begun to imagine how lovely it would be to be so close to him, to freely explore him. Now that I could, it seemed that my need for him was as insatiable as it was relentless.

"Maddie," he protested, his voice ragged, "I'm trying to go slowly, but you're making it difficult."

He was still cupping my breast with one hand, and now he caught the peak in his thumb and forefinger, shaping and tugging. I moved against him, wanting more.

"Please."

It was as if I had come to life, everything new. My boldness grew, and this time, I kissed him. He answered readily, his mouth moving tenderly over mine. He grasped a fistful of my night rail and dragged the hems higher. I felt suddenly desperate to remove the gown, twisted up in too much cumbersome fabric. He seemed to understand what I needed without words. My night rail glided up to my thighs and paused, along with the kisses.

"Do you want your night rail off?" he asked softly.

I instantly knew the answer, but I was keenly aware that I didn't know precisely what was expected of me. More than anything, I wanted to please my husband.

"Is that the proper way of things?" I returned hesitantly.

"I can lift it high enough to make love to you with it on if you would prefer it. I want you to be at ease, Maddie mine. I want you comfortable."

"What if I don't prefer it?" I dared to ask.

He hummed. "Then my lady shall have what she wants." Alexander tugged the night rail higher, pausing when my bottom prevented him from removing it further. "Lift."

I did as he commanded, lifting my bottom, and then the cotton slid silkily along my stomach and breasts. I sat up with his aid, lifting my arms so that he could finish removing the fabric entirely. My skin was bared to the cool night air. But I wasn't cold. I was aflame.

I reached for him, wanting him to be as naked as I was. More buttons came undone until his banyan parted entirely and I could sweep my hand lower, over his lean stomach. He shrugged the garment away and took in a shuddering breath.

I paused, feeling hesitant and shy again. "May I?"

"Oh yes. I cannot promise I will be able to restrain myself if you do, but there is nothing I like better than your hands on me."

Emboldened, I continued, my fingertips learning the contours of his body. The more I touched him, the more the feelings within me grew. I loved the way his body rippled and moved, the play of muscle, the way his skin grew taut when he inhaled sharply as I brushed my fingers against that male part of him, which jutted forward. I hesitated there, uncertain.

"Go on," he urged, his voice rough.

The moon's brightness enabled me to see, though not as well as I would have preferred. Enough to see that he was thick and long. Lightly, I trailed my fingers over the length of him. His skin was soft and smooth as velvet, an intriguing discovery, and as I investigated him, he seemed to grow.

"Is it…growing larger?" I asked, intrigued but also a bit concerned.

I was small. Alexander was a big man. Everywhere, it seemed.

He chuckled, a low, pleasant rumble. "That is the effect you have on me, Maddie mine."

I stroked him with a firmer touch, my fingers naturally wrapping around him. He made another sound deep in his throat, one that sounded almost like pain.

I withdrew my touch at once. "Have I hurt you?"

"Goodness no. I love your hand on my cock. Does it please you to touch me so?"

"Yes." The word was hardly sufficient to describe what was happening inside me. Yearning, longing, desperation melded as one. "I like the way you feel, so soft and silken and yet so firm."

"Give me your hand."

I placed my hand in his, and he guided me back to him, shaping my fingers around his length. As one, we stroked him from the base to the tip. "Be firm," he added. "Like this."

I liked touching him. Pleasing him. His cock was weighty and insistent, slick at the tip. I circled my thumb over the blunt end.

"Just like that," he praised.

He allowed me to continue touching and exploring him, his cock, the heavy sacs at the base, until he groaned again and took my lips, his kiss growing less polished now, almost as if he were overcome with need. His tongue sought entry, and I granted it, kissing him back, my own tongue meeting his.

His hands returned to my body, cupping my breast

again, this time without the barrier of the night rail. I moaned into his mouth as he gently guided me back so that I was lying on the bed again. When his lips left mine, I was about to protest until I felt them elsewhere, raining kisses down my body. My throat to my breasts. He dipped his head, and he took my nipple into his mouth, sucking.

I cried out, back bowing from the mattress, sliding my fingers into his hair. I held him to me, greedy for more as he moved to my other breast and licked and sucked. For a moment, I had been too distracted by the divine feeling of his mouth at my breast—shocking, yet wondrous—to take note that his hand had coasted to my hip. Slowly, he moved my legs apart until he found the center of me, where I longed for him most.

His touch was sure and knowing, parting my folds, seeking the knot of pleasure that was hidden within. Gently, he swirled his fingertips over my swollen bud. My hips jerked, and a cry left me as he continued sucking on my breasts, alternating between the two all the while. I was so overwhelmed, buffeted by a maelstrom of desire and new sensations.

"Alexander." I moaned and writhed, shameless for him, forgetting about my nervousness.

All I knew now was that I wanted—nay, needed—more. He seemed to understand, his fingers moving on me with greater insistence, faster, the pressure increasing. My body moved with a mind of its own, my fingers grasping his hair, my breasts arching to meet his lips, my lower body pumping furiously against his hand.

The pleasure, when it grabbed upon me, was sudden and intense. Something within me seized, and I trembled beneath the force of my release. Bright pinpricks of light seemed to speckle my vision, and my breath caught in my lungs. Spasm after spasm rocked through me.

But Alexander wasn't finished. He withdrew from me, and I mourned the loss of his touch until he moved over me, positioning himself between my spread thighs. I reached for him, clutching at his shoulders, clinging to him. He lowered his head toward mine. Our lips aligned as if they had been made for each other. He kissed me sweetly, deeply, and brushed his cock over my folds, lingering to tease my bud.

"I don't want to hurt you," he murmured.

"You never could," I reassured him without knowing if it was true.

I understood that there was pain a woman's first time. But I trusted Alexander. I entrusted myself to him. He was mine, and I was his.

"Tell me if I should stop." He slicked himself up and down my folds, the smooth sound of my wetness rising in the hushed stillness of the night, accompanied by our ragged breathing.

I was sure I would never want him to end. And I opened my mouth to tell him so, but then his lips returned to mine, sealing over them, and he fed me his tongue. In the next instant, I felt him press against me below.

Then into me.

The initial give of my body to his was difficult. As I had thought, I was small and he was large. I stiffened with discomfort.

He stopped. "Concentrate on me, love. On the pleasure. Relax for me."

His fingers were on me again, teasing the already swollen bud. I did as he told me, concentrating on the pleasure sparking through me, on his big, protective body against mine, on his lips, so firm and skilled, angling over mine. He thrust into me with painstaking slowness, my body stretching. There was another pinch, but this time, it was drowned out by the steady pulse of his fingers over me.

I twisted into him as the second wave of sparkling bliss hit, beginning in my core and exploding through my body as he pushed the rest of the way inside me. He was lodged deep, his chest pressed to my breasts, his mouth on mine.

"That's it, Maddie," he murmured. "Let me love you."

I held him tightly as he moved, his hips pumping, then retreating, then thrusting forward again, filling me anew. Nothing could have prepared me for this. I was raw and yet so incredibly fulfilled. I ached, pleasure to the point of almost pain, as he moved in and out of me, claiming me, making me his wife in deed.

And he hadn't been wrong. This was nothing like the animals. This was so much more, the exhilarating union of heart and body and even soul, or so it seemed to me as another shudder rocked through me. I was coming undone yet again, the driving glide of his cock taking me to the edge. He stiffened and moaned my name, throwing his head back as he surrendered to the sweet oblivion of desire. I felt the hot rush of his seed, and I reached for him again, pulling him back down to me for a kiss as his cock throbbed deep within me.

It was in that moonlit moment, our hearts pounding and bodies joined, that I knew I was in love with my husband.

CHAPTER 15

MADELEINE

"Is the proposed menu for the week to your liking, Lady Wheaton?" Mrs. Dougall asked as we were seated in the cheerfully sunlit room I had chosen as my sitting room.

We met once a week so that I could review the meals Cook would prepare. I was still new to managing a household, and I was grateful to the housekeeper for her kindly guidance as I learned all the responsibilities I now had as mistress of the house.

"You know better than I what his lordship prefers," I demurred. "Do you think these will please him?"

To be sure, being the Marchioness of Wheaton was vastly different from being a lowly chambermaid at Cliffwood. My days had become a happy blend of tending to the needs of the house and spending time with Alexander whenever I could. And my nights—well, I didn't dare think about my nights just now, seated before Mrs. Dougall. I'd likely turn red as an apple.

They were my favorite part of every day.

"I do believe these will all be suited to Lord Wheaton's

tastes," Mrs. Dougall told me, smiling. "He is especially fond of Savoy cake."

"I shall have to remember that." My husband possessed something of a sweet tooth. "He never wishes to make requests when I ask him. He tells me that he will be happy with whatever I choose."

Mrs. Dougall's smile turned fond. "I do think there are perhaps a few dishes he might turn up his nose at. He never has cared for pickled figs or fricassee of rabbit, for instance."

I committed these dislikes to memory as well, knowing I still had much to learn about my husband as well as my household duties. But I looked forward to both. I had settled into my life here at Wheaton with a graceful ease, and I was heartily grateful for it.

"That is excellent to know, Mrs. Dougall. As I've never particularly cared for either of those, I shan't miss them." I paused to peruse the list I had made in anticipation of our meeting. "How is the airing out of the music room progressing?"

"The music room will be ready for you and his lordship this evening," Mrs. Dougall informed me. "I know his lordship was looking forward to you playing for him on the pianoforte. It was tuned earlier this morning by Mr. Winthrop in the village."

"That is wonderful news," I said, though a hint of worry laced my delight at the news.

The music room at Wheaton Hall had long been closed up, the furniture and pianoforte hiding under coverings. When Alexander had suggested that I make use of it once more, I had been overjoyed at the prospect of having a music room to myself and the leisure to be able to play again. But it had been years since I had last had lessons, and I worried my husband was doomed to disappointment.

"If I may be so bold, my lady," Mrs. Dougall added, a glint entering her eyes. "I must say how pleased I am to have a mistress in this house. I had begun to despair that Lord Wheaton would never take a bride. To see him so contented with you now warms my heart. He is such a fine gentleman, none better."

"Yes, he is," I agreed without hesitation, even if I did feel my cheeks going warm.

It made me happy to think that Alexander was contented in our marriage. I thought he was, but neither of us had yet spoken words of love. It was my greatest hope that, in time, he may return my feelings. Hearing someone who knew him as well as Mrs. Dougall did suggest I made him happy boosted my spirits, making me forget my dismay at potentially harming his ears with my poor pianoforte skills later.

"Forgive me, my lady. I don't know why I've turned into a watering pot." Mrs. Dougall dabbed at her eyes with a handkerchief.

"There is no need to apologize," I assured her. "It pleases me to know that you care for my husband as you do."

The housekeeper sniffed, regaining her formidable composure once again. "Well, then. Before I turn maudlin, is there anything else you require of me today, my lady?"

"I was also hoping to hire a few more maids and footmen from the village if you think it prudent," I said. "Now that we are residing here at Wheaton, with, God willing, the promise of a family beckoning, I believe some more domestics would be helpful."

Mrs. Dougall nodded. "The nursery will have to be aired out next, I should think. A few more hands to help would be just the thing."

The nursery.

I didn't allow myself to linger overly long on that room. I had long dreamed of becoming a mother, of having a family. And now, that dream was at last within my reach.

"Thank you, Mrs. Dougall," I said, "I will entrust the matter to your capable hands."

As she was more familiar with the needs of Wheaton, I would defer to her.

The housekeeper beamed at me, clearly overjoyed to be holding the reins. "I would be more than happy to do so, Lady Wheaton."

We finished our discussion, and I decided to inspect the music room just down the hall. No servants were lingering within as I crossed the threshold, amazed at the difference that had come to pass over the last few days. Like my salon, the music room had a bank of windows that allowed a cheerful amount of natural light to filter into the chamber. The pianoforte was handsome, fashioned of satinwood and tulipwood with inlaid floral decorations spanning the sides and front. A comfortable-looking bench had been placed before it, with a harp, flute, and violin.

I never learned to play the violin, but I had tried my hand at the flute and harp. My mother had taught me. Perhaps I might play a simple tune for Alexander this evening after dinner. I moved to the pianoforte first, running my fingers lightly over the keys. The sound was clear and loud, perfectly in tune. Mr. Winthrop had performed his job well.

I missed making music. Listening to music. I missed what music had meant to me, what seemed a lifetime ago. My mother had been a talented singer and a skilled musician, and I had grown up watching her play before learning from her when I was old enough. Hearing the random notes I had played took me back to a different time, when I had been protected and comfortable. When I had never worked or feared. When I had never gathered reeds and awaited my punishment.

A stunning rush of grief sliced through me.

"I miss you, Mother," I whispered aloud.

A song returned to me, one of her favorites, called "Shepherds, I Have Lost My Love." To my amazement, I realized I remembered it, each note coming to me as I hovered over the pianoforte, my eyes filmed with the wistful mist of my tears.

When I reached the final, haunting note, the sound of applause startled me. I whirled about, heart leaping into my throat, to discover that I had an audience. Alexander watched me from the door to the music room, gazing at me with such blatant affection that I had to swallow hard to maintain my composure.

"Husband." I offered him a curtsy, feeling foolish for not realizing he had been watching and listening. "I hadn't realized you were at home, or else I wouldn't have been picking at keys."

He sketched an elegant bow and then strode into the room, bringing the vitality of the outdoors with him. He was dressed for riding, and I knew he had been out tending to the estate again with Mr. Warwick. What a dashing figure he cut, his long hair held in a queue at his nape, his breeches outlining muscular thighs, his boots gleaming. As he approached me, I caught his familiar scent of leather and fresh country air.

His dark eyes were warm upon me as he reached for my hand and brought it to his lips for a reverent kiss. "Then I am glad you didn't realize I had returned, or else I might have missed the opportunity to hear my beautiful wife play."

He chased my sadness with such ease. How happy he made me.

I smiled at him as he delivered lingering kisses to my knuckles. "I believe you are being far too gallant. I haven't played in many years."

"Time has not diminished your talent."

"My fingers are not as agile as they were in my youth." I thought of the reddened skin, the scars I bore from years of drudgery as a maid and suffering punishments from my father.

Here at Wheaton, I had grown accustomed to occasionally foregoing my gloves over the last few weeks. But reminders such as this brought back my shame over the state of my hands.

"Your fingers are perfect. As you are." As if to prove his point, Alexander delivered a new round of kisses to my knuckles.

"My hands will never be the soft, beautiful hands of a lady."

That had been taken from me. But I didn't mourn the loss so much for myself as for my husband. I wanted to be the wife he deserved.

"I adore your hands." In demonstration, he turned mine over, exposing my palm where the damage was worst, and kissed me reverently there. "They are beautiful and soft, and they most definitely belong to a lady. To the finest lady I am privileged to know." He kissed me again, his eyes burning into mine. "I especially love them when they touch me."

Longing hit me. "Then perhaps they should touch you now."

A slow, wicked grin curved his lips. "Why, Lady Wheaton, you do surprise me with your offer. What am I, your humble servant, to do but accept?"

"Surely you must be hungry from your travels this morning," I suggested thickly.

"I am starving, Maddie mine," he murmured, drawing me into his arms and holding me against his big, broad chest.

I felt safe. Comforted. I also felt desired. I wrapped my arms around his neck, the lingering sadness gone. I may have lost the old life I once had, but this was my new life, and it was brimming with hope.

"Then you must have your repast," I told him, tilting my head back and offering him my lips.

"Oh, that I shall." His mouth teased mine in a gentle kiss that left me yearning for him. "Come to my bedchamber with me, and I'll have my fill."

"In the midst of the day, my lord?" I feigned astonishment.

But in truth, we didn't relegate our lovemaking to the nights, and I didn't mind one bit. My husband's appetite matched my own in that regard.

"I can't wait another minute." He kissed me again.

"But what will the servants think?"

"That I cannot resist the incomparable Lady Wheaton." He nuzzled my throat. "And they would be correct. Now, come with me, wife. I don't think that piano bench is robust enough for what I have in mind…"

I laughed, feeling giddy, and allowed my husband to lead me from the music room, our hands entwined. We made our way through the main hall and up the curved wooden staircase to the floor housing our adjoined rooms. It occurred to me that Lydia might be within my bedchamber, sorting through some of the laundry that would have been brought up from the washhouse. But Alexander led me to his room, sparing me the need to fret.

We made our way over the threshold, and the door had

scarcely even clicked closed before I was in his arms and his mouth was on mine. We undressed each other with trembling hands. Buttons and hooks and tapes opened. It didn't matter that we had been married and making love for weeks now. I was even more caught up in my feelings for him. I knelt on the floor and helped him to tug off his boots. He rolled down my stockings, his lips trailing a reverent path over the bare skin he newly revealed.

At long last, every last stitch of clothing had been removed, and Alexander guided me to the bed.

"Sit, Maddie mine."

The bed was high and my legs were short. A stool had been discreetly placed by the bedside for my use. I used it now, leveraging myself onto the mattress and turning to face him. Although I was growing ever more comfortable in my nudity and the passion between us, I nonetheless felt a bit shy, pressing my thighs together as I devoured my husband's form with my gaze. If I had thought him magnificent in the moonlight, he was ten times more glorious by daylight, with every inch of his powerful body lovingly illuminated by the sun shining in the windows.

His chest was broad, his arms strong, his legs lean and muscular. I remained fascinated by the dusting of masculine hair covering him, by the way it felt against me. And also by his cock, which stood proudly erect, a pearl of moisture already seeping from the slit at the tip.

He approached me slowly, his eyes frankly admiring in a way that made me feel boundlessly beautiful, as if I were the loveliest woman he had ever beheld. I didn't know if it was true, but when he looked at me thus, it was easy to imagine that it might be.

"How sweet you look, sitting naked on my bed, waiting for me," he said, stopping before me and bending down to press his mouth to mine.

I kissed him with a moan, my own need for him already embarrassingly acute, opening for his questing tongue. His hands moved to my aching breasts, cupping them, his thumbs moving unerringly over my stiff nipples. I kissed him harder in response, threading my fingers through his hair. They caught in the leather thong he had used to tie his dark locks back, and I pulled it away, casting it to the carpet. He kissed a path down my throat and then lower, over my breast until he found the peak, his lips fastening over it to suck.

I watched him in fascination, this handsome man who was somehow mine. His eyes were closed, his lashes fanned out, his cheeks hollowing as he suckled the other breast. The pleasure was so sharp and wondrous that I moaned, arching my back. He withdrew to run his tongue over the pink tip, licking and teasing until I felt an answering wetness between my thighs.

But instead of returning to my lips as I had supposed he would, Alexander continued kissing down my body, over my stomach. He sank to his knees before me, gently caressing my thighs to part them as he went. His lips fluttered over my navel, then pressed to my hip bone. He was alarmingly close to my center in a way he had not been before.

"Alexander," I protested. "What are you doing?"

He kissed my thigh and glanced up at me, the heat in his eyes enough to take my breath. "I want to taste you. Will you let me?"

Taste me? I didn't know entirely what he meant, but my body was thrilled by the notion, my cunny clenching at his words.

"How?" I managed breathlessly. "Where?"

His left hand guided my thighs apart a bit more, whilst

his right tenderly caressed my mound. "Your pretty cunny. I'll put my mouth on you here."

Liquid desire pooled deep within me. His suggestion certainly felt sinful, but Alexander was a patient, attentive lover. He had shown me how to find my pleasure, how to revel in the things we did together in the marriage bed, all of it so new to me and yet so incredible. I trusted him. Trusted him with my body, with my heart.

"Is that very wicked?" I asked, tempted to pump my hips against his hand, desperate for friction.

"No more wicked than anything else we have done together as husband and wife," he reassured me, the tender smile on his lips banishing my hesitation. "If you aren't ready for me to do so yet, you need only say so, Maddie mine. All I want is to please you."

Still, I hesitated. The notion of Alexander's mouth between my legs thrilled me. I felt a bit dizzied.

"Would you like it?" I asked, wanting to be sure.

He removed his hand and slowly trailed his middle finger along my seam, parting my folds until he found the pearl hidden at the top and swirled his touch over the swollen, eager bud.

"I would love it," he told me, his voice hoarse with desire. "I've been dreaming of licking you until you spend on my tongue."

He teased me with that lone finger, making me ache for more. The longing evident in his voice and countenance couldn't be denied. His eyes were on me, feasting on me as he gathered the moisture from my opening and painted it over my lower lips. He wanted this, and I wanted it too.

"Then yes," I murmured, feeling a streak of delicious anticipation burst through me and settle between my legs. "I want you to."

He made a low sound reminiscent of a growl, not

wasting any time in removing his touch from me and replacing it with his mouth. He kissed me there, on my mound. A chaste kiss, then another. And then there was the hot, wet swipe of his tongue.

I cried out and shifted, nearly falling from the edge of the bed.

Alexander was there to catch me, to keep me planted where I was. His big hands held me in place as he licked me slowly, languorously, as if he were tasting the finest, most decadent confection. Sensation arced through me like lightning in a night sky. He flicked his tongue over my bud, his eyes on mine.

I couldn't look away. There was something so sensual about this big man on his knees just to bring me pleasure. About his hot stare.

"You are delicious," he told me, his lips glistening with my dew.

And then he lowered his head again, licking faster, making my hips rock as I instinctively thrust myself against his face. He made a deep sound of approval and sucked on my nub as he had my nipples, drawing hard.

The most exquisite burst of desire hit me, nearly splitting me in two. I reached my pinnacle, a shudder tearing through me that I was helpless to stop. He hummed, the rumble vibrating through my cunny and intensifying my release. As bliss radiated from my core, he strummed a lone digit over my entrance. He teased me with the shallow dip of his finger, still sucking hard as he sank it deep.

I clenched on him instantly. His hands were confident and strong. He knew how to use them to prolong my pleasure and bring me more. And he was determined, it seemed, to wring every drop of it from me. His clever tongue played over me as he alternated between licking and sucking, and when a second finger joined the first, I lost control again, a choked sob emerging from me.

I was still breathless, my heart pounding as Alexander rose to his substantial height and gently arranged me on the bed. He joined me, the protective weight of his body covering mine. I wrapped my arms around him, holding him to me as he gripped his rigid cock and directed it to me. Tipping my hips upward, I met him in a thrust that had him seated to the hilt. We both cried out at the rightness of it, our bodies moving together in a stirring rhythm.

"Maddie mine," he groaned, pumping into me, his face a study in ecstasy.

I committed every moment to memory, the ripple of his arm muscles as he leveraged himself on the bed, the strength of his broad chest, the way his mahogany hair hung around his handsome face. His brown eyes met and held with mine as he moved within me. My love for him rose along with my desire to a searing crescendo. I wanted to cry out my feelings, to reveal what I had been keeping to myself these last few weeks of our marriage.

But then he slanted his mouth over mine, taking my lips in a voracious kiss, and words were lost to me. I tasted myself on his lips, felt my nipples grazing his chest, the sensual glide of his cock in and out of me. It was too much. I was flying again, high above the clouds, soaring along with him. My body contracted on his length, and with a groan, he buried himself deep, filling me with the hot rush of his seed.

I clung to him afterward, holding him tightly, burrowing my face into his neck, feeling our hearts pound together as one. Our bodies were still joined, slick with perspiration, fully sated.

"I'll crush you, love," he protested.

"I like you here," I countered, holding him tighter.

He chuckled. "But you're so small compared to my big, beastly frame."

I kissed his throat. "I love your big, beastly frame."

And I love you.

But I didn't say it. Not yet. For now, I was content to hold him.

Gently, he rolled us to our sides, so that I faced him, still locked in each other's embrace.

Alexander smiled tenderly. "I'm glad I had the opportunity to come back for a repast today. I've been leaving you far too much."

"I know you have an estate to run," I protested, admiring him for the devotion he showed to the people who depended upon him.

"Yes, but I also have a new wife." He brushed a tendril of hair from my forehead, making me realize that in our haste, I hadn't unbound my hair.

The lock must have slipped out during our frenzied lovemaking.

"Not so new any longer," I teased, turning to kiss his palm as he had done to mine earlier in the music room.

He chuckled. "Nor so old, yet. I've been remiss, Maddie mine. We haven't even had a honeymoon."

He was always thinking of me, looking after my happiness.

"I don't require a honeymoon. I'm happy here at Wheaton."

He caressed my cheek. "I am well pleased that you have found your footing at Wheaton and that you've made it your home. Mrs. Dougall tells me that you have taken to being the mistress here with a natural aplomb that is a credit to you, and I heartily concur. You are, as ever, a source of wonder to me."

Warmth crept over my cheeks. I wasn't sure I deserved Alexander's praise.

"Mrs. Dougall has been helping me," I said. "I'm grateful to her tutelage. Being belowstairs for so many years at Cliffwood hardly prepared me for such a responsibility."

The moment the words left me, I regretted them. Alexander's face darkened with anger toward my father.

"You were born to this," he told me fervently, "and you never should have been made to suffer. Your father deserves to rot in Hades for eternity for what he did to you."

"Let's not speak of him," I suggested, for I didn't like for my thoughts to linger on the wretchedness of that part of my life.

My dreams were plagued by my father with far less frequency these days, and I had no wish for that to change.

"Agreed." He kissed the tip of my nose. "Let's speak of happier things. I want to take you to London."

My eyebrows rose. "London? Whatever for?"

"To spoil you. To show you off. To give you a hint of what you deserve."

"To show me off? Why would you wish to do so?"

"Because I am proud of you, Maddie mine."

"And spoil me? My goodness, Alexander, you have already spoiled me richly."

"Not nearly enough." He kissed me softly, lingeringly. "It is time you had the honeymoon you deserve. We leave tomorrow for a few days in Town."

"But what of Wheaton? You've been so busy with your tenants."

"Edward will take over in my absence. While the weather is yet good for travel, I'm going to take my beautiful wife to London. What say you?"

I had not been shopping in years, and I had to admit that the idea held appeal.

"I say that sounds lovely."

"Then it's settled," he proclaimed, grinning at me like a boy who had a secret he could scarcely contain.

He kissed me again, and I felt him stirring within me. I held him tighter, giving him my tongue, and he rolled me onto my back once more.

CHAPTER 16

MADELEINE

"Another book of poetry," I exclaimed, staring in delight at the small bound leather volume in my gloved hands.

"If my lady wants it, then she shall have it," Alexander said gallantly as he approached me, bearing an armload of books I had already chosen from the shelves.

"Oh, but your arms are already quite full," I protested, thinking of how dear the tomes were.

Alexander wished to spoil me, but we had already been to the jeweler, the haberdasher, and the dressmakers on Bond Street. He had been adamant that no expense was to be spared. I had no notion of the cost of what he had already bought for me—gowns that would be custom made for me and delivered to his London town house later, an exquisite parure of emeralds and sapphires, and enough sewing notions and bonnets to keep me occupied for at least the next year. Still, I knew he must have spent a fortune.

"I will deliver these to the desk and be at the ready to hold more," Alexander told me.

I bit my lip, feeling guilty at the expenditures.

"I'll be back in a moment," he said with a wink, not waiting for my approval. "Carry on with your book shopping."

I sighed as he left, juggling the stack of books with ease, and then turned back to the book in my hands. I hadn't had books of my own in years. The jewels and gowns were lovely, but nothing made me happier than the thought of books that were mine alone. And this one was so very handsome. I could read the poems to Alexander in the evening by the fire. He could rest his head in my lap.

It was settled. I *needed* this book. Another spine caught my eye, and I slid it from the shelf.

Alexander returned, dutifully collecting another armload before I was finally contented. As we returned to our waiting carriage with the promise that the books would be delivered to the town house later that day, I sighed in pleasure.

"I could have bought the entire shop," I told him.

Alexander grinned. "I thought you might enjoy the bookseller. Now I know the true way to your heart. I had believed it would be jewels and finery, but it is merely ink on paper, bound in leather."

Warmth stole over me. "I think you have already found the way to my heart, my lord."

It was the closest I dared come to a declaration.

"Then perhaps we should return to the town house and skip the last stop I had planned."

The lightness in his tone suggested he was teasing me.

"What is the last stop?" I ventured, curious.

He grinned. "It is a surprise, Maddie mine."

Each shop we had visited thus far had been chosen by him. Some of them, he had informed me, with the help of Lady Beckett. For, as Alexander had confided, he hadn't an inkling which mantua-maker to choose. We had paid a call upon Lady Beckett and her husband the day before, and I had been grateful to see familiar faces amidst the bustle of London.

"I suppose I shouldn't ruin your surprise," I told him, curious about where else he could have planned to take me. "Although I am already extraordinarily spoiled."

"You deserve it, wife."

"I don't know if I deserve it, but I shall accept it just the same."

He smiled, looking pleased. He cocked his head, studying me, then spoke.

"Maddie mine, I want to tell you something."

ALEXANDER

The impulsive journey I had brought Maddie on was going splendidly. Watching her take in London was a treat. She loved the same things I did. Had the same dislikes.

Spoiling her was a joy beyond compare. She was as astounded and grateful by a small bowl of cream ice as she was the lavish gifts I bestowed upon her. When the jeweler laid the trays before her of the items I had picked out, she had stared at them, bewitched and shocked, for a full five minutes. When I slipped the ring I had chosen to add to the simple gold band I had placed on her finger on our wedding day, she gasped. It was delicate and lovely—much like my wife, the tiny sapphires twinkling in the lights.

"I wanted to add to my token," I explained.

She gazed up at me with such adoration, my breath caught.

"Nothing you give me is a token, my husband. Everything has great meaning to me."

Unable to control myself, I bent forward and kissed her.

I watched, fascinated, as she tried on the pieces I had selected for her to choose from. I could tell which pieces pleased her simply by the expression on her countenance. When she was in utter delight, her lips curled up without her knowing. Her beautiful eyes brightened. When something did not suit, although she smiled, it was different.

At my behest, the jeweler brought in more pieces and, finally, she sat back.

"If I may," she murmured, "I should love the sapphire and pearl set."

I glanced at the tray holding the necklace with a matching set of earrings and a bracelet.

"And the ring, Maddie mine? You liked that as well."

"If it is not too much."

I chuckled as I slid the chosen items, plus all the other pieces I knew she loved and I preferred, toward the man waiting anxiously to find out how much I was spending.

"All these, if you please. Have them delivered to my town house. My man will attend them."

I felt Maddie's shock as he hurried away, pleased beyond his expectations.

"Alexander," she protested. "It is too much. One set will do me."

"No, it will not. I am buying you everything, Maddie.

We will not take the coral or the jade, as they did not please you. But everything else is yours as my wedding gift to you."

Her thanks was beyond enthused, both in the way she kissed me before the jeweler returned and later that day in our home.

The memories of that passion still roamed freely in my head. I had never experienced the rush of sensations I felt with my wife. How her smile brought me happiness. Her laughter made my chest lighter. Her mere presence calmed something in me I never knew was lacking. She had become more than I ever imagined another human being could be.

The feel of her hand on my arm brought me out of my musings. I shook my head to clear it, seeing her looking anxious after I spoke.

She drew herself up. "Is it bad news, Alexander? Have I done—"

I shook my head, taking her hands. "Nothing. You have done nothing, my love. Do not fall back into fear with me."

I waited as she took a deep breath, calming herself. "No. I will never fear you."

"Good." I regarded her fondly. "Never is good." I leaned forward, keeping my voice low.

"I spoke with my solicitor yesterday and made some arrangements."

"For?"

"I have established a trust for you. It will be added to annually for as long as I live."

"Whatever for?"

"For you. Money of your own. I want you to have it. To use as you wish."

She blinked, no doubt feeling stunned and overcome by my statement.

"Alexander," she whispered. "You already provide for me so generously."

I leaned closer, shaking my head. "You had years of nothing, my wife. Of being denied. I wish for you to have everything. I have the means to provide that."

"If I have you, I have everything," she replied, breathless.

I smiled at her words. What they implied. I prayed they meant what I hoped they did. That perhaps, she, too, was feeling the same tender feelings for me as I was for her. I had come to the realization that I was in love with my wife and was waiting for the right time to declare myself. I reached out and stroked her cheek.

"And I have everything with you. But this is for you. Use it how you wish. The money is yours. You do not need to ask permission to spend it. It is simply a gift to you from your husband. It means you will never have to ask anyone's permission again." I sat back, pleased. "We will discuss all the particulars when we return to Wheaton. I only wanted to tell you of it."

Her eyes shone with unshed tears, and she grasped my hands tightly. "You are the most generous, thoughtful man," she whispered. "I am honored to be your wife."

I smiled, lifting her gloved hand to my lips and kissing it. "I am the fortunate one, Maddie mine. You make me happier than I deserve."

"You deserve everything," she replied.

I met her eyes, a silent conversation flowing between us. It held promises of the future for both of us.

MADELEINE

I was stunned by what Alexander said to me. The way he bestowed yet another unexpected, thoughtful, extravagant gift on me. I had never known anyone like him. This tall, strong, powerful, yet incredibly gentle man who was generous, capable, giving, and so loving toward me.

The gifts he handed to me were numerous and expensive, but none was as worthy as the man himself.

Could he, I wondered, love me the way I had fallen in love with him?

Across from me, he chuckled. "One more surprise today, Maddie mine, then we shall be done. We will head home to Wheaton on the morrow and start our life together, yes?"

"Yes."

The carriage rocked on through the steady traffic as a companionable silence fell. I would be contented to return to Wheaton and the quiet stillness of the countryside soon, but I had to admit that our jaunt to Town had been more than pleasant. Not just because of the vast spoiling Alexander had done of me either. But because of all the time we had been able to spend together. There were no tenants, no estate matters to take him away from me in London. It was only the two of us.

The carriage rocked to a halt again.

Alexander leaned forward and peered through the Venetian blinds on the window. "Ah, we have arrived at our next destination."

A groom opened the carriage door. Alexander exited first and turned back to offer me a hand. Feeling as giddy as a schoolgirl, I placed my hand in his and alighted from the carriage. The tall, elegantly appointed building before boasted a sign that read Bellingham and Co. Two banks of windows showed off the wares within. I recognized it at once as London's most prestigious shop.

"Lady Beckett told me about Bellingham and Co.," I said delightedly. "She told me there are various departments, with everything from clocks to bonnets and fans."

Alexander smiled down at me, offering his arm. "I am acquainted with the owner, Mr. Tarquin Bellingham, and he has been kind enough to procure some special items for you that I think you may find of particular interest."

I settled my hand in the crook of his elbow, wondering what special items Alexander could have possibly thought of. Already, he had plied me with stockings, gowns, undergarments, bonnets, sewing items, jewels, and books.

We ventured within and were instantly greeted by an affable gentleman who offered to provide us with a tour of the varying departments. Alexander accepted, which was just as well because I was too busy craning my neck to observe the vast array of goods the store sold as we moved about. Furs and fans, haberdashery, fine furniture, jewels, clocks, and even perfumes. I had never seen the like, and certainly not all in one place.

The establishment was a fine one. I had no doubt that everything within was quite costly.

"Mr. Bellingham has gathered the goods he felt may be of interest to you, and they are arranged in a private shopping room, Lord Wheaton," the clerk said when the tour of the expansive and impressive store was finished. "This way, if you please, my lord, my lady."

"Thank you, that would be most agreeable," Alexander said.

The clerk guided us to a door on the periphery of the haberdashery department and bowed. "If you require assistance, I would be more than happy to provide it, my lord."

Alexander gestured for me to precede him into the small, paneled room. And the moment I was within, I couldn't contain my cry of pure happiness. I rushed forward, instantly recognizing pencils and crayons for drawing, along with papers and brushes. A handsome mahogany box was on the table at the room's center.

I turned back to Alexander, finding him watching me with an affectionate expression on his face. The clerk had discreetly closed the door behind us, leaving us alone, and I had been too caught up in the drawing supplies that I had failed to take note.

"What is in this box?" I asked.

"Open it and see," Alexander invited.

I lifted the lid and discovered cakes of watercolor within, along with a glass for water and a palette in a lower drawer. Ultramarine, Prussian blue, Carmine, Purple Lake, Venetian red, and yellow ochre were lined up neatly, their bright hues beckoning for a paintbrush.

"It is a painting box," I exclaimed softly. "It's beautiful."

I had never seen anything so fine. After so many years of making the ends of pencils and scraps of paper my father had cast off suffice, the sight of so many new, glorious implements was like something from a dream.

"Do you like it?" Alexander asked.

I turned back to him. "I adore it. Thank you for arranging for me to see it. Perhaps I will have a few small pencils. Enough to last me until another trip to London."

"I'm afraid not," Alexander said. "You're to have it all, Maddie mine."

My mouth fell open. "Everything?"

He nodded, grinning. "Everything. And more, too. Bellingham will procure anything you like. All we need do is ask."

I pressed a hand over my heart. "But this must be a small fortune."

"I told you that I intended to spoil you, and I meant it."

Tears pricked my eyes, and I had to take a moment to blink furiously to keep them from falling. He had remembered our first conversation in the carriage, the day he had brought me to Wheaton from Cliffwood.

"I don't know how to thank you, Alexander," I managed. Nothing had ever prepared me for this man. For this life.

"It isn't your thanks I want," he told me. "It's your happiness."

"You have that," I told him softly, love for him swelling in my heart. "More than I ever imagined possible."

He took my hand in his and brought it to his lips for a kiss. "Good. Now come along, wife. We have some furs, fans, and furniture to peruse."

"We shall fill your house," I protested.

"Our house, Maddie mine," he corrected, pulling me into him for a kiss.

"Alexander," I protested against his lips with a delighted squeak. "What if someone comes upon us?"

"Let them."

His lips moved over mine, and I forgot to care.

"I don't think London agrees with my constitution," I told Lydia just before I retched for the second time in my chamber pot.

My stomach roiled, and the room spun around me.

I was meant to be getting dressed for a final call upon Lord and Lady Beckett before Alexander and I returned to Wheaton, but after rising from Alexander's bed and venturing next door to my bedchamber, I had quickly begun to fall ill.

With a violent heave, I emptied the remnants of my stomach into the porcelain vessel.

Lydia calmly soothed me, her hand rubbing between my shoulder blades. "I've never heard of London making anyone bilious."

"Then perhaps I ate bad fish." I passed the back of my hand over my mouth in an indecorous swipe, trying to recall what our meals had been the day before and where we had taken them.

My stomach violently rebelled at the very notion of fish, and I wished I hadn't spoken the concern aloud. I moaned, hanging my head back over the chamber pot as another heave went through me. Blessedly, nothing emerged this time. Apparently, I had emptied my accounts entirely.

"I don't believe there was a fish course at all yesterday," Lydia mused. "Cook prepared a roast, haricot verts, white soup…"

My stomach surged again. "Please, don't speak of food."

The mere thought of any sustenance at all made me want to vomit anew.

"Forgive me. I'll fetch you a cool cloth for your brow. Perhaps that will help."

I was on my knees on the Axminster in my chemise and stockings, which was as far as Lydia had been able to get with my toilette before I had grown sick. My knees ached and I still felt faintly dizzied. What unexpected misery after such a wonderful trip to Town. I remained where I was as Lydia returned to me with calm efficiency, bringing me a cloth she had dampened and wrung of excess liquid and setting it over my brow.

"Thank you, dear friend." Wincing, I held the cloth to my head and closed my eyes to keep the walls from dancing. "I have been feeling a bit odd for the last few days. Yesterday, I was so tired that I needed to nap in the afternoon, and my head ached terribly. Perhaps I've been coming down with an ague and didn't realize it."

"Perhaps," Lydia said, a strange note entering her voice.

I opened my eyes, staring at her, noting an odd expression on her countenance as well. "Why are you looking at me that way? Have I something on my chin?"

Good heavens, what a dreadful mess I must look. I took the cloth from my brow and used it to dab the area around my mouth, the nausea slightly subsiding.

"It isn't that," Lydia said, her voice strained.

"Well, what is it, then? Tell me what you are thinking. I know you well enough by now. There is something you aren't saying. What is amiss?"

Lydia bit her lower lip. "It is only that… Well, I haven't taken notice of when you had your courses."

I frowned. "What has that to do with catching an ague? I don't recollect the two ever being related. And besides, I had my courses back at Cliffwood."

"Precisely." Lydia was still looking at me with that same, wide-eyed expression. "And it has been more than two months since you were last at Cliffwood. You should have had your courses by now."

"You think that is why I'm ill, because I haven't had my courses?"

"No, Maddie," Lydia said gently, hovering over me and patting my arm. "I think you're with child."

I was finally dressed.

I had rinsed my mouth, washed my face.

Lydia had helped me into a beautiful new morning gown that I had received the day before from the dressmaker on Bond Street. A white sprigged muslin, it hugged my figure perfectly. My hair was secured in a simple chignon.

But all I could think as I tapped at the door connecting my chamber to Alexander's was that I was going to have a babe. Alexander's babe. I was going to be a mother.

My knees went a bit weak as I listened for his voice tinged with surprise.

"Come."

He had expected to meet me at the breakfast table as we had planned when I'd left him naked and sated in bed. But I wasn't certain that my stomach could withstand the sights and smells of so many foods just yet.

And besides, I had two bits of very important news to impart.

With a deep breath, I opened the door and entered his room. Alexander was dressed, shaved, and handsome as ever, his hair already brushed and confined at his nape. His dark eyes swept over me as I crossed the carpet to him.

"Is something wrong?" He wanted to know, striding toward me. "You look pale, darling. I thought I heard some odd noises a bit ago coming from your room."

My cheeks went hot. He had heard me retching. That hadn't crossed my mind before now, but there wasn't anything I could do about it. And according to Lydia, I would have more mornings like this one to come.

"I was feeling a bit…ill earlier," I admitted, glancing over his shoulder. "Where is your valet?"

"Off tending to his duties for the day," Alexander said, frowning mightily as he took my hands in his. "Do you need to sit? I expect I am to blame, running you ragged as I have all over Town."

"You aren't to blame," I hastened to reassure him. "I have loved every moment of you spoiling me here in London."

And he had spoiled me mightily. We would return to Wheaton with a carriage laden with gowns, art supplies, shoes, jewels, books, and more.

"And I have loved spoiling you, Maddie mine." He studied me intently. "Are you sure you wouldn't like to sit?"

"No." I swallowed hard, summoning my courage. "There is something I must tell you, Alexander. Two things I must say, actually."

"Of course. Tell me what it is that troubles you."

I inhaled deeply, looking up at the man I had married. The man who had saved me. The man I loved. The father of the babe growing within me.

"I'm not ill," I told him. "I *am* in a delicate condition, however."

Somehow, telling him I was having his child was easier than saying those three words that continued to elude me.

He stilled, his expression shifting from surprise to awe to happiness. "You're going to have a babe?"

I nodded. "Yes."

A magnificent grin curved his lips, and he took me into his arms as if I were as fragile as Sèvres porcelain. "Oh, Maddie mine. You're going to be a mother, and I shall be a father."

"Does the news…please you?"

"Need you ask?" The corners of his eyes crinkled as he stared down at me as if I had just performed some manner of miracle before him. "I am thrilled, my sweet. Elated. I am the happiest man in all England."

I smiled, pleased to see him so taken with the notion already. "Good. Then I must tell you the other news as well."

He raised a brow. "Whatever can it be?"

"That I'm in love with you."

I held my breath, awaiting his reaction, and stared at the painting on the wall behind him, too afraid to look. A hint of dizziness returned, making me sway. A sudden burst of nervousness assailed me.

Perhaps this was too soon.

Or he didn't return my feelings.

He had married me out of pity, for heaven's sake. I had been naught but a maid when we met. What had I expected? Oh, what I fool I was to think the time had come to confess my feelings. He desired me, but love and desire were two discrete feelings. Could one be had without the other?

"Maddie."

His voice was deep. Beloved.

I still didn't dare look at his face for fear of what I'd see.

"Maddie mine, look at me."

It was the gentleness in his tone and the endearment he

used for me that granted me courage. I tore my gaze from the wall.

And my heart leapt.

Alexander was looking at me with raw admiration. With such tender caring. With love.

"You love me? Truly?"

I was sure my answer was already written on my face and likely had been this last month at least.

"Yes. I've fallen in love with you."

He drew me against him and cupped my face in his hands, hands that touched me with such worshipful reverence. "My darling wife, now you have made me the happiest man in all the world. For I love you too."

I had to cling to his shoulders to keep from swooning. Perhaps it was my condition, or perhaps it was simply the joyous surge within me.

Alexander loved me.

This man. This beautiful, caring, compassionate, wonderful man. My husband. My lover. The father of this precious babe I carried. The Marquess of Wheaton. He loved me.

"Oh, Alexander." My vision blurred, and suddenly, hot tears were rolling down my cheeks as I sobbed.

"Why are you weeping, my love?" He dotted kisses over my cheeks, drying my tears with his lips.

I sniffled. "Because I am also the happiest woman in the world."

His mouth found mine, and we kissed furiously, feverishly, laced with the salt of my tears.

When I was breathless, he raised his head, gazing down at me with dark, glistening eyes. "I shall have to buy you pencils and watercolors more often."

I laughed. "I would be happy without another pencil or

paint for the rest of my life as long as I had you and our babe."

"Our babe," he repeated softly, wonder in his voice.

He dipped his head, his lips unerringly finding mine, and I kissed the man I loved.

For the first time in my life, I had everything I had ever wanted.

CHAPTER 17

ALEXANDER

I woke in the early morning, blinking my eyes open to the dawn breaking through the large windows.

Maddie had begged me to allow her to move the bed to the wall that faced the arched panes and remove the heavy draperies that covered the glass. Although I felt it unneeded, I was unable to refuse, and now, I had to admit she was correct. The view when we woke in the mornings was spectacular. She loved to lie in our bed and see the stars and the sun. Having spent so many years in a windowless room under the neglect of her father, I understood her longing. The joy on her face as she stared outside brought a boon to my chest I could not explain but no longer denied.

Her happiness was now my happiness.

I turned my head slightly, smiling at the sight of my little wife asleep beside me. Neither of us could fathom not being in the same bed every night. She was a small bundle of warmth curled next to me, her hand resting on my heart, the heat of our bodies melding and comforting us. The lace strap of her shift hung from her shoulder, the pearl of her creamy skin glimmering in the growing light. She was peaceful and content in her repose, a slight smile on her face as she slumbered. The feel of her beside me brought me great peace. A sense of belonging.

Another benefit of our sharing a bed was that her bad dreams no longer plagued her. She told me she felt safe for the first time in many years with me next to her, and I was determined she never feel unsafe again.

Reaching over, I stroked her cheek, smiling as she leaned into my caress even in her sleep. I drifted my hand down to her stomach, feeling the slight swell of her belly under my fingers. Knowing our child, my child, was growing inside her gave me a thrill I could not describe. I cared not if it was a boy or a girl, only that it was ours. A symbol of the love we shared. I had never thought of children that way before. They were simply something I knew I had to do in order for my line to continue. But with Maddie, the meaning of them, of family, had become so much more.

I was grateful the morning illness that had plagued her seemed to have passed. She was tired, requiring naps at odd times of the day. I often found her asleep over a book, even over her partially eaten luncheon. Once while tending her garden, I discovered her asleep on the bench, her small bucket of flowers still clutched in her hand. She hadn't stirred as I carried her upstairs, settling her on the counterpane of our bed and watching her, feeling the love she stirred within me grow. Every time I thought my heart could not possibly contain more love for her, it developed and expanded with more affection.

A small hand settled over mine, and I looked up, meeting her loving gaze. I was thrilled to see nothing but happiness and peace in her eyes as she smiled at me. None of the worry or trepidation lingered.

"Good morning, husband," she whispered. "How fare you?"

I smiled, widening my fingers over her belly. "I am filled with joy, my love," I replied. "How could I not be? Waking beside the most beautiful woman in the world, knowing she is carrying my babe? Recalling how they were created?"

Color flooded her cheeks, a soft rose blooming in the sun. "Sir, you are impertinent," she scolded mildly.

I stroked my hand up her body, stopping to run my thumb around the stiffened nipple under the thin cotton of her shift, then cupped her face, bringing her mouth to mine. Her lips were pillows of softness, her mouth a feast for my senses. I kissed her until she was breathless, her hand gripping my hair as she made low, pleading sounds in her throat. I dropped my face to her neck, swirling my tongue over the flesh. "Would you have me any other way, wife?"

"No," she gasped as I lowered my head to her breasts, sucking a nipple through the cotton and pleasuring the other with my fingers. I loved that her pregnancy made her even more responsive, more vocal, and definitely needier than ever. She had no qualms seeking me out in the day in my study, the garden, or even the stable. The smile on her face told me everything I needed to know before I let her use me in any fashion she wished.

I enjoyed them all.

"Are you needing me again this morning, my sweet?" I whispered as I pulled down her shift, returning to her hard nipple and licking.

"Please, Alexander," she moaned, arching her back.

"Tell me," I demanded. I loved to hear her say it. To tell me what she wanted.

"Please fill me. Take me." She paused. "I want to feel you inside me. Feel your cock."

I rose over her, staring down at her flushed cheeks. Without a word, I grasped her shift, tearing it in half, exposing her to me. Her large breasts were high, the nipples tight and begging for my mouth. Her eyes were wide with desire. Need. Her breathing was rapid, and she clutched at the sheet, her hands fisting the material tightly.

My cock was rigid. Hard and aching for her. Desperate to be inside her. But first, I needed her taste in my mouth. I shifted, lifting her legs to my shoulders. She cried out as I licked into her heat. Latched on to her pearl and sucked it as I slid two fingers inside her. She was wet and ready, her desire evident. But I wanted to prolong the pleasure for her. To worship her a little more.

I worked my fingers in and out of her cunny's tight grip, curling them as I probed deep. Her soft sound of need spurred me on. The sweet taste of her was on my tongue, her bud swollen and demanding as I suckled harder. Her fingers sifted through my hair, grasping handfuls and holding me where she wanted me. She came with a cry, her body trembling beneath me from the force of her spend.

Withdrawing from her, I rose on my knees between her parted thighs. The glistening pink of her cunny beckoned. My cock was desperate to be inside her. I kissed my way over the gentle swell of her belly to her breasts, taking a nipple in my mouth.

She moaned again as I notched myself against her entrance, the sweet heat of her as my guide. I sank my cock into her, gliding easily through her velvet grip. She was soaked. Another pump of my hips, and I was fully seated. Her silken cunny wrapped around me, warm and perfect.

She began to undulate her hips beneath me, too eager, spurring me on.

I released her nipple and glanced up at her, giving her a slow, deliberate thrust. "Patience, Maddie mine."

She tugged at my hair, the pull a delightful mix of pain and pleasure. "More. I need more."

"Greedy darling." I continued to move with agonizing torpidity, sinking deep and then withdrawing, only to sink inside her again.

I was tantalizing us both.

Maddie's skin was flushed, her eyes glazed with passion, her lips full and parted. Her hair was a wild tangle on the pillow. She had never been more beautiful than this moment, filled with desire for me, a new life growing within her.

"Now," she demanded.

And I obeyed, because I couldn't last much longer myself. She felt too good, and the urge to lose myself inside her was strong. I thrust harder, faster, guiding her legs around me as I found the pace we both wanted. When I dipped a hand between us and strummed over her pearl, she clamped down on my cock, crying out my name. I moved, groaning, desperately on the edge, plunging into her slick heat one more time until white-hot bliss exploded within me. I thrust deep and filled her with my seed as she held me tightly to her as she always did, our hearts beating fast.

I remained as I was until my breathing steadied and my wits returned, and then I rolled off her, gathering her up into my arms. She nestled into me with a sigh of contentment, and I pressed a kiss to her crown. "Ah, Maddie mine, what you do to me."

"I like this part of marriage," she mused, making me laugh.

"As do I."

"Do all couples share this feeling?" she asked, curious.

I cleared my throat. "I think it depends. Not all couples have the connection we have built, my wife. Many marriages, especially those among the higher-ups, are matches that are made with lineage and connections in mind. Not love."

"I would not like to do this with someone else."

"And nor will you ever," I growled.

She laughed, slapping my chest. "How can one enjoy it if there is no love?" she asked, looking at me.

I sat up with a sigh, leaning against the headboard, the wood feeling cold. I gazed down at her with a smile as I ran my knuckles over her cheek. "People, especially men, can perform with or without love." I paused. "In fact, most men prefer it that way. It is simply a release."

"And women?" she asked, pulling herself up into the same sitting position and drawing her legs to her chest.

Absently, I pulled up the covering so she didn't get chilled. I chose my words carefully, reminding myself she was still so innocent in the ways of the world.

"Some women, yes. Others do it as their duty, with little pleasure."

She was quiet for a moment. "How sad."

"Yes, I imagine so."

She turned her head, meeting my eyes. "And you?"

"I beg your pardon?"

"Before me," she explained. "Did you give your, ah, lovers pleasure?"

I was shocked at her question, yet somehow proud of it as well.

"I tried." I lifted her hand and kissed it. "Sexual congress was empty before you, Maddie. A meaningless pleasure my body craved. No one ever touched my heart the way you have. With you, it means more. But yes, I wanted my lover to experience the same pleasure—I have never been selfish in that regard."

"Good."

"That's all?" I teased. "You are not jealous?"

"Oh, terribly so," she retorted. "I want to find any woman you had, ah, relations with and scratch her eyes out. But you married me and you say you love me. So I have won."

"I do love you," I retorted. "With all of my heart." Then I grinned. "You don't feel that you've won when I vex you," I said with a wink, enjoying the conversation with her.

She smiled softly. "We don't vex each other much."

"No."

"Have you ever loved before?" she asked.

That question caught me off guard, and I took a moment to gather my thoughts.

"When I was in my youth, I fancied myself in love. She was a young maid, and she was sweet and lovely. We grew close, and I wanted to marry her. Lift her out of the drudgery her life was."

"What happened?" she asked gently.

"We were found out by my father. He was furious. Informed me that peers of the realm didn't marry maids. That she was simply using me for my wealth and title and I was an idiot. I remember how frightened she appeared to be, how terrified her eyes were as he dragged her from me, sending her away. The look in her eyes haunted me. The look in your eyes that night reminded me of that dread."

"Is that why you took me?"

"Yes," I replied honestly. "I had seen that frightened expression before, and I refused to leave you to the life you had." I sighed. "The look of terror in your eyes that night will never leave me. I strive to ensure you never appear thus again."

She was silent for a moment, her gaze locked on mine.

"What occurred after?"

"My father and I argued, and he beat me. Locked me up in the attic for weeks on end."

She grasped my hands. "Alexander," she breathed. "How terrible."

"Once I recovered, I searched for her. It was as if she had disappeared. I was beside myself, feeling as if I had let her down. Terrified that she was alone and what she was doing for employment. How she was caring for herself."

"Did you find her?"

"It took a whole year, but I did."

"And?" she prompted, as if I were telling her a fairy tale and she couldn't wait for the ending.

"In this case, my father was right. When I found her, she was married to a blacksmith. Happy and with child. She had to recall who I was, then laughed off my concern and walked away. I realized then how little I had meant to her. She had been more concerned about losing her position in the household."

"Oh, Alexander," she murmured, stroking my jaw. "You must have been distraught."

I shook my head as I recalled how I'd truly felt. "I felt foolish and angry that my father had been right. I swore never to put my heart in danger again." I squeezed her hands. "Until you came into my life, my sweet, and changed all that."

"Another maid," she whispered.

"No," I almost snarled. "You were never truly a maid. You were raised as a lady."

"But not seen as such. Even if my father hadn't reduced my life to that of a servant, I would only be a miss."

I shook my head, not caring. "You are a lady now. My lady. My marchioness." I smiled at her. "My beloved wife."

She returned my smile, but I saw a touch of worry in it. I lifted our joined hands and kissed her knuckles. "The only woman I have ever truly loved. The only woman I will ever love."

Her smile became bright again. "As I love you."

Her stomach chose that moment to grumble, and I laughed. "I believe our child needs nourishment, my wife. Shall we go downstairs and see what Cook has made for you today?"

The domestics adored her, and my cook loved to spoil Maddie with treats and special meals. Now that she was feeling better, she loved breakfast and ate well most days.

"Yes," she sighed happily. "I am hungry."

"I have not upset you with my story?" I queried.

"No, Alexander. It is part of your life, and I want to know everything. I am sad to hear how your father treated you and of that woman's careless disregard for your feelings, but I am pleased you told me." She colored prettily again. "Especially since I know you love me as you do."

I leaned forward and kissed her. "I do, my love. I do."

CHAPTER 18

ALEXANDER

A few days later, I sat across from my wife, breaking our fast. She wore a pretty morning gown in a pale blue, gathered under her breasts, the material flowing over the small mound of her belly. I loved touching it, cupping my hand over the growing swell, anxious to feel its movement, although Maddie had informed me it would be a while before that occurred. She looked further along than she was, due to her small stature, and I could only imagine how appealing she would be as she blossomed.

Her hair was up, tendrils escaping around her ears and neck, the small ringlets bright in the morning sun. I loved her curls, and when I heard her and Lydia bemoaning the fact that they could never get them to behave, I informed them I liked it when they escaped. I found them charming and beguiling.

Much like my wife.

She was eating slowly, methodically—the way she liked to do. Enjoying every morsel. I knew she'd been denied so much for so long, and I enjoyed watching her savor her food.

I simply liked watching her, if the truth be told.

She looked up, coloring slightly at my stare.

"Sir?" she asked, impertinent and demanding. "Might I ask what you are so boldly looking at?"

I smiled as I set down my cup. "You, my wife. I am boldly looking at you and enjoying your beauty. You are glowing this morning." I refilled my cup, the aroma of the strong coffee I liked so much rich in my nose. "Perhaps you have had a good morning so far? I know I have enjoyed it immensely."

Her eyes rounded, knowing I was referring to our earlier lovemaking. I had woken this morning to her mouth around me, pleasuring me in ways I had never fathomed she would. She had licked and sucked my length, taking me to the back of her throat before I had reluctantly cried surrender, wanting to be inside her cunny when I reached my crisis.

After, she had ridden me, finding her pleasure quickly, then again moments later as I spent inside her. She collapsed on my chest, exhausted and slipping back into sleep for a short time. I had held her, content to let her rest, pondering how quickly she had become paramount in my life.

She blinked, her cheeks darkening. "How imprudent you are," she admonished with a smile playing on her lips.

"Only for you, my sweet."

"I would think so," she replied cheekily with a toss of her head, causing her curls to bounce.

"Would you enjoy a picnic today, Maddie mine?" I asked. "It is supposed to be fine all afternoon."

"Do you have time?" she asked eagerly.

"I can make time for you. Perhaps by the brook again. I'll have a footman take a comfortable chair down under the shade of the trees." I winked at her. "Perhaps I can persuade you to swim with me today."

She looked away, the color extending down her neck and to her ears. I had tried to convince her to shed her clothing and join me in the cool water of the brook once. She had looked scandalized, refusing my invitation, but I had a feeling she was curious. Perhaps today was the day I could coax her. I could show her how pleasurable the water could be.

"How brazen you are today," she murmured primly, taking a small sip of her tea—but she did not refuse my idea.

Just then, Edward strode in, looking anxious. He glanced toward Maddie, offering her a quick bow. "My lady. Forgive the interruption."

"We were planning our day," I said firmly. "We can speak shortly." Whatever it was could wait. A roof needing repair or a dispatch could be handled quickly so I could be with my wife.

But Maddie was ever the lady and frowned my way before looking to Edward.

"What is it?" she asked. "You look upset."

"There is a situation," he replied. "A serious one."

"Pray, then do tell," I insisted.

He glanced toward Maddie, then leaned close, lowering his voice.

"Her father is at the gate, demanding an audience. He has others with him."

Maddie gasped in shock, and I rose, standing behind her, placing my hands on her shoulders in comfort.

"The devil he does," I swore. "What does he want?"

"Should we discuss this in private, my lord?"

"No," Maddie protested. "I need to know."

I nodded at him to speak.

Edward drew in a long breath. "He says you spirited his daughter away in the dead of the night and dishonored her and his name. That you stole her. He is demanding satisfaction."

"He put her up as an offering," I snarled. "As if she were a piece of furniture. I stole nothing. There were witnesses."

Maddie spoke, her voice quavering. "The servants heard him. They knew how I was treated."

Edward smiled sadly. "The word of a peer will take precedence over that of an underling."

"What about my word?" she demanded.

"He will say you have been turned against him," I murmured. "From what Edward found out, he has dismissed his remaining servants, so we cannot question them."

"Lydia?" she whispered, referring to her lady's maid.

He shook his head. "Not even Liddy's word would be taken as truth."

Even with the situation, I noticed the way he referred to Lydia. As if he were familiar. But that was a subject for another time.

Maddie stood suddenly, turning to me. I loathed seeing the fear back in her eyes, the expression of worry on her face.

"Will he take me?" she asked, her voice trembling, her body beginning to shake. "Alexander, will he take me from you?"

I gathered her in my arms, holding her close. "No. You are my wife, and you will remain with me. I shan't allow him near you," I stated firmly. "I will deal with him."

"He will try," she said, sobbing. "He is violent and vindictive. He hates me—he has always hated me, and I have never known why. He doesn't want me to be happy."

I held her closer, meeting Edward's gaze over her head. He regarded her with sympathy and understanding.

"Why?" she cried. "Why after all these months?"

"I asked him the same question," Edward informed us. "He said it took him time to trace you here."

"Damn his lies. He knew," I cursed. "There is something else to this." I pressed a kiss to my trembling wife's head. "I believe you are right. He knows you are happy, and he seeks to destroy that happiness."

"Alexander," she whimpered. "Help me."

I bent and scooped her into my arms, and her head fell to my chest. "You are going upstairs, my love, and resting as I rid our home of this infestation of vermin. This stress is not good for you or my unborn child," I murmured as I carried her up the stairs. I laid her on the bed, brushing away the tears falling. "Do you trust me, wife?"

"Yes."

"Then know I will handle this. Your father will not come near you, and you will not leave this estate with him. Ever."

She nodded.

Lydia stood at the foot of the bed. "Should I accompany you, my lord? I can attest to the truth, even if they will not hear it."

"Yes. That is a good idea. Fetch Mrs. Dougall and have her sit with my wife."

I turned to Maddie. "I shall return shortly, and our pleasant day will continue."

More tears fell down her cheeks. She had become white and fearful-looking again. I was furious and ready to draw arms against the man at the gate. Strike him down where he stood for causing her anguish once again. I strove to calm myself, knowing I needed to keep a cool head and banish him.

I bent and kissed Maddie. "I will be back."

"Promise me." She gripped my waistcoat. "Do not let him near you either. He is like a snake and will strike when you least expect it. I could not bear it," she sobbed.

That was when I understood her greatest worry. Not her father taking her away, but me being hurt or killed.

I cupped her face. "Ah, Maddie mine. My love. No one on this estate shall be hurt. He is the one who should be fearful of my wrath for being here. Causing you pain. Trust me and know all will be well."

I waited until she nodded hesitantly.

I passed Mrs. Dougall in the hall. "Watch over her."

"Mr. Dougall is downstairs too, sir. None will get past him."

"Very good."

Downstairs, Edward was waiting, silently handing me my pistol. I tested the weight in my hand, pleased with the balance of the grip.

Edward's gun was already in his hand. I saw him touch his side, and I knew a knife was at the ready. We were prepared for the worst and hoped for the best. Not that I expected anything good to come from this encounter.

We mounted our horses and trotted to the gate. I refused to hurry and composed my features into what I hoped to be a look of annoyance and boredom. I allowed no concern or worry to leach into my countenance.

As we drew close, I narrowed my eyes, seeing Barnett pacing. He was even thinner than the last time I saw him, his clothing showing wear and neglect. He required a good meal, a proper haircut and shave, and no doubt a valet. As well as the funds to pay for it all.

None of which I would offer to him.

With him were three men. One I recognized as a gentleman who had been at the card game, Baron Fine.

One was his old butler. The third was familiar, but I could not place him. Something about his hawklike nose and cold gaze struck me as memorable, but how, I wasn't certain.

We dismounted, strolling toward the small group. Two of my grooms stood in front of the gates refusing them entry. I called out, telling them to open the gates, and Barnett stormed through, bellowing, red-faced, and furious. Edward held up his hand, stopping his progress, and I stood my ground, placing my hands behind my back and glaring at him.

"What is the meaning of this unwelcome interruption? Tell me. Now," I demanded.

"You leave me at the gate? Like a beggar coming to ask for a crust of bread?" Barnett shouted. "Nowhere in polite society would this be acceptable!"

He froze as Edward cocked his gun, his arm straight, his grip firm. "Nothing about this damned situation is polite. Answer his lordship's question."

"I came to rescue Madeleine. You absconded with her in the dark of night. Taking her away like a thief. You, sir, are no better than the lowest of criminals. You have ruined her and smeared my good name."

It was all I could do not to laugh at the absurdity of his words.

I crossed my arms over my chest, drawing a deep breath. "Absconded with her?" I repeated. "You put her up as a bargaining chip in a card game. Demanded I take her. Your words, I believe, were that *I was to do with her whatever I wanted, then discard her.*"

I glared at him. "Instead, I chose to marry her and give her back her rightful place in society. Is that what you are so angry about?" I paused. "That her rank is now higher than yours?" I asked snidely.

He ignored my question. "I have a witness who will swear otherwise."

I looked at Baron Fine and laughed. "As I recall, the good baron lost early that evening and was in his cups an hour later. He wasn't in the room when you led your daughter out as a sacrificial lamb to slaughter. And his reputation is highly questionable. A scenario with several married women and a sudden flurry of familiar-looking babes, I think?"

Baron Fine flushed, his face an angry shade of red. "I am done," he muttered, climbing into the carriage and slamming the door.

"Next witness," I stated, my sarcasm evident. Beside me, Edward chuckled low in his throat at my tone.

Barnett indicated the old butler. "He has signed a document with my solicitor, indicating his truth. That you left in the night, taking my daughter and her elderly companion against their will."

Now I recognized the solicitor. Known for his underhanded ways and rewriting laws to suit his own purpose, he was the lowest of the low.

"Mr. Leigh, I believe. Your reputation precedes you," I stated dryly.

He bowed. "How kind, my lord."

I barked out a laugh. "That was not meant as a compliment to you, sir. Your reputation is even darker than that of Fine's."

His thin mouth became a line of displeasure, and he stepped back, saying something to Barnett. Behind me, I heard a wagon arriving and knew Lydia was there. From the quick glance over my shoulder, I noticed Geraldine had accompanied her, and I was grateful Lydia had thought of that.

Edward stepped away, hurrying toward the wagon, and

I again glanced behind me, seeing him assist Lydia down, with Geraldine remaining in the back. I noticed how he walked beside Lydia, his hand on the small of her back. His gaze was focused on Barnett and his motley crew, but his stance was directed toward her. Protective. Assertive. Ready to defend.

Interesting.

I saw Lydia stumble, then pause, saying something to Edward, who turned back in my direction and hurried to my side.

"I have Lydia and Geraldine who will both swear my word is true," I announced.

"Servants," he spat.

"As is yours."

"Mine is trustworthy. That girl—" he pointed to Lydia "—disappeared from my household without a trace. Several items went missing at the same time. She is a thief and a liar."

"I am not a thief! I took nothing!" she protested.

Edward hushed her, his words low. "We are aware of that, Liddy. Calm yourself."

She huffed an angry sigh but remained quiet.

"And the old woman is mad!" he continued. "Not to be trusted!" Then, in a total turnaround, he shouted again. "I demand her return as well!"

I was weary of his gesturing. His ugly words and his outrageous demands. He was giving me a headache, and I was worried about Maddie. She couldn't hear what was being said, but she would be upset nonetheless by his presence.

"Leave my estate. You are not welcome here."

"I demand to see Madeleine. She will speak the truth once I am allowed to see her."

I stepped forward, furious and wanting to kill him.

"You demand? You *demand*? You forget your place. Do you really believe I would allow you to see her? Are you of sound mind? You truly think that I would leave you with my wife so you can beat her again? Make her pick the reeds and the rose to bleed on so you can strike her for your own sick pleasure? Threaten her so often and scare her so she does as you say?"

He paled and stepped back, and I kept going.

"Allow you to take her and lock her away? Work as a servant in her own home? Listen to your berating and insults?" I shook my head in anger.

"You will never see her again. You will never be allowed to touch her, hurt, or frighten her again. I will see you dead first."

"Is that a threat?"

"I will do whatever it takes to protect my wife. You, Barnett, have forgotten your place. You no longer have authority over her. I am her husband, and she stays with me."

"Which is exactly where I want to be." Maddie spoke from behind me.

Spinning on my heel, I saw her approaching, clutching Geraldine's hand. I had neglected to look past Geraldine in the wagon, and Maddie must have been beside her, hidden by Geraldine's larger frame. Maddie was pale, and I could see her trembling even from where I stood. But her head was high, and although I could hear the tremor in her pitch, I doubted anyone else could.

"I will not leave my husband or the life I have here. I have no wish to speak with you, nor be alone in a room where you are."

She stopped next to me, and I slipped my arm around her, holding her tightly to my side. I knew I should be angry with her for disobeying my order to stay in the house. For risking herself by being close to that awful excuse for a father. But I also felt a grudging admiration that she was standing up for herself—against the man who caused her so much pain and torment.

I squeezed her hip, letting her know I wasn't angry.

She lifted her head higher. "You are not welcome here. Lord Wheaton speaks the truth. I was in the room that night, and I am neither a servant nor an old woman. You gave me away. Treated me like an animal after my mother died. My life was nothing but toil and pain. There is nary a thing you could say or do that would persuade me to leave my husband's side."

I was proud of her. I felt her strength and saw her grace—the traits he had tried to break but failed.

Geraldine spoke. "My senses are perfectly fine. I know what I saw and heard." She paused. "And witnessed over the years. I will speak the truth to anyone who asks."

Barnett whitened further at her barely concealed threat.

"I believe my wife has spoken. Leave or I will be forced to make you."

He glared at me and Maddie, his eyebrows pulled down, a sneer on his face.

"Trained you well, has he?"

I felt her anger growing. "Unlike you, he has shown me nothing but kindness and love."

The breeze stirred her skirts, and his eyes widened. "Bred you like an animal too," he mocked.

I was finished with him and his words. I wanted him nowhere near my wife and unborn child. I lifted my arm, pointing my gun. "You dare, sir. Be gone and do not return."

"I demand satisfaction."

"What is it you seek?" I roared, startling Maddie, who tensed beside me.

"A duel," Barnett announced.

Maddie gasped softly, her trepidation getting the best of her.

I wanted to roll my eyes and scoff. The coward wanted his minute of satisfaction. Another lie to add to his story. How he defended his name. He expected me to refuse, to give him the chance to smear my name even more. I refused to give him that gratification.

"Weapons?" I queried.

His surprise was obvious, but he recovered quickly. "Pistols."

"Dawn. Tomorrow. Name your second," I replied, my tone one of boredom and dismissiveness.

"I will be his second," Leigh spoke.

Edward stepped closer. "And I will be Lord Wheaton's."

Barnett had the audacity to address Maddie again.

"Soon, you will come to me. I will make sure of it."

"She will never return to you. Of that, I assure you." I narrowed my eyes. "And you will never return here either, after the morrow."

Edward pointed his gun. "Leave."

Maddie's shaking legs gave out as they turned to depart. I bent and lifted her into my arms, striding to the cart. I placed her on the back, cupping her face.

"You were to stay inside."

"I wanted to face him."

"You are pale and upset now. Risking yourself needlessly. Risking our child," I rebuked her mildly.

"I was already pale and upset. I made Geraldine and Lydia bring me. Do not punish them."

I sighed, pressing my lips to her head. "I will punish no

one, my love." I drew back, meeting her worried gaze. "I am proud of you for standing up to him."

"He cannot take me." Her words were breathless, laden with worry, requiring my reassurance.

"I will never allow it."

"I do not wish this duel," she whispered, clutching my wrists. "It frightens me, Alexander."

"He wishes to embarrass me. To somehow make me look the coward. We will meet, draw our pistols, and shoot into the air. I will refute his claims and send him away. He is angry, no doubt having hoped I would offer him money for stealing you. It is his way to save face." I kissed her again, my lips lingering on her soft skin. "Nothing will happen to me, my sweet."

"What if he takes it further?"

I pondered her words. "Would you have me strike him down, my love? Kill your father?"

"I would have you unharmed, no matter the consequences," she replied promptly.

"It will not come to that. He is too much of a coward, and killing me would only cause him further trouble. It is all gesturing and noise."

If anything, my reassurances seemed to upset her more than comfort. I stepped back, pausing to drop kisses to her fists. "I will follow you to the house. You will rest, then we will have our picnic. We will not allow that cretin to ruin our day." I smiled at her, hoping to see her smile back. But she looked troubled. Lydia climbed into the cart, lifting the reins. I assisted Geraldine into the wagon beside my wife.

"I tried to dissuade her, my lord."

I smiled in reassurance. "My wife is, at best, stubborn. That she refused does not surprise me." I patted her hand. "Rest well, madam. All will be fine."

Geraldine nodded, still looking troubled.

"Take her to the house, and I wish her to rest," I instructed Geraldine. "I will follow."

I watched as the wagon moved away, Geraldine holding my wife's hand, speaking to her, hopefully comforting her.

Edward appeared at my side, handing me the reins.

"I wish to walk a moment," I muttered.

He fell into step with me, our horses trailing us. "Not the day you planned," he observed.

"No. I doubt my plans will continue. Maddie is too fraught now." I glanced over my shoulder, seeing the empty lane and closed gate. "What is he about? Nothing good will come of this for him. Did he truly think I would give him money to make him go away? That the word of a drunken card player and a butler so old would frighten me?"

"He is desperate," Edward observed.

"Yes," I mused. "But why? What is his plan?"

Edward sighed. "Liddy told me when she was in the village a few weeks ago, she saw the solicitor—Leigh. She recognized him today, and it surprised her to see him here with Barnett. He was questioning people, but she didn't stop to listen since she didn't know him."

I frowned. "Of course not. She is not one to gossip."

"I fear…" He paused. "Dash it, Alexander. I fear somehow word has gotten out that you set up Maddie with her own funds. Her father wants them."

He was referring to the trust I had created for Maddie. It was a large amount, ensuring that she would never want for anything should something happen to me, and it had been drafted in a way that ensured only she could access the money.

"The funds are not his. They belong to Maddie. The way it is set, he could never get them—no matter what."

He stopped, facing me. "Do you think he is of sound

mind? He doesn't care about her reputation or scandal. He doesn't care about her. It has to be about the money. He was drowning in debt before—God knows how much further he has slid into the deep. I believe he has made some sort of nonsensical plan he imagines will work."

I scrubbed my chin, frustrated. My day had been ruined, my wife upset, our fragile happiness threatened, and I didn't understand why.

I hoisted myself up onto my horse. I needed to return to Maddie, then think this through.

"Post men at the gates in case they return to sneak about. Fetch me Higgins from the village—I require some answers. He established the trust for Maddie's funds, and I need to know we are indeed sound in our knowledge." I paused. "Ask around the village. See if we can find out what Leigh's inquiries were regarding."

"Right away. I will return with Higgins shortly."

I nodded and urged my steed forward. I needed to check on Maddie.

CHAPTER 19

MADELEINE

I paced the floor of Alexander's bedchamber, fretful and terrified. I knew I should be in my own chamber, but this room smelled of him. I inhaled, long, greedy breaths, desperate to calm the swelling panic.

A duel. My father wanted a duel with my husband.

He intended to do him harm. I knew this as strongly as I knew my husband would refuse to ignore the challenge. His honor was very important to him.

I needed him to be alive more than I needed the memory of an honorable man.

Suddenly, the room began closing in on me. It was too hot, too confining. My clothing was too tight, my hair bothersome. My hands felt caged in the light gloves I wore.

I yanked off the gloves, discarding them, then I pulled at the pins in my hair, casting them to the floor, uncaring. My hair fell down my back, the length heavy but feeling better not wrapped around my head. I wished I could easily reach the tapes on the back of my dress and rid myself of the fabric that stifled me.

I needed air.

I needed Alexander.

How would I survive without him?

"Maddie mine." His smooth voice interrupted my panicked thoughts. I looked up, seeing him approaching me. He held out his hands. "Please stop tearing at your gown, my love. Let me help you."

"I cannot breathe."

He reached me, pulling me into his arms. He ran his hands up and down my back in soothing passes, and I felt his nimble fingers untie my tapes. The air felt good on my skin as he helped me undress, peeling away the layers until I was only in my chemise.

He rested his hands on my shoulders, his gaze tender and his voice low and comforting. "Breathe, Maddie mine. I am here, and all is well."

I shook my head, my anxiety choking my reply. "It is not. *He* is here."

"He is close but not here. Never here. He will never be near you again. He will have his moment, then be dispatched tomorrow, and you will never see him again. I swear it to you."

"I cannot go on without you, Alexander. I am not strong enough."

"Maddie mine, look at me."

I lifted my gaze and met his dark, warm eyes. "You are the strongest woman I know. If I died right now, you would carry on for the sake of our babe. You would find a life."

"No," I sobbed.

"Yes," he insisted gently. "After how you persevered all those years, I know this." He paused. "You would do it, because I would ask you to."

"Alexander," I pleaded. "No."

"But you will not have to, my love. I promise you."

He pulled me into his arms, cradling me and

whispering reassurances. He bent and lifted me, carrying me to the bed where our most intimate of moments occurred. Where our love was consummated and blossomed. It held our secrets and our story. He lay down, still holding me, whispering stories of our future. How our family would start and grow. How the years would slowly pass for us.

How we would forge our life together for years to come.

I let his words wash over me. Clung to them in desperate belief.

I needed to believe him now more than ever.

ALEXANDER

"No, my lord. No matter what occurs, Madeleine's father cannot get access to those funds."

I sat back, satisfied, but still frustrated. My little wife was beside herself with worry, which wasn't good for her or the babe. I was furious at Barnett and the fact that he had instilled terror into her again. He needed to be gone and his memory erased. Forever.

"Confounding," I muttered. "Why would he be doing this?"

"If I might speak plainly?"

I waved my hand. "Of course, Higgins. I trust you."

Higgins had been one of my solicitors in London. When his wife fell ill and required country living, he had moved to the village but maintained his standing within the legal community. He traveled to London when needed, his wife happy to be left behind. He was honest and shrewd, dealing with my businesses with a swift hand and a great eye to detail.

"I know of Lord Barnett. Many do since he owned the estate beside your father's. It was once lovely before he allowed it to fall into decay."

"He acquired the piece of land between the two estates from my father in the same fashion I obtained it back."

He pursed his lips.

"Speak."

"They were once friendly neighbors. Lord Barnett won it in a game from your father after your mother passed, then when your father changed his mind later, refused to allow him to purchase it back. It had become overrun, unused, much like his estate. They had a large falling-out over it and became bitter rivals."

"Until I won it in the same game in which he demanded I take Maddie."

"His reputation at one time was of a decent man. After his wife passed, he became known as angry and bitter. Harsh with servants. Unwelcoming to visitors. There were rumors of cruelty. Drinking. Excessive gambling. He was banned from his gentlemen's club over dishonoring his debts. He fell out of favor with many."

I barked a laugh. "He still had enough pull that he could draw them out for a card game."

He cleared his throat. "Many opportunists. Those who wished only to win, my lord. Not for the sake of friendship."

I chuckled. "Myself included."

He bowed his head. "Extenuating circumstances."

I blew out a long breath. "I can attest to his desperation. I saw the poor state of his estate. I have seen with my own eyes the marks he left on his daughter. She has told me stories of his temper." I clutched the glass in my hand tightly, recalling some of her words. "He put her up for offer to satisfy a gambling debt, wanting me to ruin her."

"She is fortunate that it was you, my lord. Another less noble man would have done exactly that and left her badly off."

I turned in my chair, staring out the window. I could not even begin to think of my Maddie used and cast aside in that fashion. Her beauty diminished and faded, and her gentle spirit crushed. Simply the thought made me ill. It also filled me with rage. Fury at an unknown I could not fight.

I turned back to Higgins. "My affairs are in order?"

"Completely, my lord," he assured me.

I looked to Edward, who had joined us. "And you will follow my wishes?"

"To the letter, my lord. Your wife and child will never want for a thing." He shook his head. "Not that this is necessary."

"No," I agreed. "But I feel at ease knowing all is well."

"It is," Higgins repeated. "Is there anything else, my lord?"

"No. Thank you for your speedy arrival."

He bowed. "My time is yours, my lord."

He departed and Edward sat.

"Any news?"

"Leigh was asking about Lady Wheaton. Your life. The villagers refused to talk about you or her. The tavern owner and his wife felt as if he were trying to find out how loyal they are to you." He smirked. "He wasn't pleased to see how deeply it ran. The villagers are aware of how good you are to them. To your tenants. The prosperity you bring to their village. Much more than other estates here."

"The village has always been good to me," I replied.

"They adore her ladyship."

I felt a grin pull on my lips. "As do I."

He returned my smile. "I am aware. She has brought your smile back, my friend. She fills this house with sunshine." He paused as he took a sip of brandy. "Your heart as well, if I might be so bold."

I sat back, observing him. "And what of Lydia?" I asked. "Or, should I say, Liddy?"

He remained calm, although his cheeks flushed. "What of her? She is very good to Lady Wheaton. They are close."

"As you appeared to be with her, Edward. You looked ready to murder Barnett for his accusations."

"He is a bastard," he spat. "The world would be better off without his kind."

"I agree, but you are changing the subject."

"Leave it be, my lord."

"You are enamored with her?"

He looked away. "It is complicated."

"Only if you choose for it to be. Neither of you is titled, and even if you were, it is your choice."

"She feels she is my inferior."

"How do you feel?"

"I am unsure at this moment. I did not expect to feel anything for the young lady. Especially, ah, tender feelings."

"I see."

"She is kind and gentle. Loving. Her life has been one of difficulty and loneliness."

"And you wish to change that?"

He scrubbed his hand on his face. "I do not know."

A knock at the door ended our conversation. Edward rose and opened the door, revealing Geraldine. She looked worried, clutching a small bundle of linen in her hands. I rose to my feet.

"Is her ladyship well? Is something amiss?"

"She is fine, my lord. Sleeping finally. Lydia is watching over her."

"Good. Is there another concern?"

She hesitated, and I indicated that she come inside. "Please sit. Be at ease."

She sat in the chair Edward had vacated. He withdrew, leaving us alone.

"What have you there?" I asked.

"May I tell you some history, my lord? It has to do with Lady Wheaton."

"Of course," I replied, intrigued. "You have known her all her life."

"Yes."

I nodded for her to continue.

"I was her mother's lady's maid. I had been with her most of her life. I was with her when she escaped Paris. When Lady Wheaton was born, she wasn't a usual mother. She wanted to be very involved in her babe's care the way her mother had been. I assisted her in caring for Lady Wheaton as she refused a nursemaid. I became one of sorts." She paused, her eyes becoming misty. I rose and fetched her a glass of Madeira. She thanked me, took a sip, and placed the glass on the desk.

"When my mistress died, I became her ladyship's nurse for all intents and purposes for a short time. Lord Barnett had never bothered much with her. He had been disappointed she was not a boy, but he had tolerated her. At least until her mother died. She—Lady Wheaton—was very young."

"Ten and four, I believe?"

"Yes." She paused to take another sip. "He informed

me I would be in charge of her upbringing and making sure she was prepared to be presented when she was ready."

"What changed?" I asked. "He treated her as a servant. Worse than at times, I believe."

"Not long after my mistress passed, he discovered something." She placed the small linen-covered bundle on my desk. "Something I will entrust to you, my lord."

I opened the linen, lifting two small leatherbound books. Opening one, I saw the feminine penmanship and a name written on the first page.

"These are Lady Wheaton's mother's journals?" I asked.

"Yes."

"And how do you have them in your possession?"

She lifted her chin, meeting my eyes. "I stole them from the baron's desk. He kept them in a hidden drawer."

"Why?" I queried. "Why did you take them? For Lady Wheaton?"

"Yes. So she knew the truth."

"Which is?"

"How deeply her mother loved her." She swallowed, lifting her head. "That Lord Barnett is not her father."

I sat back, shocked. "What?"

"I was very close to her ladyship's mother, and I was her only confidante. I was sworn to secrecy and remained loyal to my mistress even after she passed. But I believe it is time to speak."

I nodded again, indicating for her to continue.

"She was newly *enceinte* when she met him—Lord Barnett—after fleeing Paris. He quickly became obsessed with her, desperate to marry her. Knowing the life she faced as an unmarried woman with child, she agreed. Her family would disown her, and she would be out in the streets if they discovered her secret. She liked the baron well enough and thought they would make a good match. He knew she had loved another but didn't care. He was besotted. They married hastily and remained in England. He doted on her. Was thrilled when she told him she was with child. Lady Wheaton was a small baby, and her being early was accepted easily." A smile pulled on her lips. "Even then, Lady Wheaton cooperated since she was past her time, in truth. Helpful, as always."

"I see."

"The baron never had much to do with her ladyship, and there were no more babies—no heir for him to dote on. When her mother died, he found the journals. Read them. Destroyed her rooms and shredded all her clothing. Burned it. Sold all the jewelry. Tore down the paintings he'd had purchased for her." She met my eyes. "And punished Lady Wheaton for it from that moment on."

"That bastard."

"My mistress was prepared to be with him all her life. Give him other children. Set aside her own happiness for his. She wrote of how fond she was of him. How her life was so much better because of him. His wonderful gifts. But none of that meant anything. All he saw was her mistake. Her lies. He called her terrible names. And then took his anger out on the one thing she loved more than anything. Her daughter."

"But you stayed?" I asked.

"I moved to the kitchen. He never saw me—it was as if he forgot about me most of the time. But he took delight in making sure I knew when she was being punished. How much I loathed it. But I had to stay close and help her as much as I could. Protect her, if possible."

"You were the one to make the gloves for her hands."

"Yes. She needed to cover her hands for protection,

and the gloves the baron forced her to wear were insufficient." Once again, her eyes filled with tears. "I tried as best I could. As much as I was able. The older servants all did at the beginning, but as they passed or moved on, it became harder. Soon, it was only Lydia and me."

"You have my eternal gratitude and a home with us until you no longer wish it. Lydia does, as well."

"You are a good man, my lord." She paused. "I worry for your lordship with the baron tomorrow. If he can take away her happiness, he will."

"He will not. I assure you. Be at peace with that."

"He will try. He is an ugly man."

I looked at the journals. "Does Lady Wheaton know?"

"No."

"I will tell her once I have dealt with the baron. It might ease her mind in many ways." I lifted a journal. "What of her real father?"

"A young nobleman, deeply in love with my mistress. They planned to marry, then he was killed by a footpad. My Felicity—my mistress—was beside herself with grief. A few weeks later, she was introduced to Lord Barnett..." She trailed off. "The rest you know and can read in greater detail in the journals."

I ran my hand over the dull leather.

"Inside the second book is a likeness of Lady Wheaton's mother. It was all I could save before the baron destroyed everything."

I flipped open the pages, staring at the small image tucked into the back.

"She is like her," I said quietly. "He should have found comfort in that instead of hating her."

"He is not of sound mind, my lord. Once she died, I don't think he ever was. Grief and anger destroyed him."

"No, he is not." I glanced up. "This will mean the

world to my wife. She has said often she wishes she had an image of her mother."

"I have been guarding that image, knowing one day I would give it to her. I removed the journals from the desk before we departed. They should belong to Lady Wheaton, not the baron. I felt today was the day to give them to you and you were the person to trust to tell her this story." She reached into her pocket, withdrawing a small brooch. "I found this after his rampage. It had fallen under the dressing table. I have kept it hidden for her ladyship all these years."

I studied the delicate brooch. The dull gold glinted in the light, the sapphires and small diamonds twinkling. The center stone was surrounded by filigree and tipped with matching jewels, enhanced with the tiny diamonds at each of the four tips of the oval brooch.

"It is lovely."

"It was a gift to Felicity from Lady Wheaton's real father. It was all she had of him."

"She will treasure this." I looked up. "Do you recall the name of her father?"

"Louis Dupont." She sighed quietly, then finished her glass of wine. "He was the last of his line."

"So she has no family left," I mused. "She will be saddened by that."

"I have heard there is a much younger female cousin somewhere in England, but I don't know if that is true." She reached over and patted my hand. "She is more than happy with you, my lord. Her own family. And I think knowing the truth will only add to her happiness."

"I am in your debt once again for telling me all this, Geraldine. Thank you."

She left, drawing the door shut behind her. My mind was ablaze with what she had shared. Barnett was not

Maddie's natural father. For some men, it would be a blow, but they would move on. However, he became so twisted with his own anger and grief that he took it out on her. A defenseless, naive child who had just lost her mother. He had punished her for years for something that was no fault of hers. She had tried her entire life to be the daughter she thought he wanted. Obedient. Subservient. Anxious to please.

Only, you cannot please a monster filled with hate.

And now, he was back, wanting once again to destroy her. Dissolve the happiness she had found. He didn't want the information these journals contained to be known.

That was the reason for this duel.

He thought I knew. That Maddie knew.

And he wanted us both silent.

I stood and bellowed for Edward.

This changed things.

CHAPTER 20

ALEXANDER

Edward stopped his pacing, facing me and gripping the back of the chair.

"You cannot face him."

"I must, Edward."

"He will kill you."

I had told Edward the contents of the journals. He agreed with me on the fact that Barnett wished me silent. That Maddie be under his rule once again. I had no plans on divulging this information to anyone other than Maddie and Edward. And I knew she would never breathe a word of it, in order to protect her mother's reputation. Barnett was not thinking clearly—that was evident to me.

I shook my head. "Surely even in his addled mind, he knows killing me would bring down hardship on him. Jail. Possible hanging."

Edward leaned forward. "Perhaps to him, that is better than a debtor's prison—which is where he will end up, given how his funds have vanished. You did not offer him funds to leave Maddie and depart. I believe he was certain that you would. He is grasping at thin air for another way to come up with the coin."

I huffed a laugh. "I offered him a solution—an honest one—to purchase Milton Manor. He refused it. He wants blood." I drummed my fingers on the desktop. "I must carry through with this."

"No!" A gasp came from behind Edward. Maddie stood in the doorway, grasping the frame, her eyes wide, her face pale. "If he is determined to kill you, you cannot!"

I rose from the chair, making haste toward her. "Hush, Maddie mine. All will be well." I drew her trembling form into my arms, cursing myself for not making sure the door had shut behind us.

She gripped my waistcoat, staring up at me. "You cannot," she repeated. "Please, Alexander. Our child." A sob caught in her throat. "Do not leave me alone again!"

I hastened to reassure her. "I will not."

I carried her to the large wing chair I liked to sit in, settling her on my lap. "Edward and I will make sure all is well."

"Of course we will, my lady," he assured her, his voice firm, although his eyes were filled with doubt.

"I must do this, Maddie—for my honor."

"I don't care a whit about that. I know how honorable you are."

"Your father will label me a coward, and we will be ostracized. You will suffer. Our child will suffer because of my cowardice."

"He wishes to destroy me."

"His wishes will be denied."

I met Edward's worried gaze over her bent head, stroking along her soft curls gently. How, I did not know, but I had to survive this.

"I will do everything in my power to bring your husband back to you safely," Edward assured her.

"You saw the state of your father," I said, tilting up her chin. "He was barely able to stand upright. He does not have the fortitude to hold a pistol straight and shoot me. I doubt he will even try," I lied. "He will aim for the sky, and we will part ways."

She didn't respond, her alarm a living, breathing thing that surrounded us.

I cupped her face. "I will return to you."

She dropped her head to my shoulder and cried, and I realized nothing would comfort her. We both had to suffer the worry until the morning.

And that made my hate for the baron burn even hotter.

MADELEINE

The hour was late, and I was beyond weary, but there was no hope of sleep tonight.

Curled on my side, I faced the windows that framed the gently twinkling stars of the night sky. It was a sky I had admired many nights before. A sky that had borne witness to the hideousness of the day. A sky that would also bear witness to the wretched spectacle of tomorrow.

If any harm befell Alexander, I didn't know how I would survive. Even thinking of the possibility of my father hurting him or—God forbid—worse, made my breath freeze in my lungs. It made my stomach churn and ache.

Tears threatened my vision, blurring the brilliance of the silvery stars. I closed my eyes tightly, willing them away.

Weeping would solve nothing, and I had already sobbed enough to fill a lake this day.

But I couldn't banish them. They slipped past my lashes, traveling in hot streaks across my cheeks. This was all my fault. I had brought the danger upon my husband. And if anything happened to him, I would own the blame. My father had come to Wheaton for me, and the only way he could have me was through hurting my husband.

A sob escaped me. I bit my lip, trying to hold in my sorrow. Alexander was a large, beloved presence at my back. But he had fallen into a steady slumber after he had slowly, painstakingly made love to me earlier, and I had no wish to wake him. He would need all the rest he could get to face my father in the duel on the morrow.

"Maddie mine."

Alexander's deep voice cut through the silence, laden with caring and concern.

Another sob emerged. He faced possible death in the morning, and it was he who was worried about me.

"Forgive me," I said.

"For weeping?" He stroked his hand up my spine beneath the bedclothes, warm and reassuring. "Never, my sweet. You are in a delicate condition, and it heightens your emotions."

I sniffed, eyes fluttering open, as I stared back into the night, wondering how it could be so glorious, so perfect, so calm, when my world was about to be torn apart. The sky that had been my comfort these past few months had become a traitor. I longed to claw each star from the black velvet night. I was furious, and I was terrified. How dare those stars shine so brightly upon my misery?

"Maddie?" Alexander prodded softly, his hand splayed between my shoulder blades.

"I'm not crying because I am with child," I said quietly. "I'm crying because I am responsible for all this."

"What?" Gently, he grasped my shoulder, rolling me toward him. "Why should you think you are to blame?"

I was on my back now, gazing up at the ceiling, trying not to dissolve into a new fit of tears. It wasn't easy. They scalded the backs of my eyes, threatening to pour forth.

"Because I am the reason my father came to Wheaton," I managed, barely keeping my composure. "You brought me here, you saved me, made me your wife, granted me every happiness, and look at what has happened in return. It is my fault that your life is now in danger."

"Nonsense."

"It is hardly nonsense. It's the truth." The tears won, escaping my eyes and slipping down my cheeks again. "What is the thanks that you receive for saving me, other than the possibility that you will meet an untimely end at the hands of my father?"

"Look at me, Maddie."

I couldn't. I was silently sobbing. I didn't wish to distress him, but I couldn't bear to have our precious, fragile happiness shattered. I couldn't lose him.

"Maddie mine."

I closed my eyes again, loving the way he said my name, the endearments for me that were his alone. What if this were to be the last night I would ever hear them? The last night I was blessed enough to lie with my husband in our bed?

I choked on my anguish, a wretched sound emerging from me that was scarcely even human.

"My love." Alexander reached for me then, pulling me into his lean, solid strength. "None of what has happened is your fault. Not that bastard's despicable treatment of you, not his appearance here at Wheaton, and not whatever shall happen in the morning. There is one person who will forever bear the burden upon his soul, and that is Lord Barnett himself. Not you. *Never* you."

"What if he shoots you? What if he k-kills you?"

I could scarcely form the words.

"I won't let him. Have faith in me."

I buried my face in his neck, breathing deeply of his scent. "I do have faith in you, but I am also scared of losing you."

"You won't lose me. You'll never lose me. No matter what happens on the morrow, Maddie mine, I am always here." He flattened a hand over my chest. "In your heart." He slid his hand lower, cupping the swell of my belly where our child grew. "And here, in the life you will soon bring into this world."

"Our babe needs a father," I said.

"And so our babe shall have me." He kissed my crown. "You must never think that you are at fault. You are, and will forever be, the light of my days and the stars in my night sky. You are the best part of my life, Maddie mine, and I would meet your father at dawn every day until my last to keep you safe and to love you one day more."

I was weeping again, but it was because of his words. "I love you, Alexander."

It was a poor declaration compared to his, but it was all I could manage past the emotion constricting my throat.

"And I love you and our babe." He caressed my belly fondly. "I have every intention of returning to you both and of putting this behind us for good. Now, get some rest, my love. You need your strength for the babe's sake."

I wrapped my arms around him. "I will try."

I knew it would be useless, but Alexander needed sleep

far more than I did. I wanted him as well rested as possible when he dueled. I wanted him safe.

"Sleep, Maddie mine," he murmured, resting his cheek on my head.

But I lay there awake just the same until the faint streaks of light began to fracture the night sky, listening to the steady thrum of my husband's heart.

ALEXANDER

Dawn was barely breaking when I left my solemn wife in the great hall. The long night had left her bereft of any tears, her pale cheeks and red eyes attesting to her heightened state. "Do not leave this house, Maddie mine. I will not risk you being anywhere near him on this day."

She didn't lift her eyes but nodded. I had spoken at length to her, telling her if she were there, I would be distracted and certainly injured, if not killed.

"Come back to me, Alexander," she whispered, her voice thick with tears.

"I will return to you, my wife. I swear it."

"I love you," she added.

I slid my fingers under her chin and kissed her softly. "As I love you." I laid my other hand on her expanding belly. "And our little one. We have much to look forward to."

"Please be here to do so."

I kissed her again. "On my honor."

I walked away from her, shocked at the dread building inside me. Terrified I would never again see her lovely countenance. Hear her voice. Feel the touch of her gentle hands on me or her mouth on mine. I met Edward's gaze, his filled with sympathy and worry. I straightened my shoulders. I was an excellent marksman. I refused to let Lord Barnett take away the happiness I had found. I loathed the idea of killing a man, but if it was him or me…

I chose myself. Maddie. Our child.

I chose my life.

CHAPTER 21

ALEXANDER

As we rode toward the field at the edge of the estate, I inhaled deeply. The air was resplendent with the scent of spring. I glanced around, taking in the beauty. The dew was heavy on the long grasses that swayed in the early morning breeze. I knew that, later, the sky overhead would be so blue it would remind me of my Maddie's extraordinary eyes. A niggling thought worried at me, and I wondered if this perhaps might be the last time I would be able to gaze on such beauty. Unusually overcome, I offered up a prayer for my safety. For my wife and our unborn babe.

I paused my horse, taking it all in. Edward turned in his saddle, regarding me.

"Alexander?"

"Promise me one last time."

He rounded his steed and drew alongside me. "She will be looked after. Always. As God as my witness, she and your babe will want for nothing. I will watch over both of them as if they were my own and care for them. He will never again touch her life."

I reached over and grasped his forearm. "Thank you. You have been the truest, most loyal companion a man could ask for to walk beside him."

"Until the end. That was our vow as young men."

I nodded. "If the end be today, I am grateful to have you with me."

"It will not be," he stated firmly. "You will return to your wife shortly and put this behind you."

"Let us get on with it, then."

We urged the horses forward, and I took in some deep breaths, settling my nerves. I dismounted, drawing myself up to my full height. I refused to show any hesitancy or worry in front of either man. I glared at Barnett, focusing my loathing in his direction.

Our eyes met, mine angry and determined. His were rheumy, bloodshot, and I noticed he was holding on to the cart, as if to steady himself. He looked even older than he had the day before.

All pluses for me.

As was customary, my physician was present, ready to come to my aid if necessary. I prayed he would not be required. I nodded my thanks to him, and he dipped his chin in return.

The weapons were checked, and Edward nodded in satisfaction. The rules were laid out, clear and concise. Ten paces. One shot.

"Gentlemen, your places."

Time felt as if it were racing. My pulse beat rapidly, my heart pumping. I reached for my pistol, once again catching Barnett's eye.

"We can end this peacefully. As gentlemen," I urged, offering him one last reprieve.

"We will end it completely." His voice was raspy and thick, indicating his own nerves.

"I have no wish to kill you. Allow me to purchase Milton Manor and erase your debts. Be done with this vendetta."

He didn't reply, continuing only to glare at me in distaste.

"As you wish."

I held my head high as we counted off our steps.

I turned, pausing. I intended on firing my pistol into the air, hoping he would follow suit. But he was determined. His arm shook as he aimed, firing in my direction. As honor stated, I remained in place, his bullet whizzing past me. I felt the heat as it went by, the sound a low, dull hum in my ear.

I pointed my gun, but I didn't engage until he did the unthinkable, breaking every rule of engagement.

He fired again.

Edward shouted out in fury as I shot my pistol for the first time. In my head, I imagined the bullets passing each other, a fury of heat and steel, seeking their targets. I felt the burn of the bullet as it tore through my flesh, and I stumbled back as the pain exploded in my left arm.

I dropped my pistol, clutching my limb. Barnett fell back on the ground, Leigh kneeling beside him. Instantly, Edward was at my side, grasping my shoulder.

"Alexander, where are you hurt?"

I grimaced. "My arm. His aim is as bad as I thought." I looked over. "The bastard took a second shot. That was not what was agreed upon. He broke his word."

"The coward," he seethed. "He has no honor."

"Is he dead?" I asked, seeing he hadn't moved.

"If there is a God."

Dr. Atwood appeared, pulling off my jacket. "You are lucky," he muttered. "It's a through and through."

"Bandage it and tend to me later."

"My lord—"

"Check on Barnett," I demanded. "Now."

He wound a bandage around my arm and walked toward Barnett.

"What will you do, Alexander?"

I huffed, feeling relief, anger, and the need to see my wife coursing through me.

"Get him off my property. He is a coward and a cheat. I will make it known to all."

Dr. Atwood came back. "He is hit in the left quadrant, but the bullet is lodged inside. I will have to remove it."

"Will he live?"

"I am unsure at this point. He is losing a lot of blood and—" he cleared his throat "—he is not in the best of health."

"Take him to the inn and see to it. Not here. Return when you are done."

He bowed. "My lord."

"Take me home, Edward. I need to see my wife."

"With pleasure."

We waited as Barnett was loaded on the cart and it rambled away.

"Can you ride?"

"Yes." I was determined to return as I departed. Head held high, shoulders straight, my pride intact. Besides, it would give Maddie great comfort to see me riding to the house.

At Knight's side, I shook my head. "I believe I require assistance."

Edward chuckled. "It will be gladly given, my lord."

Once in the saddle, I grimaced again. "Damn it all to hell, that hurts."

"Lady Wheaton will tend you."

I thought of my wife's gentle touch. All at once, my

adrenaline left me, and I felt the sheer magnitude of what had occurred hit me. My body seemed to deflate, and I felt my limbs shaking.

"Alexander?"

"I think perhaps I might—"

I couldn't speak, unable to form words.

Edward grabbed my reins. "Shut your eyes, and for God's sake, don't fall off your mount."

IT WASN'T the glorious return I had imagined. I was barely able to remain upright. I heard Maddie's voice, strained and upset. Edward's assurances. I opened my eyes, meeting Maddie's terrified gaze.

"I am well, my love."

"You, sir," she replied, her eyes bright with unshed tears, "are a liar and an imbecile."

I wanted to laugh. To hold her and assure her that all was settled. But it was difficult to achieve when my legs refused to hold me up and I required Edward's assistance and his strong grip to get me inside.

"Take him to his chamber," Maddie ordered.

Upstairs, I was shocked when I realized it was my wife who tore away my sleeve. She muttered and tutted while attending me, ignoring my low groans of pain and discomfort.

"The baron?" she asked Edward, who was assisting her.

"Alexander shot him after he took a second attempt at hitting him."

"I thought you said it would be one shot!" she exclaimed, horrified.

"We did."

Her eyes grew round with anger, and she muttered something under her breath. It was most unladylike and something I was certain she had heard me say.

"That pigeon-livered cad. As useless as a flaccid cock."

I was shocked and delighted at her anger and choice of words.

"Dr. Atwood is seeing to him at the inn," I informed her. "I did not want him in this house."

"Good. But he should be here tending you."

"It's just a scratch, my sweet," I assured her. "Although if you insist on wrenching my arm one more time, it may detach."

"Hush."

I gasped as she poured something on my arm, the burn almost as bad as the wound.

"Damnation!" I yelled. "What was that? Brimstone?"

"Whiskey. It will clean the wound. Be still."

"The whiskey is for my throat, not my arm," I argued, but did as she requested. I wasn't used to this demeanor from Maddie. No-nonsense. In charge. It was rather unsettling.

Dr. Atwood walked in, and I heaved a sigh of relief. He would take over now. Except he looked at what Maddie was doing and nodded in agreement. Even the herbs she had brought out from the healer in the village. Together, they wrapped my arm, and Dr. Atwood stood back, satisfied. "We will watch it and make sure it drains and does not become infected. I believe your wife has this well in hand."

Maddie lifted my head, letting me sip some liquid. It

was sweet and light with a slightly bitter aftertaste, but the cool was welcome on my throat.

"And the coward?" Edward demanded.

"I dug out the bullet and left him to his butler and solicitor." He shook his head. "I asked the innkeeper's wife to check on him and send for me if needed." He met my eyes. "I turned after the first shot, thinking it was over. I saw what he did. You had no choice but to fire, my lord. He was aiming to kill you—of that, I have no doubt."

Maddie gasped, and I reached out my hand to comfort her. The room seemed too hot and bright, and I struggled to reach her, the distance seeming to grow between us.

"I believe he will rest. The draught you gave him will help," Dr. Atwood stated, nodding. "I will look in on him tomorrow."

My eyes refused to stay open. I fought the heaviness, needing to talk to Maddie. To reassure her. I was home. I was fine. I would heal, and we would move on from this unpleasantness.

But I lost the battle and drifted.

CHAPTER 22

MADELEINE

"You should rest, my lady."

The voice, with the gentle French accent, was Geraldine's, interrupting the vigil I kept over my sleeping husband. Seated in a chair at his bedside where I had been ever since he had arrived this morning, I turned to find her hovering at the threshold, a look of concern etched on her face.

"I *am* resting," I told her. "I'm sitting here by his lordship's side."

"Perhaps you will take some sustenance, then," Geraldine suggested. "Mrs. Dougall said you didn't break your fast this morning, and it is afternoon now."

I hadn't the stomach to eat this morning. I had been fraught. And my fears hadn't been for naught. My father had proven a dishonorable liar and fired a second shot at Alexander, wounding him. Had his aim been any better…

I shuddered, not able to think of the consequences had my father's bullet hit its intended mark. I would have lost my husband. I would have been devastated, weeping on the floor, screaming at the heavens, instead of sitting by a peacefully slumbering Alexander. I was incredibly thankful that the outcome of the duel had been a mere grazing for the man I loved.

For my father and his injury, I hadn't spared a thought. He was dead to me.

"My lady," Geraldine repeated gently. "You must eat."

I shook my head. "I find that I'm not hungry."

"For the babe's sake, if not for your own," she pressed.

I gently caressed the swell of my stomach. "I will eat later."

"It isn't good for the babe, my lady. You must have something, perhaps some honey cakes or a bit of jam and bread. I will fetch you a tray."

My stomach rumbled.

I relented, nodding. "If you must."

"I must." Geraldine dipped into a curtsy before disappearing.

When she had gone, I turned back to Alexander. It hurt my heart to see him brought low. He was so still, so very unlike himself. My sole reassurance was in the steady rising and falling of his broad chest, proof that he was merely resting.

He had been in more danger than I had even known today. Rage grew within me anew at the knowledge that my father had attempted to kill Alexander. Did his hatred for me know no bounds? Or had he merely been so intent upon regaining control over my life that he had been willing to do anything to take my husband from me and force me back under his roof?

I would never know, for I had no wish to speak with him ever again.

I reached for Alexander's hand, which was lying on the counterpane with such serenity. His skin was warm and vibrant, a reminder that he had survived as he had promised he would.

"I am sorry, my love, for calling you names," I murmured, feeling guilty for my reception of him.

I had been terrified and then relieved and then worried again when I had spied his wound.

He had been in good spirits, however, insisting it was just a scratch, and I had understood at once that the greatest of the danger to him had passed. He would live.

That was the most important thing.

But I would still be breathing much easier when he was awake and smiling at me again and when I knew that no infection had set in.

Geraldine returned then, bearing a tray laden with far more than she had suggested, beaming at me with an encouraging smile. "Here you are, my lady. An assortment from Cook."

She settled the tray on a table, and I spied sweets and tea. "Thank you, Geraldine."

"You needn't thank me, my lady. I am happy to be of some service and comfort."

I stood from the chair, stretching as I did so. Although I wasn't heavy with child yet, my small frame meant that I felt the weight of our growing child already, and it was more than I had expected. My back ached from sitting in the chair for so long.

I went to Geraldine and laid a hand on her arm. "You have been so loyal and good, first to my mother, and then to me."

"It is the least I can do, my lady. Your mother would have wanted me to look after you, and it wasn't much, but I did as best as I could. I'm pleased to see you settled and contented with the marquess now. Your dear mother would have been happy too."

I liked to think that my mother would have adored Alexander. I wished the two of them could have met. But fate hadn't allowed such a meeting.

"I am indeed settled and contented," I agreed softly, casting another glance at Alexander, who still slept on, unaware of the bustle around him.

"You love his lordship very much, don't you?"

"I do. He is the first man who has ever shown me kindness and love. My father never did."

Thoughts of the baron made me frown. He had hurt me for the last time, and I would never allow him to harm Alexander again either.

Geraldine's countenance shifted. "I think he would have loved you very much, my lady."

Her words took me by surprise. It took me a moment to realize just what she had said, for it made no sense.

"He would have," I repeated. "Do you mean if my mother had not died?"

Geraldine looked torn. "I've said more than I ought. Forgive me, my lady. You should ask Lord Wheaton when he wakes."

Before I could ask anything further, she bobbed in a hasty curtsy and left the room.

I stared after her, wondering what she had meant.

My stomach grumbled at me again, so I picked up a honey cake and took a bite, my mind churning with the possibilities of what Geraldine's cryptic words could have meant. And then suddenly, all at once, the truth sank its claws into me. The honey cake fell from my numb fingers.

Could it be?

ALEXANDER

I woke in the dim of the evening. The windows were open, the breeze drifting through the room. I blinked in confusion, uncertain as to events I could recall. My head felt unclear, as if I had imbibed too many brandies over an intense chess game with Edward. Except my arm didn't usually feel as if it were on fire.

A noise startled me, and I looked over, meeting my Maddie's tired gaze.

"Hello, my love," she whispered. "You are back."

The evening light cast a glow around her, accentuating her delicate features. She smiled at me, but I could see she had been weeping.

"Come closer, Maddie mine," I pleaded. "I wish to see you."

She perched on the mattress, her slight weight hardly making a difference on the thick pad. I reached for her with my good hand, holding her palm in mine. "I am parched," I whispered.

Maddie lifted the jug, pouring me some water. It was cool and delicious on my dry throat, and I drank deeply. I relaxed back on the pillow and took her hand again.

"I am back. And, despite the baron's best efforts, alive. I will send him back to his estate, and you will never have to see him again."

"I was so frightened. I didn't care what happened to him, but to have lost you…" She trailed off and swallowed. "I could not even bear to think it."

"I am here and safe. And thanks to your tending me, I will recover fully. Tomorrow, I will be up and ready to face the day."

A tear splashed on my hand, the drop making my chest ache with repressed emotion.

"I, too, was afraid," I admitted quietly, sharing with her emotions I could only admit to my wife. "Terrified I would never again see your beautiful face or hold our babe."

Her startled gaze flew to mine. "Truly? You never showed it."

"I could not. I refused to let him see I was unsettled. I would not give him that satisfaction. I tried to get him to stop the madness, but he refused."

"Why does he dislike you?" She paused, her soft voice dropping even lower. "Why does he hate me so much?"

I hesitated, and then she spoke again.

"Geraldine said something to me earlier that caused questions to begin to form in my mind. He is not my father, is he?"

"No, Maddie, he is not."

"I suspected. I know I certainly wished for it often enough. I searched my features, but there was nothing of him. None of his temperament. Often, I wondered if he had discovered that fact and punished me for it."

"Yes," I agreed. "It was nothing you did."

Briefly, I told her what I had discovered and how. She wasn't shocked by my words, nodding as I finished.

"How does this make you feel?" I asked.

She sighed. "If I am being truthful—relieved. I feel nothing but loathing for him. Any family feelings I might have had, he beat and starved from me long ago."

"Never again, my love. You are safe here with me always. And should there come a day I am not here, Edward will ensure you are protected."

"Please don't speak of that."

A low knock on the door interrupted us, and Edward came in.

"Ah, the victor is awake."

I smiled at his attempt at levity. I met Maddie's eyes.

"My love, might I ask for some sustenance? Something to rid my stomach of the empty ache?"

She slid from the bed. "Of course. I should have thought of that."

"No. I was enjoying gazing on you and hearing your lovely voice. A whiskey would be a welcome addition. To drink this time and not poured on my arm as a sacrifice."

She pursed her lips, prepared to say no.

"A small one. It has been a trying day," I coaxed.

"A small one," she conceded.

"If you would fetch my valet as well. I require some assistance."

Edward stepped forward. "Allow me to help, Alexander."

I was too tired to argue. Maddie leaned down and pressed a kiss to my cheek. "I shall return with your tray."

"Let a footman carry it."

She glided away, her silk skirt drifting along the floor. I admired her carriage and the way her hips moved. The curls framing her face. My cock twitched in my pants, and I was grateful to know all was working. I would show her I was indeed well when we were once again alone.

Edward approached the bed.

"I need the water closet and to get out of these clothes," I told him. "Give me your flask."

He pulled one from his jacket and offered it to me. The bite of the liquor was what I needed to face moving. I handed it back to him and, with his aid, stood from the bed. The burn in my arm increased, and I groaned in frustration.

"Remind me not to get shot again."

"Good plan. Now, let us get this over with, shall we?"

MADDIE REAPPEARED A SHORT TIME LATER. "Your tray will be here soon." She looked at my bare chest and arm, frowning. "I want to check the wound."

I was growing weary, the simple act of undressing and relieving myself almost too much. I nodded, and she efficiently undid the bandage and hummed, sounding pleased.

"It is clean and cool," she informed me. "I will rewrap it, and Dr. Atwood can check in the morning." She went to the washstand and wrung out some cloths, returning to the bed and wiping down my face, chest, and arms. She was proficient and quick, and I enjoyed her tender ministrations.

She allowed me to sit in my favorite chair, and I sipped the whiskey and ate the food offered. Edward spoke, filling me in on the day I had slept through. The farmers were doing well, the crops planted. Missives had arrived for me to look over but nothing urgent.

"Tomorrow or the day following will be fine, my lord," he assured me.

"I will go to the village tomorrow," I informed him. "If Barnett is well enough, I will dispatch him back to his own estate. I don't want him even remotely close to my wife," I said quietly, watching as Maddie bustled around with Mrs. Dougall. The bed was changed, fresh water brought in, and a banyan laid out for me. They conferred in quiet voices, and I stared in wonder at my wife.

"She knows the truth of the baron," I told Edward, my eyes never leaving her.

"It would appear she has taken the news in stride. She is a strong woman."

"She has had to be with all she endured." I paused. "She humbles me."

"Love can do that," he mused, causing me to eye him closely.

"Oh? You know this from experience?" I asked.

"Words I have heard."

I snorted in derision, but he ignored me.

"I wish to find out as much information as possible about her real father," I informed him in a low voice. "I think it would bring her comfort."

He nodded in agreement. "I have already started inquiries about the possible cousin."

"Thank you."

"I will be ready in the morning to escort you to the village," he said, standing. "If, of course, her ladyship permits it."

"Let us not allow her to think she has that power," I murmured.

He smiled as he clapped a hand on my good shoulder. "She already knows, Alexander. She already knows."

ALEXANDER

The sky was overcast and dark the next morning as we rode into the village. Under the guise of collecting some supplies, we took the cart. The truth was, my arm ached constantly, and the thought of swinging up into the saddle was unpleasant. Especially knowing I would be watched.

At the inn, we entered, surprised to see Dr. Atwood there talking to the innkeeper.

"What is the news?" I asked.

"He is awake, complaining, and cranky."

"Is he well enough to travel?"

My physician sighed. "He is breathing and the wound is clean, so in my estimation, yes." He lowered his voice. "He was not of good health before this incident, my lord. How he will fare, I do not know. It is up to his physician when he arrives to his own estate."

"Good enough." I looked toward Edward. "Settle the account, and I will go speak with him."

I headed upstairs, knocking on the door of the room I was told Barnett was in. I didn't wait for his summons before entering and shutting the door behind me. The room smelled of piss and unwashed flesh, and I grimaced, crossing to the window and yanking it open. "Good God, man, have some pride."

Barnett glared at me, his hatred on full display.

"Your account is settled as of today. Take your unctuous little crew and leave. Do not return."

"I will sell you Milton Manor now."

"No. You had your chance. Many of them. I no longer want it," I lied.

He cursed me, calling me several names. I remained silent until he was done.

I raised my voice so he could hear me clearly, having no wish to get closer to his person.

"I have no idea why you hate me. Or why you treated Maddie as you did. You could have chosen to see all of her mother in her. To celebrate that she lived on in a clever, loving woman, instead of punishing her for something she had no control over." I shook my head in anger. "Did you think that made you a bigger man? Hurting a child? Beating her into submission?"

"How I raised her is none—"

I cut him off. "Everything about her is my concern. She is my wife. My marchioness. I hold due any past transgressions to this day. Any slurs you say against her, you say against me. I will drag you through the mud so deeply, you will never recover. Not one word, Barnett. You will leave, you will never return, you will never so much as speak her name, or I will ruin you so thoroughly that not even the lowest of moneylenders will allow you in their door. Even those who wish to profit from you will stay clear."

He remained silent.

"And you will cease in this tirade of proclaiming I stole

her. You gave her away, and I will not hesitate to prove it. I have the funds and the witnesses." I crossed my arms. "You seem to think you hold something over me, and you do not. I am not a child you can beat into silence. I will use my position and whatever other means to destroy what is left of your life."

I eyed him with dislike.

"Any funds Maddie possesses, any gifts I choose to lavish on her, belong to her. Not to you. You will never benefit from the love I bestow upon her. And she has ceased to care about your indifference. She now knows what love is, and she has blossomed. You, in your uncalled-for rage—your heedless vendetta against a dead woman—have turned someone who would have loved you throughout your entire lifetime into a stranger who doesn't wish to know you."

I shook my head. "You will never truly understand that loss since I believe your heart no longer exists."

I curled my hands into fists to stop myself from hitting him. Giving him a taste of his own medicine.

"You hated my father over an insignificant argument, so you punished me by refusing to sell me a piece of land you knew I coveted. You hated Maddie's mother, so you punished her daughter by stripping her of her life. Your hate and bitterness overtook you. And you lost. Now you are alone, penniless, and without a friend. I wish you gone from my sight and that you spend any time you have left in misery. It is all you deserve. You are a despicable man."

He stared at me, then spoke, his voice almost pleading. "I need help."

"So did Maddie when her mother died. So I will give to you what you gave to her. Nothing."

And I walked out.

THE SUN CAME OUT, brightening the sky and sending its rays over the fields. I breathed in lungfuls of clean air. The cart creaked under the weight of our purchases. Sugar, tea, sweets for Maddie. Coffee, brandy, and cheroots for me. A fine joint and sundries for the kitchen. Seed and tools for my farmers. I tore through the small shops like a madman, picking up anything that caught my eye.

In my pocket were two pairs of gloves. Lacy, delicate, soft. Fingerless. Maddie loved the style, and I knew she was most comfortable still when her palms were covered. These would please her. I had also purchased a small pair of pearl earrings I decided I wanted to see her wear. A lovely dressing gown from the dressmaker, long soft silk in a creamy violet trimmed in lace and pretty. Like my wife.

None of it needed, but it somehow took the edge off my anger. I didn't leave the village until Edward quietly informed me Barnett was gone.

"Snuck away like the rotter he is. He and that slimy solicitor. His butler barely made it into his seat when they were moving. Whatever you said to him sent him away quickly."

"I spoke only the truth."

Wheaton came into view, the rolling hills and neat fences making me smile. Tenants worked in the fields, smoke rising from the chimney stacks in the tidy little cottages where they dwelled.

"I wish to walk in the fields later. Speak with the tenants." I sighed deeply. "But first, I wish to lay my eyes on my lovely wife and hold her in my embrace."

"Of course, Alexander. I understand."

"If I am able to purchase Milton Manor, I wish to present it to you."

He pulled the cart to a stop. "My lord?" he asked, sounding incredulous.

"For your future."

He shook his head. "I cannot accept that, nor would I possibly need so much land or so grand a house."

"It is not a large parcel, but perhaps part of it, then. Build your own house. Have land to tend."

"You said you told him you no longer wished to buy it."

"I did, but only to anger him. I will have Higgins make the proper inquiries under a different name." I clapped him on the shoulder. "Perhaps yours."

"Alexander, what has come over you?"

"I could have died," I replied simply. "You have been loyal and constant. A true friend and never once have you ever asked me for anything."

"You are more than generous with my wages."

"And you earn them and more. This would be a gift. We will work out the details and how the estate could be managed. You would receive part of those earnings."

For a moment, he stared.

"You need a home of your own, Edward. A wife. A place to call yours. You would be close. Still able to assist me, and together, we can run the estates." I looked around, feeling the pull of the land. "Wheaton is home. Where we will raise our family. I would like to think of my closest friend as my neighbor."

"You would sell the town house?"

"No. I will need to return for business and Parliament on occasion. But it can be run with fewer servants. My visits will be brief." I chuckled. "Until my daughters, should I have some, wish to see the city and be presented.

Or my sons long for city life." With a laugh, I clapped him on the back. "That, my dear friend, is years ahead. For now, let us plan. Let us return to Wheaton and build our future. Think about what I have said. We will discuss it on another day."

He returned my smile. "Another day."

CHAPTER 24

ALEXANDER

Maddie was outside, waiting for me. I could see her nervous pacing as the cart moved toward the house along the winding road. Edward spoke, his voice low and steady.

"She will be relieved this is done. That he is gone."

"Yes. The worry is not good for her. Or the babe. I wish that I could erase the past few days."

"Just be there for her, Alexander. She draws her strength from your love."

I glanced at him. "When did you get so wise about love, my friend? Since you found your own?"

He shook his head. "This is not about me."

I chuckled. "Somehow, I think it may be."

He ignored me, pulling the cart to a stop. I jumped off, ignoring the jarring pain in my arm, desiring Maddie to see me fit. She hurried forward, and I embraced her, holding her close with my good arm. Behind her, the footmen began their work of emptying the cart. Edward watched over them, instructing them where some items were to go. He handed Lydia the presents I purchased for my wife, and I saw how he bent low, speaking to her, and the way she gazed up at him. I didn't miss the way he grazed his finger over her cheek as he sent her inside. He looked at me, raised an eyebrow, and turned his back, making me want to taunt him, but I refrained and concentrated on my anxious wife.

"All is well, my love." I drew back and met her eyes. "He is gone and will stay gone. You have no need to be fearful."

"Are you certain?"

"I have made sure he understands the consequences should he choose to act foolishly or talk needlessly. He will not risk my anger."

"How is your arm?"

"I stopped at Dr. Atwood's. He said you are a miracle worker. It is healing well, and he has no doubt of my full recovery."

She smiled, looking relieved and joyful. But I saw traces of exhaustion under her eyes. She had not slept well, trying not to disturb me but failing, as I, too, could not rest.

"I believe our plans the other day were rudely interrupted. I feel as if a picnic is in order today. The sun is shining, and the breeze makes it most agreeable. I will visit my farmers, then we can spend the afternoon together in the sun, enjoying the day." I touched the end of her nose affectionately. "Just the two of us."

"I would like that."

"Yes? Some delicious morsels to feast on, some of your favored drink, a comfortable chair, and perhaps your favorite sonnets? I will read to you as you relax. We can be naughty and roll up our hems and splash in the brook if you wish."

"What if I wish to be even naughtier?" she whispered, a small glint appearing in her eyes.

I lowered my head and touched my mouth to hers. "Then I shall be happy to oblige my wife in any way she pleases."

THE BREEZE RUSTLED Maddie's hair that hung down her back in ripples of dark silk. I had convinced her to remove her bonnet and the hairpins keeping it tethered to her nape.

"It is one of my greatest pleasures—to see your hair down," I had urged, knowing she could not resist my plea. She wished to indulge me in any fashion I wanted, and I was prepared to take full advantage of her soft feelings.

I had discarded my waistcoat and cravat, loosening the buttons on my shirt and rolling up my trousers, letting the breeze kiss my skin. I had also persuaded Maddie to remove her gown, the petticoat, and her stays, remaining only in her chemise, in order to be comfortable. She was leery at first, but I could see she was enjoying the freedom. Her chemise was loose and fairly modest, and I assured her no one would see her but me. The servants would not appear until we returned to the manor and they came to clean up. I did not tell her how much I enjoyed the view of her unencumbered breasts and the way they moved under the thin linen of her shift. We had both removed our stockings and shoes, letting the breeze play over our toes. It made her giggle, and I enjoyed watching her happiness. She laughed as I lifted her hems to her knees then kissed the dimpled swells, telling her how much I loved her legs and instructed her to leave them on display.

"You present such a delicious tableau for my eyes,

Maddie," I whispered with a lingering kiss to her lips. "Please stay as such."

She rested in a comfortable wicker chair the footmen had brought out and placed in the shade beside the brook. I sat on a stool beside her, the picnic basket in front of us mostly empty now. Cook had packed a feast for us, and I had plied Maddie with all the tempting morsels, feeding her from my hand. Pork pies, cheeses and breads, savory meats and the choicest of cakes and tarts were enjoyed by us both. The delicious lemonade and fresh fruit rounded off the repast.

I smiled at her, pleased to see the color returning to her face and the strain around her eyes easing. My arm was hardly paining me at all, thanks to Maddie's care. We did not talk about her father, but rather the babe and the room she wished to prepare for the arrival of our child. The drawing she had been working on. A new idea I had for the farmers.

"Did you always love the land?" she asked, sipping her lemonade and resting her head back.

"Yes. Even as a child, I spent time out of doors. When I was old enough, Edward and I would sneak down to the farms and watch. Learn. Eventually, they allowed me to toil with them, although we made sure my father didn't see."

"You have a strong bond with Edward."

I nodded, sipping the claret I had chosen for the meal. It was rich and decadent, the flavor bursting on my tongue as I drank it. "We have been like brothers. I know no finer man than he. We experienced so much of life together. Good and bad. We made an oath as young men we would stand by each other until the end, and I believe we both mean to stick to those words."

"It is good you have him."

"I think so as well."

We were silent for a moment. I slipped my hand into my pocket and laid the delicate gloves on her bare knee. "I saw these and thought you would like them."

She gasped in delight, slipping one on and admiring the lace. "Alexander, they are beautiful!"

"I have no desire for you to cover your hands, but if you wish to, I should like it if you wore those, not heavy leather ones." I picked up her hands and studied the palms. "The salve the healer made for you has lessened the scarring, and they are no longer rough."

"It has. But it will never be totally gone."

"These light gloves will help hide them."

She leaned forward and kissed me. "Thank you. I will wear them. I would feel better in mixed company if they were covered. And these are so lovely!"

I touched her ear where the small knot of pearls lay I had given her earlier. "I am pleased you are happy with my gifts."

"I am spoiled by all your gifts." Her eyes glowed. "Though none is as dear to me as the gift of your love."

I dropped to my knees in front of her, wrapping my hand around her neck and pulling her face to mine. I pressed my lips to hers, groaning as she immediately opened for me. She tasted of sweet berries and lemon. Of life and love. Of Maddie.

She sucked my tongue, as desperate for me as I was for her. I kissed her deeply, exploring the sweet recesses of her mouth as though it were new to me. And it was—every time. She flung her arms around my neck, tearing away the band of leather holding my hair back and delving her fingers into the heavy strands, pulling and twisting them. I slid my hands to her knees, pulling them apart and pushing the fabric of her chemise out of the way, feeling the warmth of her bare skin under my fingertips. I stroked up her legs slowly, still kissing her. She mewled in frustration as I teased her thighs, throwing her head back. "Please, Alexander. I need you."

I smiled against the heat of her neck, licking, kissing, and biting along the delicate arch of her throat. "You want my hands on you, my sweet? My fingers inside you? Are you wet for me?"

"Yes to all," she panted, shivering as I bit down at the juncture where her neck and shoulder met. "Can it be done here—outside? Is your arm—"

I stopped her words. "My arm is fine. And as for doing it outside, yes, my sweet. I will happily show you." Impatiently, I tugged at her bodice, wanting her nipples in my mouth. She wiggled, exposing her luscious breasts, and I wasted no time in drawing a stiff pink nipple into my mouth, teasing and sucking, then doing the same to the other one. She gripped the back of my head, whimpering my name. The low, hungry sounds she made in her throat made me frantic. More desperate for her. I slid my fingers up her legs, finding her silken heat, wet and ready for me.

"Ah, Maddie mine," I groaned. "How good you feel," I praised as I stroked her, my thumb strumming her pearl as I slid two fingers inside her. She gasped, sliding down in the chair, widening her legs. She reached blindly for me, and I aided her in unbuttoning my falls so she could reach in and pull out my cock, stroking it perfectly as I worked her. Our mouths never separated as I passed circles over her clit, slowly increasing the pressure until she was trembling and moaning, her breasts rubbing on my chest, the material of my shirt abrading my skin. I wanted to feel only her—only us—but I wanted her to succumb first.

I moved my fingers faster, curling them the way that always made her come. She stiffened and inhaled quickly, her sweet cunny tightening around my digits as she climaxed. Her grip on my shaft loosened, and then to my utter shock and delight, she pushed on my chest, sending me down to the blanket. Faster than I expected, she climbed over me, settling herself on my thighs and once again grasping my cock. She drew me inside, her walls still quivering from her spend. She was wet, ready, and began to move. She braced herself on my chest, then frowned and pushed her hands under the linen to my skin. With a grin, I grasped the middle and tore it in half, exposing myself fully to her. She traced over my muscles and chest, lingering on my flat nipples, pulling and teasing them, making me groan. She undulated her hips, rocking slowly, taking her pleasure and giving me mine. My cock was bathed in her heat. Saturated in her wetness. Delirious with passion and rejoicing in her taking charge.

"Ride me, Maddie," I pleaded. "Harder. Take me as deeply as you can."

She leaned over me, gripping my thighs as her head fell back, her hair tickling my knees. I was as deep inside her as I could possibly be, the sensation incredible. We moved like a wave, flowing and ebbing, rising higher and higher. The pleasure grew, expanding and rippling down my spine, sending shards of ecstasy throughout my body. Nothing in my life had prepared me for this woman. For the passion I felt for her. The love.

With a roar, I sat up, wrapping her in my arms. Covering her mouth with mine. Swallowing her cries of pleasure. Drowning in my own. I spilled inside her as she gripped my cock, milking me. Taking all I had to give. Until we were spent. Exhausted.

Blissfully wrapped around each other.

I FLOATED in the cool water, Maddie's arms around my neck, her voice still shocked. "Alexander, I still believe you lie! This is not done."

I laughed quietly, pressing a kiss to her crown. "But we are doing it, my sweet."

"Naked in the water. What if a person came by right now? They would be scandalized beyond comprehension!"

After our frantic, passionate coupling, we were both hot, sticky, and a mess. I convinced Maddie to swim naked with me in the brook, assuring her I did it all the time and we were fully protected by the trees. When she had protested, uncertain and worried, I had laughed and drawn her into my arms.

"You just rode me on this blanket for anyone to see, my love. Let me suck your breasts in the open. Think of how cool and refreshing the water will be against our hot skin."

I knew her to be overheated and uncomfortable and the offer too tempting when she gave in quickly. I laughed as I watched her remove her chemise, her gaze seeking the trees and fields constantly. She moved swiftly to the water's edge and let me tug her in with me, her low inhale of air as the water lapped around her waist and chest almost a sigh of relief.

"If someone happened by, all they would see are our heads. Far less than they would have seen only a short while before."

"Oh," she replied.

"Is it not cool? Wondrous on your skin?"

"Yes." She frowned. "I worry about your arm."

"The water is clean and feels good on it. Cease to worry, my love. It is fine. It hardly pains me at all."

She glanced around again. "Do others make a habit of this?"

I laughed. "Probably not. I love the outdoors. I enjoy how the water feels on my skin with the sun overhead. The freedom. I have always enjoyed it."

I pulled her closer, feeling her breasts press into my chest. "I find it invigorating," I murmured, reaching low and pulling her legs around my waist. "Stimulating, even."

Her eyes widened as she felt me hard and pressing against her again. "Alexander," she whispered. "Again?"

"Yes," I assured her. "Lean back in the water," I coaxed. "Relax. I will support you."

She did, her hair streaming behind her. Water dripped off her skin, her nipples hard points that glistened in the sun. Bending, I took one in my mouth, warming it and making her moan.

"I can show you another way to enjoy the water, Maddie," I growled against her breast, sucking hard. "One so scandalous you will cry out my name repeatedly."

"I would like to try that," she murmured, arching her back. "Alexander," she pleaded as I bit down gently, then blew over her nipple.

I smiled against her skin.

Swimming naked had never been so stimulating, and I liked the added benefits. I would assume that my wife did as well.

Repeatedly.

THAT EVENING, I laid out the new dressing gown I had purchased for her and waited impatiently for her to finish her nightly routine. I heard her exclamation of delight when she spied my gift. A moment later, my wife appeared before me, wearing the gown and nothing else. We both enjoyed sleeping skin to skin, and she found herself too warm these days with a nightgown. The violet silk glowed in the firelight, clinging to her form. I held out my hand, drawing her to me.

"You are a vision," I murmured.

"Alexander, it is so beautiful," she whispered. "You are too generous to me."

I shook my head. "I don't think I am generous enough. I love spoiling you, but my love, I believe getting to see you in that dressing gown is more a gift to me."

She laughed and twirled, a froth of lace and silk circling her. "Exquisite," I mused, placing a hand over the swell that grew a little every day. "Our babe grows," I added.

"Hmm," she replied. "Perhaps it is more I am full of lake water this evening than babe." She paused. "I believe much entered my body earlier today through your vigorous, ah, actions."

I looked up at her, her mischievous smile making me throw back my head in laughter. I loved it when she teased me.

I pulled her to my lap and lifted my knees, jostling her. "Shall I shake it from you, wife?"

She joined me in laughter, nestling her head to my shoulder. "No, I shall recover, my lord."

We were quiet for a moment, and I enjoyed the peacefulness of the evening, holding my wife and appreciating a fine snifter of brandy. Often, Maddie would chat about her day or talk about something she was working on for the babe, but tonight, she was silent.

I pressed a kiss to her head. "Did I exhaust you today?"

"Perhaps," she said, sounding sleepy.

I had looked forward to removing her pretty dressing gown. Making love to her. But it had been a day filled with many "vigorous actions," as she phrased it. I knew there would be many nights ahead of us when I could indulge my wish. For tonight, I would be happy to hold her in my arms and sleep next to her.

After our swim earlier, we had dried in the sun, then dressed and returned to the manor. My waistcoat covered my torn shirt, and Maddie carried the blanket in front of her, hiding her disheveled appearance and the fact that her clothing wasn't proper. Half an hour after returning, we had met in the library, both put to rights, my arm rebandaged, and looking dignified again. She had blushed prettily when I informed her I preferred it when she looked tousled. She had lifted her chin, trying to appear stern.

"You, sir, must learn to behave."

I grinned, lowering my head to hers and pressing a kiss to her sweet mouth. "What fun would that be, my wife? I think you like me just as I am."

She had smiled. That beautiful, wide smile she had only for me. "I do."

I glanced down, seeing she was asleep. Her eyelashes rested on her skin that was slightly rosy from the sun today. I ran a hand over her head, feeling the silk of her hair. Liking how she relaxed against me, knowing I would keep her safe. I rested my hand on her stomach, pleased to know it wasn't the only place she was growing. She was no longer thin and malnourished-looking. Her skin glowed, her hair was luxurious, and her body had filled out well. Add in her condition, and she was glorious.

I finished my brandy and carefully lifted her from my lap. My arm pulled a little, but it wasn't overly painful and I ignored it.

I sat her on the bed, carefully divesting her of the pretty silk gown and laid her down. She slept through the entire happening, obviously more tired than she allowed me to see.

I stretched out beside her, smiling as she rolled into place with her head in the crook of my neck and her arm flung over my chest. I lay in the dark, the stars outside bright in the night sky. I was thankful for this day. For every day. Perhaps more aware now of how precious they were.

Then I slept.

CHAPTER 25

ALEXANDER

Three days later, I strode into the library, taking note of the cheery blaze in the fireplace. Maddie was on the chaise, reclining against pillows, a blanket draped over her feet. She was staring out the window at the stormy sky, heavy with rain. It had begun to cloud over the day before, and my farmers predicted it would last for a few days. Lydia was in the window seat, looking despondent. I had a feeling it was due to the fact that Edward was in London on a task for me. He had looked rather grim when he departed the day before, his mouth turned down in an unfamiliar frown. He usually enjoyed the missions I sent him on, but then again, he'd never left behind someone he cared for.

They looked up as I entered, Lydia immediately standing. Maddie held out her hand. I took it, kissing the palm and holding it to my face. "Are you well, my love? You look sad."

"No, I am fine. The weather is gloomy and makes me somewhat melancholy."

"Edward has sent word he has arrived and will

conclude his business swiftly." I glanced at Lydia. "He plans to return as soon as possible."

She smiled, looking pleased.

"Would you be so kind as to fetch tea, Lydia? I should like a moment with my wife."

She departed quickly, leaving me with Maddie. I sat beside her, and she watched me with a confused frown. "Is something wrong?"

I stroked her cheek. "No, Maddie mine, but I am pleased you regarded me so calmly and without worry when asking that question."

"I know you would never hurt me."

"No, I wouldn't. I would rather cut off my own arm than to cause you pain."

"Yet, you look serious. Something is amiss, I fear?" she asked.

I set the small bundle I was carrying on her lap. "These were given to me."

"From?"

"Geraldine. They were your mother's."

She eyed them with caution. "How did she come to have them in her possession?"

"She stole them from the baron's desk. They are how he discovered he was not your father. Geraldine felt they should be in your possession, not his. I thought you might like to read them."

"Have you already done so?"

"Yes. There is a great love story there of your true father. And many thoughts of your mother on her love for you. Even fondness for the baron. Your mother seemed to be of a determined nature, wanting to find the good everywhere." I touched her cheek. "Much like you, my sweet. You take after her in many ways."

"I wish I could remember her face clearly," she whispered.

I opened the bundle and handed her the small portrait. She inhaled sharply, staring at it, tracing her mother's features with a trembling finger.

"You resemble her very much."

A tear ran down her cheek. "Have I upset you, dearest?" I inquired gently.

"No, my dear husband," she whispered, her voice catching. "This brings me great joy. I find my emotions high these days."

I nodded in understanding. "The babe."

"The babe," she agreed.

"I thought today being dreary, you might like to read some of your mother's words."

"I would very much like that. Thank you for this gift, Alexander. It is incredibly precious to me."

I opened her hand and slipped the small brooch into her palm. "This was a gift from your father to your mother. Geraldine has been safeguarding it for you, along with the likeness of your mother."

She turned it over, studying it. "I recall her wearing this. It was small compared to some pieces the baron gave her, but she always said it was her favorite." She smiled softly, another tear running down her cheek. "She said it was a family piece."

"It was." I took it from her, pinning it to her bodice. "And now it is yours. You were her family, Maddie. Her greatest love."

She traced the sapphires, not speaking, her expression saying it all. I tapped the small likeness she still held.

"Perhaps we can commission a larger portrait of your mother from the likeness. You may hang it where you can see it every day. You can tell our little one about their grandmama when they are old enough."

"You are the most generous, thoughtful man."

I stood and pressed a kiss to her upturned mouth. "Because I love you, I find being both very easy. When Lydia returns with the tea, enjoy a cup, then read. I shall be in my study, working. If you need me, send Lydia."

She reached up and grasped my face between her hands. "Thank you for this."

I turned my face and kissed her palm. "I would give you everything if I could, Maddie."

"You have, my love," she whispered. "That and more."

EDWARD RETURNED TWO DAYS LATER, tired but filled with news. He had been caught in the still-falling rain, so he retired to his quarters, cleaned up, and presented himself shortly in my study. I poured us each a large brandy and handed him the glass. "Tell me the news."

"Everything is as Geraldine spoke. The young nobleman made no secret of his love for Maddie's mother and their plans to wed. I managed to track down the cousin on his mother's side who knew him well, but she was departing soon for the continent, which is why I made such haste in leaving. She had even met Felicity. She shared a few stories—wrote them down." He handed me a small packet of papers tied with a ribbon. "She would love to meet Maddie if you take her to London and she has returned. She gave me this as well for her." He handed me a miniature of a young man with dark hair and a serious expression. I could see Maddie in the shape of his mouth and his gentle gaze. He was handsome, and I imagined he would have been a good father to her. I knew he loved her mother with such passion.

"This will bring her much joy. I will endeavor a trip after our child has come. A short one."

"I have many other things to tell you, one piece in particular."

I lifted an eyebrow. "Do speak."

"Barnett is dead."

I gaped at him. "What? When?"

"Only two days ago. His wound healed, but he had a run-in with someone in an alley. The word is it was a man to whom he owed a large sum. A lender not known for his patience with unpaid debts. All suspicion, of course, since not a soul saw anything. A passerby found him and called for the authorities."

I rubbed my chin thoughtfully. "They never do."

"Higgins was in town while I was there. He told me the news, and he also mentioned Milton Manor will be going for sale to cover balances. Plus what was left of the estate you visited. The house in London was stripped of anything valuable and is in desperate need of refurnishing, if rumors are to be believed. Selling the lot will barely cover his obligations. You might get Milton Manor for a song."

"I will have Higgins start inquiries. I have no interest in Cliffwood, other than purchasing it and allowing Maddie to burn it to the ground if she desires it."

He chuckled. "I assumed you would not. The entailed property will revert to the crown. It was much farther north, and I understand he rarely ventured there." He grinned. "No one to play cards with other than sheep, and they loathe being fleeced."

I had to laugh at his levity.

"I told Higgins as much as well," he added.

"Excellent."

"What will you do now? Tell Maddie?"

"Yes," I replied promptly. "I believe it will ease her mind, knowing that awful man will never be seen again. That he can never again hurt her."

He nodded, rubbing his eyes.

"Retire for the evening, Edward. Tell me the rest tomorrow, unless there is anything pressing."

"No. I dealt with the matters you sent me on. I have documents for you. Some new items to discuss. But nothing urgent."

I rose to my feet and extended my hand. "Thank you for your work. As usual, you have proven to be exemplary."

He smiled and shook my hand. "I believe I shall wander to the kitchen and see if I can persuade Cook to share some of her delicious treats."

"Do. The roast joint tonight was exceptional. And the cherry tarts divine. Maddie ate three."

He laughed. "I will see you in the morning, Alexander."

"In the morning," I agreed.

He left, and I picked up the miniature and added the small package of letters, planning on reading them to her. I decided to go upstairs locate my wife. She had been emotional since reading her mother's journals, and I sensed these letters and likeness would do the same to her, so I wished to stay close.

I swallowed the last of my brandy and headed for the stairs.

MADELEINE

Curled up comfortably on a chair by a crackling fire, I was waiting for Alexander when he came to our bedchamber. The open book of poetry in my lap no longer held my attention as my handsome husband crossed the threshold. I took a moment to admire him as I oft did, still unable to believe that he was mine, that my father would never dare to harm us again, and that our future would be as bright as the morning sun that shone in our windows each morning.

He wore a dark coat and trousers, his cravat snowy white to match his crisp shirt, his waistcoat a lighter shade of gray. His long, dark hair was pulled away from his face, and his strong jaw was clenched, as if something troubled him.

Since he had sent my father away, I had observed a lightness in my husband, one that filled me with happiness. His somber countenance made my stomach tighten.

"What is amiss?" I asked him.

He closed the door at his back, striding toward me.

I moved to stand and greet him.

"Stay as you are, Maddie mine. There is no need to rise on my account. I'm sure you're tired after carrying our babe about all day."

My back and feet were tired and sore, but my joy at our impending child more than assuaged any physical infirmity I suffered. I rose despite his protest, setting aside my volume of poetry.

"Something has distressed you, and you aren't telling me what it is." I pressed a hand to my lower back, thinking that I would soon need to let out the seams of my dressing gown. Or perhaps have a new one fashioned for me, one with room for my ever-growing belly for my lying-in.

"Nothing is distressing me," he assured me, "but I do

come to you bearing news. Edward has returned from his sojourn to London."

Belatedly, I noticed he carried a stack of papers bound with ribbon and something that looked like a miniature.

"What news does he bring?"

Alexander reached me, his countenance gentling as it did for me alone. "Please sit, my love. Some of the news may overset you."

"Alexander, please, you're worrying me." I reached for his coat sleeve.

He was my anchor. My everything. We had weathered so much together. He knew me better than anyone. Sometimes better, even, than I knew myself. If he believed I would find the news upsetting, then it must be something dreadful indeed.

He kissed my brow. "Sit first. I'll not have you swooning and injuring yourself or the babe."

He was right. My pride wasn't worth such a risk.

Reluctantly, I obeyed his request, settling back into the chair I had so recently vacated.

"Now, then. Tell me, if you please."

Alexander surprised me by sinking to his knees on the Axminster before me, his dark eyes searching mine. "Edward brings news of two fathers. The one you believed was your father up until so recently, and the man who was truly your sire."

My breath caught, my heart pounding faster. "Barnett hasn't returned to Wheaton, has he? You said he wouldn't dare. Has he threatened you again?"

"He has done none of those things," Alexander told me softly. "Because he is incapable of doing anything. Lord Barnett met an untimely end in London two days ago. Or, given his vile deeds, some might say timely indeed."

Shock coursed through me, followed swiftly by relief. "He is dead?"

Alexander nodded. "Yes. Barnett is dead. He can no longer harm you ever again."

I exhaled slowly, the tension seeping from me. "I do not wish death upon anyone—"

"Then you are a saint, Maddie mine, and a far better person than I shall ever be," Alexander interrupted grimly. "But of course, I already knew both of those things."

"But I am glad he is gone," I finished. "I am glad that he can no longer hurt you, me, or our child. It is a blessing that we do not have that worry hanging over us like a storm cloud. How did he die?"

"There are whispers that he was murdered by an unscrupulous creditor. Perhaps it was a footpad. I reckon we will never know for certain."

I nodded. "Thank you for telling me." The other half of what he had said occurred to me suddenly. I had been numbed by the news of Barnett's death. But now, I recalled that Alexander had spoken of two fathers. "Mr. Warwick brought news of my true father, you said. What is it?"

"A miniature likeness of him," Alexander said, turning the object in his hand to face me.

I gasped, a face so like mine staring back at me. A serious, handsome young gentleman. One who had loved my mother deeply. One I wished I had been fortunate enough to know and meet.

"May I?" I asked, reaching for it.

"Of course, my sweet. It is yours." He gave me the miniature and then offered me the packet of what appeared to be letters as well. "Along with these. Stories of your father, that you may better know the man he was."

Emotion rushed through me, bittersweet. "Thank you, my love."

"Thank Edward. I didn't venture to London and return with spoils," he said tenderly.

"You asked him to go for me. You wanted to find the pieces of my past."

He cupped my cheek with one hand, the other going to my stomach, cradling the ever-growing swell that housed our babe. "So that you can look to the future awaiting us."

I glanced again at the miniature before reverently setting it on the table alongside the abandoned poetry book, then placed the letters there for safekeeping as well. I would read the stories of my father in good time.

Alexander frowned at me. "Do you not wish to read about him now?"

I smiled, feeling as if a weight had been lifted from me. And it had. My life was complete. I was safe. I was loved. I was married to the finest man I had ever known.

"I wish to savor them," I told him softly, love for him beating swiftly, furiously, jubilantly within my heart. "But for now, I want to savor my husband."

His expression shifted, his lips turning up at the corners. "Is that so, Lady Wheaton?"

"Yes, that is so, my lord marquess." I took his face in my hands and drew his lips to mine for a kiss.

How I loved this man.

I had been made for him, and he for me.

Of that fact, I was certain.

EPILOGUE

ALEXANDER

The sun was high in the afternoon sky as I reined in Knight and sat looking over my estate. Fields of wheat danced in the afternoon breeze of the late spring. Various crops splashed numerous hues of green around the countryside. Patches of flowers perfumed the air. The breeze was warm and smelled of the rich earth. Farmers toiled around me, their horses and plows working hard to cultivate the land.

I looked toward Milton Manor, seeing the new structures still rising from the rubble, the crops taking shape. Cottages for the tenants dotted the land, the first item of business Edward and I had concluded on the estate. We had torn down the decaying house and stables, rebuilding newer, more modern buildings in their place. Lydia had been beyond excited at the thought of residing in a home with running water. Being the mistress of a house as lovely as the new edifice was a joy to her. I had worked with Edward and the company employed to erect their home. It was more modest than most estates but suited Edward and Lydia perfectly. Maddie was thrilled her friend would be so close, and I was pleased to know Edward would be with me, still at my side, as he had been all these years. Together, we ran the already profitable estate, and I knew the riches would only grow.

I looked at the small bundles I carried on my steed, knowing Maddie would roll her eyes and tell me I was spoiling her and our children again.

And she would, as usual, be correct.

But I refused to stop.

My family was my greatest joy. My treasure.

Our son, Andrew Charles, was pure sunshine. He looked like me, but he had his mother's sweet temperament. He was inquisitive and intelligent. Tall for his age and robust. Kind and loving. He toddled around, always asking questions, constantly climbing onto my lap. I insisted he was the cleverest boy I had ever met. Barely past three years of age, he had an incredible vocabulary. He was curious about everything and loved to walk the estate with Edward and me. He enjoyed digging and farming with us. He could name seeds, plants, and birds. He knew a weed from a shrub. The tenants loved him, and I was certain one day he would be a good master.

His table manners, however, still required some polish. He enjoyed his meals thoroughly, his hands his preferred way of eating. Maddie was endlessly patient, and I had given up worrying about the Axminster or the table. We removed the carpet for the time being as the servants found it easier to sweep the wood floors, and the table was protected with a heavy cloth. Watching Maddie coax him to use a fork or spoon often made me laugh. He would smile his sunny smile, nod, eat a mouthful or two, become impatient, then discard the utensil in favor of a fistful of beef or potatoes that he would jam into his mouth and chew away on. We loved his antics. Maddie and I enjoyed his company, so he ate with us daily. Scandalous to some, but for us, it was normal. I didn't want my children to be seen and not heard. Maddie had no desire for a nursemaid to raise her children. We had help but were very involved. We agreed we had years to teach them all the manners they would require, but they were small for such a short time, we wished to enjoy them. Andrew loved his mother fiercely, gazing at her in rapt adoration when she spoke with him. He enjoyed it when she read to him or they sat together drawing. She encouraged his artistic side, and I was pleased to see it. I wished for him to know the love of arts as well as the land and his duties as a future marquess. I wanted him to have it all.

I knew it was thought that I was strange. And Maddie odd. Edward had informed me I was quietly referred to as the "eccentric marquess" in certain circles.

"Stories of your family shock the *ton*," he informed me. "Children eating with their parents. Spending hours with them daily—not just an appointment. Digging in the dirt alongside their father like common farmers. Supping with locals as if that was normal. Best friends with commoners." He opened his eyes wide. "Not wearing hats."

I had laughed hard at his imitations of the London town folk. I liked being different. And since Maddie and I went to London rarely, their opinion mattered not.

Our friends, those I had known and valued since my school days, knew me. Knew us. Knew the truth. And it was their opinions that mattered. The people of the village knew us and regarded us as their benefactors. They didn't care if I missed some dirt under my nails when I went into a shop. Or if my son rode on my shoulders and pretended

I was his steed in the middle of the street, pulling on my hair and yelling, "Go, Papa! Go!" They loved the fact that my wife drove the wagon herself into town, dropping off fresh vegetables to the villagers who needed them the most —just like my mother used to do. We were welcomed. Respected.

I urged Knight forward, suddenly anxious to see my family. As I approached the manor, I smiled, seeing my wife and children outside, no doubt waiting for me. Andrew was playing in the grass with a ball, his little sister not far from him, her arms in the air, and I assumed, demanding the ball and his attention.

Our daughter, Charlotte Rose, favored her mother in looks, but she had my dark eye color. Maddie insisted she had my temperament, and I feared she was correct. Tiny scowls and insistent demands were regular occurrences with my little girl. She expressed her displeasure with a stare that looked far too familiar. I had seen it in the mirror often. Maddie laughed, on occasion citing her sympathy for the man Charlotte fell in love with.

"He will have his hands full," she murmured. "I fear your daughter will be a hurricane."

"Is that a personal observation, Maddie mine?" I asked, linking my arms around her waist and pulling her back to me. "A comparison to her sire?"

"She will charm him the way you charmed me," she replied. "And he will spend his life trying to keep up." Then she patted my arm. "And be in heaven every day, besotted with her."

I had to chuckle. Maddie often commented on my lack of patience and how I preferred things done "my way." I had assured her it was a trait of being a marquess. She had informed me it was my own personality and nothing to do with my standing.

I hated to admit that she was correct.

Andrew doted on Charlotte—we all did. And she was a

loving child. Clever like her brother, and already walking, she was going to be the handful Maddie feared.

And I adored her.

Maddie shaded her eyes, seeing me approach. I pulled Knight to a stop close to them and dismounted, laughing as Andrew ran toward me, his arms outstretched.

"Papa! Papa!"

I bent and caught him, tossing him above my head, my heart warm as his laughter filled the air. I set him down, after accepting his wet kisses on my face. I would never deny my child affection, no matter what.

I knelt to scoop up Charlotte, kissing her plump cheek as she prattled on in her baby voice. Not quite two, she was already a beauty. She accepted my kisses then squirmed away, needing to be close to her brother. I set her down, swatting her little bum gently as she crawled away, too impatient to try to walk.

I held out my hand for Maddie, drawing her close. "Hello, my wife. I have missed you."

She laughed, shaking her head. "You have been gone but two hours, my love. Hardly enough time to miss me."

"Ah, but there you are wrong, my love. I miss you every second you are not next to me."

I rested my hand on the swell of her stomach. "Are you well?"

She covered my hand with hers. "Very. Your child has been moving quite a bit all morning. I believe they are anxious to join us."

I laughed, bending and pressing a kiss to the linen covering her stomach. "Give your mama a moment to breathe, my child. We are anxious to meet you as well."

"Did you accomplish your errands?" she asked.

"Indeed."

She peered behind me. "Did Mr. Hughes have any of

those chocolate conserves your unborn babe has been demanding?"

I chuckled. "Yes. I procured some for you and some barley sugar and lemon drops for the children."

"Oh, they will love such a treat!"

"I thought perhaps a picnic tomorrow. It promises to be a fine day. Edward and Lydia could join us."

Maddie smiled. "How lovely."

I leaned close, my lips to her ear. "We cannot partake of the joys we used to seek on our picnics, Maddie. Our clothing must remain on, and you must be on your best behavior."

She scoffed, swatting my shoulder. "I believe you have that wrong, sir. Your old age is showing. You are, and always have been, the impertinent one."

I chuckled and kissed her neck at the juncture, smiling as she shivered.

"Old age, madam? I shall have to endeavor to change your mind of that notion later." I caressed her large belly. "I do not believe old age has yet rendered me un-impertinent." I bit down lightly. "Or unable to bring to you an earth-shattering cli—"

She covered my mouth. "Alexander," she admonished. "We are not in private!"

I kissed her fingers, grinning at the way her eyes had darkened. She was still responsive and always passionate, and I love to tease her and claim her at the most unexpected moments.

"We could be," I murmured.

She shook her head and gathered her skirts. "Children, I believe Cook has a treat waiting. Come with me."

I pulled the small sacks from Knight and handed him off to a waiting stable hand. I had a feeling the children weren't the only ones about to have a treat.

I followed where my wife led.

I always would.

THE SUN SHONE high in the early afternoon sky, the breeze light and warm on my face as I chased my son, laughing with him as I caught him and tossed him high, catching him and swinging him around. I loved spending time with my family this way. Relaxed and easy. A picnic—a family favorite—good friends, delicious treats, and lots of laughter.

I tossed my son up onto my shoulder and headed toward the picnic. "I think our repast is ready, Andrew."

He yelped in excitement. He loved picnics, and Maddie was of the mind it was due to the fact that we all ate with our fingers. Our cook had begun making sandwiches with the most delectable fillings, and I knew the basket was full of them. Chicken, beef, cheese, with savory sauces and the softest of breads. Some creamed mixtures we all loved but only had for picnics would be in the mix. Maddie adored them, and I had heard the fare was becoming more popular even in London.

We reached the blanket, and I sank to my knees, letting Andrew off my shoulder gently. Edward grinned at us.

"Maybe some ball games after lunch, Master Andrew?"

He nodded, his mouth already too full to speak. Maddie chastised him gently but without rancor. It was too fine a day for anger. She handed Charlotte a sandwich with cucumber and soft cheese. Our daughter stared at it with that stubborn look on her face, then turned it in her hand as if inspecting it. She tasted it, chewed, then pointed to the platter.

"Mo'."

Maddie laughed and handed her another one. Unlike her brother, who had one in each hand and was devouring them simultaneously, Charlotte placed the second one on her plate and daintily bit into the first one.

I met Maddie's amused glance.

"At least one of them can be presented in mixed company," I muttered with a grin, taking a beef sandwich and biting into it, the strong mustard tightening my taste buds.

Maddie laughed and wiped Andrew's mouth. "He can behave when he wishes to. He is always too hungry."

We ate and chatted, laughing at the antics of the children, taking in the vistas and enjoying ourselves.

"Papa, can we swim?"

I ruffled his hair. "Not this time. I will take off your boots, and you may wade today."

"Tomorrow?"

"It is too cold. Soon," I promised.

I glanced over at my wife. She had been quiet as we ate, and I noticed she barely picked at her food.

"Maddie?" I queried. "Are you well?"

"I am fine. My back is a bit sore."

She was in a chair I had the servants bring down to the brook. It had plump pillows and a blanket in case she was chilled. A small stool to rest her swollen feet on. I had driven her and the children down in a small cart. But something was amiss.

I studied her. She looked paler than she had earlier. There were lines of pain around her eyes.

"Do you wish to return to the house?"

She waved her hand. "It will ache here or there, my lord. Do not trouble yourself."

I frowned. She only ever used the title "my lord" if she was vexed or upset.

I leaned closer. "I will trouble myself if I fear you are ill, Maddie mine."

She smiled and cupped my face. "I am not. Simply uncomfortable for a short time. In a few weeks, that shall resolve itself," she replied with a gentle smile.

"And I look forward to it. But I dislike seeing you in pain."

"I am fine. Do not—"

I lifted an eyebrow, stopping her words.

"I am fine," she repeated. "But my appetite is off."

"Then nibble. You can eat a substantial evening meal. I know Cook is making your favorite."

"Lovely."

I sat back but kept my eyes on Maddie. One thing I had learned in our years together was that she still had trouble expressing her needs at times. She still put herself last—whereas for me, she would always be first.

After we ate, Edward and I left the ladies in the shade and took the children to the brook. As promised, I let Andrew stick his feet in, and his yelp of surprise at the cold convinced Charlotte she did not want to risk it. We retrieved the balls and began a slow, fun game of kicking them, letting my little girl have her chances. She was competitive—another trait she got from me. But after a while, she became tired and stood in front of me, her arms outstretched. I lifted her to my shoulder, where she nestled in with a sigh, falling asleep. I watched Andrew and Edward kick the ball around until Andrew decided he wanted to scale the tree. We watched him as I stroked along Charlotte's back, her little puffs of air warm on my neck. I heard a shout and turned, seeing Lydia waving frantically. Without a thought, I transferred Charlotte to Edward's waiting arms and ran over to where Lydia was now kneeling in front of Maddie.

I skidded to my knees in front of her. She was pale, shaking, and grimacing in pain. "Maddie? My darling, what is it?"

"The babe," she gasped. "It is coming, Alexander. *Now!*"

I glanced down as she gripped my hands. "My waters," she gasped. "And the pangs, they are hard and fast."

I looked at Lydia, who seemed calm. She turned and spoke to Edward. "Help the children into the cart for me, then run to the house. Get the servants to send for the midwife. Tell her it is urgent." She looked at me. "Lift Maddie to the cart and hold her. I will drive us."

I nodded. She laid a hand on my arm. "Remain calm, my lord. For her and the children. Do not let them see you frightened."

I straightened my shoulders. "Of course not." I bent and scooped up Maddie, who whimpered. I pressed a kiss to her head. "All will be well, my love. I have you, and you will soon be bringing our child into this world."

She gasped as another pang hit her. She was correct— it was too fast. I only hoped the midwife came quickly.

"We cannot wait," Lydia murmured. "I must do this without the midwife."

"I will help."

I had not left the room yet. Maddie's obvious pain was

too much for me to leave her. She gripped at my hands during the more painful moments, holding them so hard, I knew her agony had to be great. Edward was keeping the children entertained and busy. I was required here.

Mrs. Dougall spoke. "This is woman's work, my lord."

Maddie shook her head wildly, her voice pleading. "Alexander. I need you."

"And you shall have me." I looked at Lydia. "Tell me what to do."

She heaved a sigh and indicated the head of the bed. "Get behind Maddie. Hold her and help her. She needs to push."

I rolled my shoulders and did as she asked, once again sending a prayer above for the safe passage of my child and the well-being of my wife.

Then I held her close, offering the only thing I could—encouragement and my strength.

"Was it...terrible?" Edward asked.

I shook my head, still trying to put to words what I had witnessed.

"Seeing Maddie in such pain was horrendous, but seeing my child born was a miracle I am still trying to comprehend," I replied, taking a long draught of brandy. My hands were still shaking.

The midwife had appeared just as the babe was born, and she took over, not blinking an eye at my refusal to leave the bedchamber. I held Maddie and rocked her, soothing her brow with a damp cloth and murmuring my love before a small bundle was placed in my arms.

"Your son, my lord."

I looked down at the red-faced little boy. Fat and wrinkly, he was one of the most beautiful things I had ever seen. Carefully, I handed him to Maddie.

"My love," I whispered. "What a gift you have given me. Look at our son."

She smiled, exhausted and pale but more beautiful than ever.

Shortly thereafter, I was escorted from the room and turned over to Edward. Mrs. Dougall took the children to the kitchen, promising tarts. I assured them their mother was resting and they could see her shortly.

"Have you chosen a name?" he asked.

"We have. He shall be called Edward Thomas." I paused. "After one of the greatest men I know."

He blinked. "Alexander. I am at a loss for words."

"I pray he follows in your example. We would like you and Lydia to be godparents." I requested.

He reached out and grabbed my hand. "I would be proud."

"Thank you."

Lydia appeared, looking tired but happy. "Maddie wishes to see you now."

I drank the last of my brandy and set down the glass, anxious to return to her.

As I passed Lydia, I paused. "Thank you," I stated sincerely. "You are the epitome of friendship to Maddie. To us both."

She blushed, lowering her eyes. "Thank you, my lord."

I touched her cheek. "Alexander to my friends," I reminded her. "And I consider you that, Lydia. You are part of my extended family. I am Alexander to you."

She smiled, tears shining in her eyes. "Very well, Alexander."

I GRINNED as I bounced my baby son in my arms, looking over at my wife. In front of us, Charlotte played on the Axminster, close to the fire, content with her dolly. Andrew ran around, his little toy soldier in his hand. Geraldine sat close to them, ensuring they were happy. She now lived in the small house Edward had previously dwelled in. She was close enough to visit daily and often took her meals with us, but she had a place to call her own. She had been beyond grateful and excited the day we moved her in, running her hand over the fresh paper on the walls and new furniture. Maddie and Lydia had done over the small house to suit her. It was a far cry from the masculine air it had when Edward was there. It was now light and airy, filled with feminine touches and soft fabrics.

She wept when she saw it, admitting she never thought she would have a home of her own.

I had kissed her hand. *"For all you did for my wife, it is the least I could do for you."*

To our children, she was Grandmama, and a beloved member of the family.

Maddie watched them both from the settee, a smile on her lips, but looking wan.

"Are you well, my sweet?" I asked Maddie. It had only been a few days since Edward's birth, and she was still recovering.

"I am well, my love. Do not concern yourself." At my glower, she laughed lightly. "It is only that I am still tired, but I feel well. Truly. The servants and the nurse you hired are not allowing me to do anything but rest and sit."

"Good."

She watched our children for a moment, then looked at me, a small furrow on her brow.

"Alexander, are you content?"

Her question caught me off guard.

"My darling?"

"Here. With us. Not living an opulent life in London with all it has to offer as a carefree bachelor? But here with children, a wife, and all that it entails?"

I felt a rush of tenderness. As with our other two children, she was overwrought at times after the births. Emotional and needing reassurance.

My reassurance.

I rose, transferring our babe into Geraldine's arms. She met my gaze with a small smile of understanding and held out her free hand. "Children, I think Cook has a treat!"

They followed her eagerly, and I sat beside Maddie, sliding my arm around her and tucking her close. I tilted up her chin, making her meet my eyes so she saw the truth.

"When I was a carefree bachelor, this was a house. You turned it into a home again. I sat alone most nights, whether in London or here. Now I am surrounded by love and laughter, and I feel more alive than I ever have in all my years. London is anything but opulent. Here, the soil is rich, the air is clean, and I am the happiest man in the world because I have you. You were made for me."

"A former maid," she teased softly.

"A beautiful woman I am so in love with it befuddles me at times. I hate what you went through, but it brought you to me. You were a maid briefly, but you will be my marchioness for the rest of our lives. Made specifically for me."

"You truly believe that."

"I do." I ran my finger down her cheek. "You make me happy, Maddie mine. Something I had long forgotten to be. You bring such joy to my life. Before you, I was empty. You and our family mean everything to me. That will never change. Nor will the love I have for you, except to grow more abundant every day. So, am I content? More than I can express." I paused. "Does that put your worries to rest?"

"Yes."

"Never doubt my love or what you are to me, my wife. You are the beginning and the end for me."

"I love you, my Alexander. Thank you for this life."

I shook my head and bent to kiss her.

"No, my wife. Thank you."

ACKNOWLEDGMENTS

From Melanie –

Thanks to Scarlett for putting up with me and making my dream come true. Working with you has been a pleasure and an honor. Your knowledge and patience as I learned was invaluable. I loved working with you. I hope to do so again.

Lisa, your red pen is legendary. Thank you for making the story better.

Karen your talent, love of this book, and support means everything. Thank you for being so much more than a PA. Bestie, right hand, everything in between. Much love.

And to the readers and bloggers. Those who post and share. Many many thanks.

And Matthew – always. Forever.

From Scarlett –

Melanie, thank you for writing with me and letting me be part of Maddie and Alexander's HEA. When you first told me about your idea for this book, I got goosebumps, and I knew it was a special story that had to be told. Thank you for entrusting your passion project with me and for being patient when my inner history nerd came out to play and when lightning literally struck and I wrote more slowly than planned. It was a true joy and honor to work with you, and I would love to do it again.

Thank you to Lisa for making the book shine.

Special thank you to Karen for the beautiful formatting

of this book and for all your hard work and cheerleading as Melanie and I wrote.

Thank you to Dar for this gorgeous cover.

Thank you to the readers and reviewers for your support--you make it all possible.

And thank you to my family for putting up with me when I'm on deadline.

TITLES FROM MELANIE MORELAND

Titles published under Melanie Moreland

The Contract Series

Marriage of Convenience- Same Couple

The Contract (Contract #1)

The Baby Clause (Contract Novella)

The Amendment (Contract #3)

The Addendum (Contract #4)

Vested Interest Series

Billionaire - Different Couples

BAM - The Beginning (Prequel)

Bentley (Vested Interest #1)

Aiden (Vested Interest #2)

Maddox (Vested Interest #3)

Reid (Vested Interest #4)

Van (Vested Interest #5)

Halton (Vested Interest #6)

Sandy (Vested Interest #7)

Vested Interest/ABC Crossover

Second Generation Introduction

A Merry Vested Wedding

ABC Corp Series

Second Generation - Different Couples

My Saving Grace (Vested Interest: ABC Corp #1)

Finding Ronan's Heart (Vested Interest: ABC Corp #2)

Loved By Liam (Vested Interest: ABC Corp #3)

Age of Ava (Vested Interest: ABC Corp #4)

Sunshine & Sammy (Vested Interest: ABC Corp #5)

Unscripted With Mila (Vested Interest: ABC Corp #6)

Men of Hidden Justice

Vigilante Justice - Different Couples

The Boss

Second-In-Command

The Commander

The Watcher

The Specialist

Men of the Falls

Canadian mafia duet - Different Couples

Aldo

Roman

The Irishmen

Canadian syndicate duet - Different Couples

Finn

Niall

My Favorite

Romantic Comedy standalones - Different Couples

My Favorite Kidnapper

My Favorite Boss

My Favorite Hero

Reynolds Restorations -

Blue Collar heroes in Small Town - Different Couples

Revved to the Maxx

Breaking The Speed Limit

Shifting Gears

Under The Radar

Full Throttle

Standalones

Tropes from high angst to romcom

Into the Storm

Beneath the Scars

Over the Fence

The Image of You

Changing Roles

The Summer of Us

Happily Ever After Collection

Heart Strings

A Simple Life

Unexpected Complication

Titles published with Scarlett Scott

Historical Romance standalone

Maid for the Marquess

Titles published under M. Moreland

Insta-Spark Collection

Low Angst and all standalone

It Started with a Kiss

Christmas Sugar

An Instant Connection

An Unexpected Gift

Harvest of Love

An Unexpected Chance

Following Maggie

The Wish List

Wrapped In Love

Wicked Dukes Society
Duke with a Reputation (Book One)
Duke with a Debt (Book Two)
Duke with a Secret (Book Three)
Duke with a Lie (Book Four)
Duke with a Duchess (Book Five)

Christmas Dukes
The Duke Who Despised Christmas (Book One)
The Duke Who Ruined Christmas (Book Two)

League of Dukes
Nobody's Duke (Book One)
Heartless Duke (Book Two)
Dangerous Duke (Book Three)
Shameless Duke (Book Four)
Scandalous Duke (Book Five)
Fearless Duke (Book Six)

Notorious Ladies of London
Lady Ruthless (Book One)
Lady Wallflower (Book Two)
Lady Reckless (Book Three)
Lady Wicked (Book Four)
Lady Lawless (Book Five)
Lady Brazen (Book 6)

Unexpected Lords
The Detective Duke (Book One)
The Playboy Peer (Book Two)
The Millionaire Marquess (Book Three)
The Goodbye Governess (Book Four)

Dukes Most Wanted

Forever Her Duke (Book One)
Forever Her Marquess (Book Two)
Forever Her Rake (Book Three)
Forever Her Earl (Book Four)
Forever Her Viscount (Book Five)
Forever Her Scot (Book Six)

The Wicked Winters
Wicked in Winter (Book One)
Wedded in Winter (Book Two)
Wanton in Winter (Book Three)
Wishes in Winter (Book 3.5)
Willful in Winter (Book Four)
Wagered in Winter (Book Five)
Wild in Winter (Book Six)
Wooed in Winter (Book Seven)
Winter's Wallflower (Book Eight)
Winter's Woman (Book Nine)
Winter's Whispers (Book Ten)
Winter's Waltz (Book Eleven)
Winter's Widow (Book Twelve)
Winter's Warrior (Book Thirteen)
A Merry Wicked Winter (Book Fourteen)

The Sinful Suttons
Sutton's Spinster (Book One)
Sutton's Sins (Book Two)
Sutton's Surrender (Book Three)
Sutton's Seduction (Book Four)
Sutton's Scoundrel (Book Five)
Sutton's Scandal (Book Six)
Sutton's Secrets (Book Seven)

Rogue's Guild

Her Ruthless Duke (Book One)
Her Dangerous Beast (Book Two)
Her Wicked Rogue (Book 3)

Royals and Renegades
How to Love a Dangerous Rogue (Book One)
How to Tame a Dissolute Prince (Book Two)

Sins and Scoundrels
Duke of Depravity
Prince of Persuasion
Marquess of Mayhem
Sarah
Earl of Every Sin
Duke of Debauchery
Viscount of Villainy

With *NYT* Bestselling Author Melanie Moreland
Maid for the Marquess

Sins and Scoundrels Box Set Collections
Volume 1
Volume 2

The Wicked Winters Box Set Collections
Collection 1
Collection 2
Collection 3
Collection 4

Wicked Husbands Box Set Collections
Volume 1
Volume 2

Notorious Ladies of London Box Set Collections
Volume 1
Volume 2

The Sinful Suttons Box Set Collections
Volume 1
Volume 2

Stand-alone Novella
Lord of Pirates

CONTEMPORARY ROMANCE
Love's Second Chance
Reprieve (Book One)
Perfect Persuasion (Book Two)
Win My Love (Book Three)

Coastal Heat
Loved Up (Book One)

Writing as Lora Whitney

Mafia Romance
Andriani Brothers
Brutal Devil (Book One)
Cruel Sinner (Book Two)

ABOUT MELANIE MORELAND

NYT/WSJ/USAT international bestselling author Melanie Moreland, lives a happy and content life in a quiet area of Ontario with her beloved husband of thirty-plus years and their rescue cat, Amber. Nothing means more to her than her friends and family, and she cherishes every moment spent with them.

While seriously addicted to coffee, and highly challenged with all things computer-related and technical, she relishes baking, cooking, and trying new recipes for people to sample. She loves to throw dinner parties, and enjoys traveling, here and abroad, but finds coming home is always the best part of any trip.

Melanie loves stories, especially paired with a good wine, and enjoys skydiving (free falling over a fleck of dust) extreme snowboarding (falling down stairs) and piloting her own helicopter (tripping over her own feet.) She's learned happily ever afters, even bumpy ones, are all in how you tell the story.

Melanie is represented by Flavia Viotti at Bookcase Literary Agency. For any questions regarding subsidiary or translation rights please contact her at flavia@ bookcaseagency.com

facebook.com/authormoreland

instagram.com/morelandmelanie

bookbub.com/authors/melanie-moreland

amazon.com/Melanie-Moreland/author/B00GV6LB00

goodreads.com/Melanie_Moreland

tiktok.com/@melaniemoreland

threads.com/@morelandmelanie

ABOUT SCARLETT SCOTT

USA Today and Amazon bestselling author Scarlett Scott™ writes steamy Victorian and Regency romance with strong, intelligent heroines and sexy alpha heroes. She lives in Pennsylvania and Maryland with her Canadian husband, their adorable identical twins, a demanding diva of a dog, and a zany cat who showed up one summer and never left.

A self-professed literary junkie and nerd, she loves reading anything, but especially romance novels and poetry. Catch up with her on her website https://scarlettscottauthor.com. Hearing from readers never fails to make her day.

Scarlett's complete book list and information about upcoming releases can be found at https://scarlettscottauthor.com.

Connect with Scarlett! You can find her here:
Join Scarlett Scott's reader group on Facebook for early excerpts, giveaways, and a whole lot of fun!
Sign up for her newsletter here
https://www.tiktok.com/@authorscarlettscott

facebook.com/AuthorScarlettScott

x.com/scarscoromance

instagram.com/scarlettscottauthor

bookbub.com/authors/scarlett-scott

amazon.com/Scarlett-Scott/e/B004NW8N2I

pinterest.com/scarlettscott

www.ingramcontent.com/pod-product-compliance
Lightning Source LLC
Chambersburg PA
CBHW070609300726
48975CB00006B/1761